kitty
GOES TO WAR

kitty
GOES TO WAR
Carrie Vaughn

The right of Carrie Vaughn to be identified as the author
of this work has been asserted by her in accordance with
the Copyright, Designs and Patents Act 1988.

First published in Great Britain in 2011 by
Gollancz
An imprint of the Orion Publishing Group
Orion House, 5 Upper St Martin's Lane,
London WC2H 9EA
An Hachette UK Company

10 9 8 7 6 5 4 3 2 1

A CIP catalogue record for this book
is available from the British Library

ISBN 978 0 575 09865 7

Printed and bound in the UK by
CPI Mackays, Chatham ME5 8TD

The Orion Publishing Group's policy is to use papers
that are natural, renewable and recyclable products and
made from wood grown in sustainable forests. The logging
and manufacturing processes are expected to conform to
the environmental regulations of the country of origin.

www.carrievaughn.com
www.orionbooks.co.uk

To the men and women
of the U.S. armed forces,
who have some of the toughest
jobs in the world.

The Playlist

JOHNNY NASH, "I Can See Clearly Now"

DEACON BLUE, "Fergus Sings the Blues"

TOO MUCH JOY, "Magic"

DRESSY BESSY, "Shoot, I Love You"

SAM THE SHAM AND THE PHARAOHS, "Li'l
   Red Riding Hood"

NEW ORDER, "Love Vigilantes"

OINGO BOINGO, "Stay"

BIG BROTHER AND THE HOLDING COMPANY,
   "Roadblock"

LED ZEPPELIN, "When the Levee Breaks"

DEPECHE MODE, "Peace"

PINK MARTINI, "Autrefois"

FAIRPORT CONVENTION, "Farewell, Farewell"

PAUL SIMON, "Late in the Evening"

Chapter 1

I SAT AT my desk, my monitor and microphone in front of me, maps and notebook paper spread over the whole surface. I was writing down addresses and marking points on the map as people called in.

"So you're saying it burned down and nobody could find out why?" I asked Pam from Lexington.

"That's right," she said. "My friend Stacy who's kind of a witch said it's because it was on a crossroads, and something demonic must have happened there, one of those deal-with-the-devil-type things, and the energy overflowed and incinerated it. Could she be right?"

"I don't know, Pam," I said. "That's why I'm discussing the topic, to find out if these events are all coincidence or if something spooky really is going on here. Thanks for the data point. Okay, faithful listeners, that gives me about a dozen independently verifiable stories about supernatural happenings at Speedy Mart convenience stores all over the country.

This is already more than I thought we'd get, so keep them coming."

After the third person suggested that something weird was going on at Speedy Mart, I started paying attention. And wondering. And remembering a couple more stories I'd heard about intersections between the chain of stores and weirdness. Then I decided to devote an episode of my call-in radio show to the subject. It turned out that maybe something strange was going on here. That didn't explain *why* the Speedy Mart chain would have anything supernatural associated with it.

"My next caller is Al from San Jose. Hello, Al."

"Hi, Kitty. I'm such a big fan, thanks for taking my call."

"Well, thank you, Al. What's your story?"

"It's more of a question: is it true that Speedy Mart hires vampires to work the night shift?"

"Funny you should ask," I said. "I once got a call from a vampire who said he was working the night shift at a Speedy Mart. Now, I don't think this means that it's a matter of policy that Speedy Mart hires vampires. I think this guy just needed a job, and there's only so many places open in the middle of the night. But you can definitely see the advantages of hiring the ageless undead to work behind the counter. I imagine they don't get too freaked out about holdups."

"But there's probably not a whole lot of career advancement for vampires there," he said.

"Does *anyone* working the night shift at Speedy Mart have a lot of opportunities for career advancement? Although with vampires it would literally be a dead-end job." I chuckled. I really shouldn't laugh at my own jokes so much. "Right, we have Chuck from Nevada. Hi, Chuck."

"Hey, Kitty! How you doing?" He was brash, a real talker. This ought to be good.

"I'm doing just great," I said, the standard line. "Where in Nevada are you?"

"Area 51."

Deadpan, I said, "Really?"

"Okay, yeah, I'm from a little town about thirty miles up the freeway from Las Vegas. *Near* Area 51. And you want to talk about weird stuff going on with Speedy Mart, I've got a story for you."

"Lay it on me."

"UFOs."

I leaned back in my chair. "Okay, now you're just making crap up."

"No, seriously, we get sightings all the time. We're one of the stops on the Southwest UFO tour. The Speedy Mart parking lot is one of the best places to see them. UFO hunters park out there with their lawn chairs and binoculars looking for them. It's, like, UFO central!"

"If you say so, but like I always say, there's weird and then there's weird. But I suppose a data point's a data point. Thanks for calling." I didn't have to tell him I wasn't actually going to mark that location on my map. We'd call it an outlier. A real far-out outlier.

I continued. "The real question here is: why Speedy Mart? Is it a coincidence? Does the supernatural really have some kind of strange affinity for this specific convenience store chain over any other? Or is it a conspiracy? Is there a guiding hand behind these stories? A dangerous hand? I'm not sure it's possible to answer any of these questions, which is always the trouble with this sort of thing, isn't it? It turns out the Speedy Mart chain is a privately owned company, which makes its records harder to get at. The owner and president of the company is Harold Franklin, who seems to have a typical upper-middle-class white guy upbringing, degree from Harvard Business School, vacation home in the Hamptons and all that jazz. Nothing to suggest he'd be behind any kind of far-reaching conspiracy. But who knows? For a company that's managed to open branches all over the country, not many people seem to know anything about it. It all seems a little strange to me."

I checked the monitor and picked what looked like was going to be a live one: the caller wouldn't give his or her name and city, but claimed to have worked at a Speedy Mart for several years.

"All right, it looks like we have someone from the inside on the line, a former employee of Speedy Mart. Hello, you're on the air."

"Um, hi." The voice was female, hushed, like she was trying to keep from being overheard.

"So you worked at Speedy Mart," I prompted.

"Yeah. For a couple of years when I was in college."

"You were a night-shift clerk?"

"I worked whenever I could get the hours. Sometimes at night."

"And did you notice anything strange during your time there?"

"I don't know. I didn't think it was all that strange at the time. I mean, I thought it was strange, but not supernatural strange or anything. These people would come in around midnight, about once a month. They'd be wearing cloaks. I just thought they were from some science fiction convention or Renaissance fair, driving home late. Strange but harmless. But looking back on it, they weren't really the Renaissance fair type, you know? These were all older guys, middle aged and clean cut, dressed normal except for the cloaks. They came in, walked all over the store, all the way to the back and every aisle, like they were looking for something. They never bought anything—total freak cheapskates. They were just some weird club. I never did anything about it because they didn't hurt anything, they weren't trying to rob me or anything, what was I going to do? I couldn't kick them out just because they didn't buy anything."

"What do you think they were doing?" I said, intrigued. I tried to imagine it, cloaked men walking around the store, every month—during what phase of the moon, I wondered? The whole thing screamed ritual.

"I don't know, that's why I'm calling. I thought maybe you would know."

"Well, that these men repeated the same action every month for—how many months?"

"I worked that shift for maybe six months. It happened every month," she said.

"And do you know if it was at the same time of the month? The same phase of the moon maybe?"

"I didn't pay attention—do you think it's important?"

"I don't know. The thing is, repetition says to me some kind of ceremony or ritual was going on. That means some kind of magic, some kind of power. Or at least they thought so—it may not mean anything. Can you tell me where this was?"

"No, I can't, I shouldn't even be calling, I—goodbye." The phone clicked off.

Dang. I'd have marked that spot on the map with a big star next to it. Of course, it could be coincidence—some weird local club had an initiation ceremony involving nothing more devious than wandering around the local Speedy Mart. Somehow I didn't think that was likely.

I checked the clock, and we had the time, so I

clicked the next call through. "Hello, Charles from Shreveport. What's your story?"

Charles from Shreveport talked fast. "You're right about Speedy Mart. And Harold Franklin. He's up to something. And someone has to stand up to him before it's too late."

I assessed the voice: male, quick, a little thin. Kind of eager, or desperate. Not laid back, not a disbeliever calling in to try to get a rise out of me, not someone with a deep personal problem. He didn't have the accent to go along with his Louisiana location. After doing this show for years, I'd become a pretty good judge of voices. Most of my callers fell into certain categories, and I could usually tell which one after a sentence or two. This guy had something to say, and he was the kind of person who thought late-night talk radio was a good soapbox.

"What's he up to, Charles?"

"I've been tracking Franklin's movements for decades. For example, in late August 2005, he spent four days in New Orleans, did you know that?"

"No. What has that got to do with anything?"

He sounded like he was reading off a list. "Biloxi, Mississippi, in August 1969—that was his first big showing. He was supposedly on a fishing trip right after college, but you know what happened next. He's only gotten more ambitious since then. February 1978 in Boston, April 1991 in Bangladesh, October 1991 in Nova Scotia."

How intriguing. My favorite kind of call—devoted and a little crazy. "How do you know all this? Have you been stalking him?" I was buying myself a little time, trying to figure out what Charles's pin markers in space and time meant. I wished I had an Internet browser on hand.

"He always leaves a couple of days before the worst of it hits. Always."

"The worst of what?"

"The worst of the storms!"

New Orleans, August 2005. Matt, my board operator, knocked on the booth window, and I figured it out at the same time I read the scrawled note he pressed to the glass: KATRINA.

Biloxi '69: Hurricane Camille, wanna bet? And if I looked up the rest, I'd probably find other epic hurricanes, blizzards, perfect storms.

I leaned into the microphone. "What are you saying, Charles? That Harold Franklin has really bad luck with the weather?"

"I'm saying it's not luck," he said.

"Do you know that experiments have shown that people have a tendency to find patterns, even when no actual patterns exist? In our attempts to make order out of the universe, we see connections where there just aren't any." Playing the skeptic—the term *devil's advocate* made me nervous when we were talking about the supernatural—usually got my callers riled up, which had high entertainment value.

But it also made them explain themselves. Made them delve, and often exposed more information.

Frustrated, he said, "If he was at any one of those locations it would be a coincidence but not noteworthy. But the fact that he was at all of them? Right around the time of some of the most destructive storms in modern history? And doesn't it make you wonder about the storms *before* modern history? That maybe Harold Franklin is just the latest in a long line of weather terrorists? Did you know that some people believe that the storm that scattered the Spanish Armada in the English Channel in the sixteenth century was created by English witches?"

"How did you get so interested in this?" I said. "How did you know to look for Franklin?"

"Have you ever met him?"

"No."

"Well, I have. And there's something off about him. I think he should be brought to justice for what he did to New Orleans."

He certainly wasn't alone in thinking someone ought to be brought to justice for happened to New Orleans. But most people were referring to events after the hurricane, not the hurricane itself.

"The thing is, Charles, science provides us lots of perfectly reasonable, natural explanations for how storms happen. Most people will say that Katrina wasn't anyone's fault. There's no need to go looking for malevolence."

"It's a nice little arrangement, isn't it? He wreaks all this havoc and everyone just writes it off on convection currents."

The guy may have been a crackpot or he may have been spot on the money. But I ran into the problem I usually ran into when dealing with the supernatural: how did we go about proving this connection?

"Charles, thank you very much for calling, but I'm running out of time and need to move on, all right?"

"As long as you listen to me. You have to listen. You're the only one who can do anything to stop him."

I highly doubted that. I highly doubted there was anything to do.

Matt gave me a neck-cutting signal through the window, then held up a finger—one minute to go. I'd been doing the show long enough that my sense of timing was pretty good—I'd given myself just enough time for a closing.

"All right, folks, we're out of time. I want to thank everyone who called in for helping me out on my little research project. I'll certainly let you know if anything comes of it. In the meantime, I've said it before and I'll say it again: you never can tell what's out there. So good night, stay safe, and until next week this is Kitty Norville, voice of the night, on *The Midnight Hour*."

The on-air sign dimmed, and the recorded closing

credits rolled, a familiar wolf howl playing in the background. My own wolf howl, my other voice, the other half of my being.

I slumped back, exhausted, pulled my headphones off, and rubbed some feeling back into my ears. Matt came in to stand in the doorway between the booth and studio. He was stocky, and he'd recently cut his black hair short. Way short. He used to wear it in a ponytail, but he'd noticed it was thinning up top and didn't want to end up like our boss, Ozzie, KNOB's station manager, who compensated for his thinning hair by growing his graying ponytail even longer.

Just another little change in the world. If you didn't pay attention to the little changes, you'd wake up one day and the whole universe would be different.

"How do you think it went?" I said.

"I think it went fine," he said. "I always like it when you do investigative stuff. But it's going to suck if you don't actually find some conspiracy. Al Capone's vault, baby."

"That won't matter," I said. "No conspiracy theory ever really dies. I'll be perfectly happy if nothing comes of this, because then I won't have to look over my shoulder every time I drive past a Speedy Mart."

"You do spend an awful lot of time looking over your shoulder, don't you?" he said, and I grimaced, because he was right.

I was sick and tired of secrets and conspiracies. These shadow groups, entire shadow worlds that seemed bent on destruction, with the rest of the world none the wiser. The worst part was how justified I was in feeling like a conspiracy-theory nut. I'd seen the results with my own eyes. I'd bled over it.

No more. No one else should have to die for shitty power games. If something was going on with Speedy Mart, I'd figure it out. If nothing was—then that was just fabulous, too. I'd be happy looking like an idiot if it meant nothing was wrong.

Matt and I said our farewells for the night. Outside the building, Ben was already parked at the curb, waiting to pick me up. My sense of relief and pleasure at seeing him in his car, looking out the window at me, was physical, a warm flush across my skin.

It didn't matter how many times we played this scene out—my crawling into the passenger seat after my shift, leaning into each other for a kiss hello—it never got old.

I leaned in for a second kiss, and a third, this one long enough to taste him.

"Hm. Hello to you," he said, when we finally broke apart. "You okay?"

"Yeah," I said with a sigh. "Just a little tired." I kept my hand on his leg as he drove away from the curb; even that light contact helped me relax. I could feel warmth through the fabric of his pants, and the flexing of his muscles as he pressed the gas pedal.

"Are we going out or going home?" he asked.

"Home," I said. "I don't want to talk to anyone else but you right now."

Ben smiled his crooked smile, and all was right with the world.

TREES MEANT safety. Forest was home. So when I felt trapped, it was in a building, an impossibly vast mansion, with corridors turning at sharp angles, floors rising and falling steeply. I ran, not knowing if I was on two legs or four. It felt like four, but my skin was smooth, furless, which meant I hadn't turned Wolf. I could smell blood, rotting blood, but I couldn't track it. It was everywhere. Sometimes blood meant food, sometimes it meant danger. Conflicting feelings of desire and terror confused me. It meant I ran without resolve, even though danger was close at hand, in the next room. Other people were here, also fleeing, and if we could only find each other we'd all be safe. But I couldn't find anyone. I couldn't save anyone. I was alone, running and cornered at the same time, and when a shot rang out, I flinched, feeling the burning pain through my body—

—and woke up, sitting up, breathing too fast, my pulse racing in my throat, painful.

"Kitty, shh, it's okay. Calm down." Ben was right there, arm across my shoulders, face close to mine, whispering comforts. I'd woken up like this before.

When I could separate myself from it, I knew what

the dream was: the building that trapped me was the lodge in Montana where I'd been hunted with a dozen others. Five of us had escaped. We survivors had all been wounded to one degree or another.

I still had nightmares, months later.

I covered my face with my hands and took a deep breath. Part of me was still flailing, terrified, furious, looking for a way to lash out with claws and sharp teeth—my Wolf side, surging to the fore. It took all my self-control to soothe her, to pull her back into the cage. I imagined all that power shrinking to a hard knot in my belly. As long as my heart kept racing it was difficult to listen to Ben, my husband.

"Keep it together," he murmured, nuzzling my neck, a wolfish gesture of comfort. He stroked my hair, and finally my heartbeat slowed, my muscles unclenched, and I could breathe without thinking about it.

Human now—mostly human—I slumped into his embrace, wrapped my arms around him, and let out a sigh. I was safe, I was home. Kneeling in bed, we held each other for a long time.

"You okay?" Ben said finally, his breath ruffling my hair.

"I don't know." My voice was muted by his shoulder, where I rested my head and took in the scent of him. "I dream about them." The ones I hadn't saved; Ben knew.

He pulled away and smoothed my hair back. "You

think maybe you should talk to someone about this? Get some counseling?"

Ben's gaze was full of concern, and maybe a little frustration. He'd skirted around the subject before, and I'd dodged because I liked to think I was a tough girl.

I scratched my head and rubbed my eyes, which ached. I needed more sleep, and I was starting to hate sleeping. "I thought I could handle it."

"I know," he said. "I would just really hate to wake up one night and find your wolf tangled up in the sheets. How would I explain the growling to the neighbors?" The condo complex had a no-pets policy. If I ever did lose it and turn Wolf—yeah, that might get a little noisy.

"That would almost be amusing enough to try it," I said, turning a lopsided grin.

"How about I let you talk to them when the complaints come in?"

"How about I just try real hard not to turn Wolf in the house?"

His brow furrowed, giving him a perplexed look. "Do other lycanthropes have house rules like that? No shape-shifting indoors? No silver in the silverware drawer?"

Ben was still getting used to being werewolf. He was good at overanalyzing the situation, which I found endearing. Even in the dark, I could make out his form and features: his lean frame, handsome face, shadowed eyes that would be hazel in the light, and scruffy hair sticking out, begging me to comb it with my fingers. So I did. That pulled him close to me, and we kissed, his warm mouth lighting my nerves. Lingering tension melted away, and I pressed my naked self to his naked self. He pulled me under the covers, and sufficiently distracted, I felt much better.

MONDAY, BACK at the office, I spread the map from the show across my desk. I'd marked a dozen spots, locations where people had told me intriguing stories about Speedy Mart. The marks were spread all over the country, in no discernable pattern. So much for that idea. I was about ready to pass it all off as some statistical anomaly—it wasn't that crazy stuff only happened at a Speedy Mart, it was just that no one talked about it when it happened anywhere else.

I was still pondering when I got a call. "Hi, Kitty? This is Lisa down in reception, I've got a letter here that you need to sign for."

"Really? Okay, I'll be right down." Now this was exciting. I wasn't expecting anything fancy. Certainly nothing I needed to sign for.

I went down the hallway from my office, and down the stairs to the lobby of the KNOB building, where a reception desk against the back wall faced the glass front doors. Lisa, a prim, professional twenty-something, was standing with a delivery guy. He looked to be from a courier service rather than from the postal service or one of the big parcel companies. He wore a jacket with a company logo, but a plain shirt and slacks rather than a uniform. They both looked up at my approach.

"Are you Katherine Norville?" the guy said. He held an nine-by-twelve manila envelope and a clipboard.

"Yeah."

"Could you sign here?" He pointed to the line of the form on the clipboard, showing that, yes, I did receive the envelope in question. Then he handed me the envelope.

"Have a nice day," he said, with kind of a leering smile, then sauntered out of the building.

"What is it?" Lisa said. "You expecting anything cool?"

"Not a thing." I'd started to have kind of a bad feeling about this. The envelope wasn't all that thick; it probably had some kind of document in it. Something official and important, no doubt, to be delivered by private courier. I opened it right there at the reception desk .

It was indeed a document, only a few pages thick, fairly innocuous looking. But the cover letter was printed on linen stationery and had an intimidating logo and letterhead with a string of names and "Attorneys at Law" after it. I read the text of the letter a couple of times and still wasn't sure what exactly it said. But I got the gist of it.

"Huh," I said. "I'm being sued for libel."

Chapter 2

REALLY, IT was bound to happen sooner or later.
I took the document—an honest-to-God sum-
mons—to Ozzie, the station manager. I thought he'd
blow a gasket, but he seemed to have the same reaction I did—confusion, colored with a tiny bit of awe.
The suit was being brought against me on behalf of
Harold Franklin, the president of Speedy Mart, for
derogatory and damaging comments made on my
program about both him and his beloved and respectable business.

"What the hell did you do?" Ozzie asked, reading
the letter for the fourth or fifth time, as I had.

"Um, I did the last show on Speedy Mart and
whether or not it's at the center of a supernatural
conspiracy."

He stared at me a moment. "So this doesn't really
come as a surprise."

"I know," I said. "But it was so fast!"

"You must have really offended him for him to move this quick," Ozzie said.

"Or maybe he really does have something to hide," I said, pointing. "Maybe there really is some kind of cover-up and he's diverting attention."

"Kitty—"

"Okay, I know. But we just hand this off to the lawyers and they should be able to wiggle us out of it. Right?"

"I think you should go pull the recording of that show for the lawyers. And what do you mean *us*?"

I escaped before having to come up with an answer for him.

The thing was, Franklin had a point. If my show somehow made people afraid of going to Speedy Mart, or damaged the company's reputation to a point where the business was negatively affected, the guy had a right to sue me. I just didn't think I was a big enough fish for him to notice. I had a decent-sized market share, but not *that* decent. This seemed like an overreaction. A cease-and-desist order and maybe a request for an on-air apology seemed more appropriate. Maybe Franklin and his lawyers were just trying to scare me, and they'd ask for the apology in exchange for withdrawing the lawsuit. I wouldn't be able to argue with that kind of deal.

While I was pulling the digital file of Friday's broadcast and burning it to a CD for the station's lawyer people, I called my own live-in lawyer for advice.

After our hellos, I launched right in. "Well, Mr. O'Farrell, attorney-at-law. Guess what? I'm being sued for libel."

"Well," Ben said. "That's a new one even for you. Who's suing?"

"The president of Speedy Mart."

"Already? That was fast, you only did that show a couple of days ago."

"I know. I'm almost impressed."

"I suppose it was only a matter of time."

"That's kind of what I was thinking," I said. "But I thought libel was when you lied about someone in print."

"Print or broadcast media," he answered. "It's libel because you have a built-in audience."

"So how do I get out of it?"

"You either prove that what you said wasn't damaging, or that it isn't libel because it's true. You were pretty good about saying that you were only speculating. I wonder what argument they're going to make."

"You think they have a case?" I asked.

"I don't know. This isn't my area of expertise. A civil suit's a long way from criminal defense. Do *you* think they have a case?"

I shrugged. "My instinct is that something really is going on. But I don't have any way to prove it. I think my mistake was bringing up the president by name. Because even if something is going on, he may not have anything to do with it."

"I assume KNOB has lawyers who can handle this?" Ben said.

"The legal side of it. I'm not sure they can do anything about proving there's any supernatural involvement."

He paused; I could almost hear him thinking over the phone. "I think I have an idea," he said finally. "You coming home soon?"

"It may be an hour or so. What's the plan?"

"We'll talk about it tonight."

"At least no one's trying to kill me this time."

"Yet," he said. "Give it time."

There was just no arguing with him. As a lawyer, he was trained to expect the worst.

WHEN I got home, Ben met me at the door and turned me right back around.

"You feel like going out to dinner, don't you?" he said.

"Um, sure?" Ben had that predatory, on-the-prowl gleam in his eye. Not the predatory gleam that came from being a werewolf, but the one he'd had long before he became a werewolf. This came from being a lawyer.

He had a plan, and I couldn't wait to see what it was. We were in the car, headed for the freeway when I asked, "Where are we going?"

"New Moon."

New Moon was a downtown bar-and-grill-type restaurant, and we went there more than anyplace else because it felt like home. It practically was home—Ben and I owned it. I'd made it a refuge, neutral territory for the lycanthropes in town. A place where we could go and not worry about territory or posturing. New Moon's manager was Shaun, Ben's and my lieutenant in Denver's werewolf pack. Any given evening, a few of us from the pack hung out there.

When we entered the restaurant, I got an inkling of Ben's plan—Cormac was sitting at our usual table in back, against the wall.

Cormac had been out of prison for five months and I still wasn't sure how I felt about him. Every time we got together, I was happy to see him. And worried, anxious, relieved, guilty, confused, and a few other emotions to boot. I could sense Ben tensing up beside me, a similar stew of conflicting emotions roiling in him. Cormac had saved our lives and ended up in prison for it. He'd had to put his life on hold; we hadn't. Cormac and I had had a thing, once upon a time. Then he'd brought Ben, his cousin and victim of a recent werewolf attack, to me. I'd taken care of him, Cormac went to jail, and Ben and I got married.

The three of us understood each other when no

one else did. No one else had the history to be able to understand us. We were like the three musketeers, but kinda twisted.

Cormac stood to meet us as we approached. He had an athletic leanness to him, and an easy, calm way of moving that could be nerve wracking. Physically, he hadn't changed so much—same rugged features, short brown hair, a trimmed moustache. But he'd aged. His face was a little more lined than it had been, a little more tired. Like even though he'd spent two-plus years behind the same set of walls, he'd seen too much.

"Hey," he said.

"Hey," I said back. And there ended our usual, laconic greeting.

Ben looked Cormac over, and he wasn't very subtle about it. He craned his neck, checked his sides, looked as far behind him as he could without actually walking around him. Looking for telltale shapes.

Cormac glanced ceilingward and said, "I'm not wearing a gun."

"Sorry," Ben said, defensive. "You can't blame me for worrying."

"I'm not stupid," Cormac said.

"So you don't have a gun anywhere? You're sure?"

"Like he could forget he was wearing a gun," I said to Ben. "You can smell him, he's not wearing a gun." That was another thing about Cormac that had changed, along with the tired expression; I was used to Cormac smelling like firearms. Gunpowder and oil. Now he smelled like soap, clean human, and the leather of his jacket. As antsy as his old collection of weaponry made me, he smelled like something was missing.

"I'm sorry. It's just that I haven't seen you without a gun since high school," Ben said. "I'm still getting used to it."

"*I'm* still getting used to it." He slumped back into his chair and took a sip of his coffee.

Cormac was a convicted felon on parole. Legally, he couldn't carry a gun. Technically, he *could* carry a gun—he just couldn't get caught with it by his parole officer or the cops, or they'd lock him up again. So he didn't carry a gun. Once upon a time, Cormac might have taken the risk. The preprison Cormac would have been confident in his ability not to get caught. But something had gotten to him.

Ben and I slid into chairs across from him. I had a weird sense of familiarity, Ben and me sitting side by side, looking at Cormac across the table from us. This was how we'd sat when we visited him in prison. Then, we'd had a Plexiglas wall between us.

"I've got a job for you," Ben said. "How do you feel about a little PI work? PI work that doesn't involve carrying a gun."

Cormac looked away, frowning. "You don't have

to give me a job because you think I need the work. I'm doing just fine without any charity." His parole officer had gotten him a part-time warehouse job—it may have been the first aboveboard job he'd ever had. He even had his own apartment. He was determined to be independent.

"Cormac, I'm not asking you to do this because I feel sorry for you. I'm asking you to do this because you're the most qualified person I know for the job."

That got his attention. He straightened a little. Ben looked at me to do the explaining.

"For the last couple of years I've been hearing weird stories about the Speedy Mart chain," I said. "Supernatural goings-on, all over the country, and all of them at a Speedy Mart. Usually at midnight. Vampire clerks, satanic rituals, intersecting ley lines. Think of every crazy supernatural angle you can, and there's probably an anecdote about it happening at a Speedy Mart."

Cormac looked thoughtful. "That vampire, the one you had me go after while you were doing the show—what was that, three years ago? Four?"

"Estelle," I said. I hadn't forgotten Estelle.

"She was hiding out in a Speedy Mart."

"Yeah, exactly," I said.

"That's stretching it even for you," Ben said. "It's coincidence."

I said, "Each of these stories don't mean anything

by themselves. It's when you put them all together things start looking weird. I need to know if there's anything to it."

The bounty hunter—former bounty hunter—gave a nod, lips pursed. "All right. I'm interested. I'll see if I can find anything."

"Stop by my office tomorrow; I can give you what I've been able to dig up so far," I said.

Business concluded, Ben looked around, craned over his shoulder. "Hey, isn't the service around here usually better than this?"

It was; if Shaun was here, he usually stopped by our table himself first thing. Ah, there he was, hiding out behind the bar. He was a hip twenty-something, short dark hair, brown skin, laid back and sensible in a T-shirt and jeans. When he saw all three of us looking over, he finally came over.

"Took you long enough," Ben said.

Shaun wilted, hurt and puppylike. "I wasn't going to interrupt whatever powwow you have going on here. You look like you're planning the takeover of a small country."

"It's not that serious. Do we look that serious?" Ben said.

"It's the body language, hon," I said. "We look like we're hunting."

"Uh, yeah," Shaun said. "But if you're all done with that maybe I can get you something to drink." He looked hopeful.

We gave him our order, and Ben tried to be nice to make up for making Shaun nervous.

"Huh. Werewolves," Cormac said, shaking his head.

CORMAC STOPPED by the KNOB offices at noon the next day. I met him at the lobby and brought him upstairs.

"Déjà vu a little, isn't it?" he said.

I glared at him, unamused. The first time Cormac and I had met, he'd been stalking me at the studio in the middle of my show, intending to shoot me. Very uncool.

"No comment," I said.

My office was more like a closet, just enough room for the desk and a couple of chairs, but it was mine. Inside, Cormac took the seat I offered while I sorted through the papers on my desk: the map, the notes, the news articles printed off the Internet that verified some of the stories. I really didn't have very much when I put it all together.

"It's not very impressive," I said by way of apology. "Ben's right, there's probably nothing there. Maybe we can settle the lawsuit out of court."

"Don't jump to any conclusions," he said, leaning forward to start reading.

I'd never seen him so studious. He usually—at least before he went to prison—cultivated this air of indifference. Not quite apathy as much as a sense of apartness, like he wasn't interested because he lived on a different plane of existence. It would have been almost Zen-like, if it hadn't been so creepy. Now, he really seemed interested. Fascinated, even. Hand on his chin, he chewed his lip.

He even smelled different. Slightly, bookishly different. Paper and ink. But this was Cormac, and I didn't have anything to worry about. Right?

The office had become so still that when he spoke, I flinched.

"I need to do some checking, but I have some ideas," he said, looking up at me, calm and steady. He was all Cormac again.

"Really? Like what?"

"Not sure," he murmured. "Maybe ritualistic magic. Maybe something else."

I was never going to find out just how much Cormac knew about the supernatural. When we'd first met, he knew more about werewolves than I did, even though I was one. He'd hunted them for half his life, after all.

"How long do you need?"

"I'll let you know," he said, standing, rolling the pages up and tucking them in the pocket of his jacket. Preoccupied, he walked out without a word or second glance. I stared at the open doorway for a minute or so, wondering if he really was okay.

Chapter 3

I COULDN'T DO much else about the lawsuit business, at least not for a while. The wheels of justice were turning, and it was in the lawyers' hands. There'd be response, counterresponse, deal making, and all I had to do was stand aside and look innocent. What were the odds?

Or maybe Cormac would come up with something interesting, in which case there might be fireworks. I didn't know which outcome to wish for more.

During my office hours the next day, I tried to stay focused and avoided calling Cormac, even though I wanted to, to see if he'd learned anything yet. It had only been a day. This would take time. My phone still sat on my desk, taunting me, luring me.

When it actually did ring, I jumped out of my chair to pounce on it. The voice on the other end wasn't Cormac's.

"Kitty, this is Elizabeth Shumacher, from the CSPB."

That was Dr. Elizabeth Shumacher, who headed up the Center for the Study of Paranatural Biology, the research clearinghouse for all things supernatural that was part of the National Institutes of Health. I'd had a long and not always wonderful association with the center, but I liked Dr. Shumacher. The center had become much more rational and useful—rather than clandestine and paranoid—with her at the helm.

I sat back down and calmed myself. "Hi, Doctor. What's up?"

"I'm afraid . . . well, there's no good way to put this. We have something of a problem, Kitty. We need your help."

I recognized the tone of voice; she sounded like someone calling into the show. "Who's we? Is it something with the lab?"

"We—" She sighed. "I guess you could say it's the U.S. government."

Okay, that sounded heavy. My impulse was to vehemently deny that I could possibly be of any help whatsoever. Then hang up and refuse to pick up the phone when her number showed up on caller ID. Then maybe flee the country so she could never find me again. That might have been an overreaction. "What is it? What's going on?"

"It would be much easier to explain this in person. Would you be willing to meet with me? The sooner the better. Today, if possible."

"I'm not sure I could get out there on such short notice," I said.

"I'm not in D.C. right now, Kitty. I'm at Fort Carson in Colorado Springs."

About eighty miles away, in my backyard practically.

"What are you doing there?" I said.

"I'd rather explain it all in person." Clearly spoken in a tone of bureaucratic stubbornness.

"Is this a werewolf problem?" I said, fishing.

After a hesitation, she said, "Yes."

Color me intrigued. "It'll take me a couple of hours to get there, but I think I can make it."

"That would be wonderful," she said, clearly relieved.

I agreed, and she gave me directions about getting to the huge army base south of Colorado Springs, then what to do when I got there. I had the impression she'd set up a temporary office at the hospital there. This made me think that her problem was military in nature—or maybe she just felt more at home at any government installation, whatever the flavor.

THE NOONTIME drive to Colorado Springs was crisp, wintery, and clear. I managed to miss rush hour.

I didn't spend much time in the Springs. It had started life as a quiet, respectable enclave for the state's nouveau riche a hundred-plus years ago, and since then had turned into an almost Lovecraftian behemoth of urban sprawl. It's also home to something like half a dozen major military bases and even more fundamentalist Christian organizations, which established a rather dubious reputation for ultraconservatism, giving the place a weird vibe. A couple of our pack members lived here, and it marked what we considered the southern boundary of our territory.

After pulling off the freeway, I wound my way along side roads to the main gate at Fort Carson, which looked simultaneously innocuous and aggressively military. Chain-link fence strung with barbed wire, then tall black fences, lined the street. But behind the fences lay normal-looking suburban tract housing. The gate looked like a toll plaza, but the attack helicopter parked on display outside it indicated that this wasn't so ordinary.

Dr. Shumacher had given my name to the security guards on duty. I still had to hand them my ID and car registration, and they inspected my car's trunk and undercarriage. I supposed it was comforting, but I still felt twitchy. There didn't seem to be any problems, though. The guy handed my driver's license back, gave me helpful directions to the hospital, and ordered me to have a good day.

Very carefully, I pulled away. Five minutes of driving on a long, winding road brought me to a modern building of tan brick and narrow windows.

Again, I might have mistaken the area for a typical suburban hospital and neighborhood, except that in the parking lot, a lot of the cars had "Army" and "Infantry" stickers in their windows.

Dr. Shumacher was waiting for me outside the building's glass front entrance.

She looked like a scientist, in a cool way. In her fifties, she was short and brisk, her dark hair going gray, cut in a bob around her ears, and had smart wire-rimmed glasses. Her gaze was intense, her expression serious. She wore a dark fitted sweater, a skirt, and sensible shoes.

When she saw me, she smiled. "Kitty, it's so good to finally meet you in person."

"Likewise." I offered my hand for her to shake.

Inside, she guided me down a hallway to a windowless conference room, with a tile floor and off-white walls, white boards, signs of AV equipment, and a table. Nothing too sinister yet, except maybe the guy sitting at the table. He wore a crisp green army uniform, with all the bells and whistles, lots of insignia I didn't know the meaning of. He had eagle pins on his shoulders. He was tall, broad, with short cropped hair and a drill-sergeant stare. He stood when we entered the room. His stance was aggressive, shoulders back, spine straight, ready to leap. He was probably never anything but aggressive.

"Kitty, this is Colonel William Stafford. Colonel Stafford, this is Kitty Norville."

As I had with Shumacher, I reached my hand for him to shake before he could decide not to offer me his. He studied me hard, assessing me, and seemed skeptical. Worried. But maybe he wasn't worried about me.

"Thank you for coming, Ms. Norville," he said, firmly and politely, and some of the tension left me. He sounded genuine. We all sat at the table.

"I'm happy to help, but what is this all about?" I said, my curiosity becoming overwhelming.

They glanced at each other, the confident scientist and assured colonel, and looked chagrined. As if they were debating over who was going to explain it. As if they were embarrassed. The colonel fidgeted with the corner of a manila folder in front of him. I waited. I could stare them down.

Dr. Shumacher started. "You remember Dr. Paul Flemming, don't you?"

"As much as I would like to forget about him, I remember." Dr. Flemming had been Shumacher's predecessor at the CSPB and one of my least favorite people ever.

"I believed that none of his projects had advanced past the conceptual stages. My intention had been to start the center on a clean slate, with complete transparency. Do some real science instead of Flemming's secret project version of it." Her half-smile was too pained to show real amusement.

I waited, keeping my mouth shut. What monster

had they discovered frozen in some forgotten NIH closet? My imagination failed me.

Shumacher continued carefully. "You remember that Flemming was particularly interested in military applications, and whether the military could effectively utilize soldiers possessing paranatural traits?"

I might not have figured it out if Stafford hadn't been sitting next to her looking guilty. But the pieces fell into place. Shumacher was talking about nearly indestructible werewolf soldiers, immune to gunfire, physically strong, possessing immense stamina and wicked killer instincts. When the CSPB went public, Flemming had been disgraced before Congress and vanished. All his secret projects had supposedly been shelved. That had been my understanding. Weaponized werewolves were such a bad idea.

I tried not to be furious. "Are you telling me Flemming's lycanthrope soldier program went forward?"

"No, it didn't," Shumacher said quickly. "At least, not officially."

"But unofficially?" I said. I was starting to understand the looks of chagrin.

Colonel Stafford pulled a five-by-seven black-and-white photo from his manila folder and slid it across the table to me. Looking like a snapshot that had been cropped and blown up, it showed a young-ish man, maybe thirty, supremely confident, his shoulders square and solid. He looked at the camera lens with an adventurous glint in his eyes and a curl on his lips. He wore a beret, a dark T-shirt, and camo fatigue pants. The colonel didn't have to tell me—this was one of the army's best and brightest. The photo radiated it.

"This was Captain Cameron Gordon," Stafford said. "Top five percent of his class at West Point, went on to Special Forces—Green Berets."

"And he did it all while infected with lycanthropy. He was a werewolf," Shumacher said.

"How did he manage that?" I said, in awe of the man. Sometimes I barely managed to keep my life functioning, my werewolf and human identities working together, without running screaming into the woods. Captain Gordon must have been superhuman.

Stafford answered. "Near as we can figure, a lot of careful planning. He always had favors to call in so he could get time off on nights of the full moon. People covered for him, he never got caught. He was careful. And he was too good for the army to let him go the time or two he did screw up."

I could also speculate that Gordon had been infected with lycanthropy young, as part of a well-adjusted, functional pack where he learned a high level of control. He'd known exactly how to handle his werewolf side.

Shumacher picked up the story. "When Flemming was exploring . . . possibilities . . . regarding lycanthropy and the military, he recruited Captain Gordon.

I don't know how Flemming knew about him, but he did. I believe the two worked together until Flemming was forced to go public. By that time, Gordon had deployed to Iraq. You know that Flemming destroyed many of his records. I've been trying to reconstruct what work the two of them did, but I haven't had much luck. Then Colonel Stafford called me."

I said, "So Flemming really did it. He really did put werewolf soldiers in the field—"

"That's just it," Shumacher said. "Flemming didn't have anything to do with this. He never authorized any implementation of his plans. He never did anything but interview Captain Gordon—but that put the idea in Gordon's head. Captain Gordon did everything else on his own. He independently created his own squad of werewolves, without authorization."

Stafford pulled out another photo, this one showing seven men, including Gordon, all fully decked out in badass army gear—helmets, backpacks, rifles, boxes of ammunition—posing as a group for the camera. They were all fit and strong, holding rifles in assured grips; a couple of them smiled confidently. If I hadn't known they were all werewolves, I might have missed some telltale signs, or attributed those signs to their military background. But studying the picture, I could tell: Gordon was the only one standing, putting him in the position of dominance— he stood like an alpha. The others crouched, knelt, or leaned around him. A few of them didn't look at the camera at all. They instinctively didn't stare, which is an expression of challenge among wolves. I could almost smell them.

"Gordon wasn't stupid," Stafford said. "He took his time and picked likely candidates from the Special Forces. He maneuvered to get his people transferred to the same base, if not the same unit. He infected them himself, and trained them himself, all on the sly. He was in Afghanistan by this time. I think he saw a need in the mission, and he set out to fill it."

I looked at the colonel. "When did you find out about this? How much did you know when it was happening?"

"Not enough. Gordon acted on the principle that it's easier to ask for forgiveness than permission. And he was right, to a point. His squad had an amazing record in Afghanistan. It was one of the most successful units we've fielded out there. They handled the terrain like it was nothing, they could travel for weeks without support, get to places nothing else could, track down damn near anything. They didn't need body armor or NVGs—"

"NVGs?"

"Night-vision goggles," Stafford said. "We had them hunting Taliban leaders in the Kunar Province, in the high country. Their success rate was . . . was worth everything, we thought."

"And then what?" I said, a chill twitching my spine. They kept using the past tense.

"There was a mortar attack," Shumacher said. "Captain Gordon was one of several people caught in the explosion.

"It turns out a big enough explosion can kill a werewolf just fine," Stafford said, deadpan.

"I know," I said, my own bitter experience tainting my voice.

"The folklore doesn't say anything about werewolves being killed by explosions," Shumacher said.

"That's because most of the folklore was in circulation before explosions of that scale existed," I said.

"After Gordon's death, everything fell apart," Stafford said. "The remaining members of Gordon's unit became unruly, I guess you'd call it. Rebellious. Insubordinate. We tried to appoint another commander—they refused to follow orders. Then Vanderman killed Yarrow." He pointed out the two faces on the unit photo. The two biggest guys there, of course. Vanderman was a burly no-neck white guy. Yarrow was equally burly, with lips turned in a half grin, half snarl.

Stafford continued. "We wouldn't have known who killed Yarrow, except Sergeant Crane reported the murder. He went to the base commander and asked for help. In the morning, he was dead, too. Ripped to pieces, same as Yarrow. That's when we drugged the rest of the unit, took them into custody, and brought them home until we could figure out what to do with them."

"That must have been some picnic," I said. I didn't want to imagine what that must have looked like and resisted an urge to look over my shoulder, as if the army werewolves were nearby, waiting to pounce. I didn't want to get anywhere near them, not if they were as dangerous as I thought they were.

Shumacher gave me a grim frown. "That's when Colonel Stafford called me. Unfortunately, I'm not much of a werewolf psychologist. I'm guessing that what happened in Afghanistan was some atypical pack behavior—"

"Gordon was the alpha," I said. "He held the pack together. As long as he was there to lead them, the others had a center, a reason to stay in control. His word was law, and without him—no law." I tapped the photo, pointing to Vanderman and Yarrow. "These two look like the strongest left in the bunch. I bet they fought it out to see who would lead them next. Vanderman won. After that, I'm thinking Crane deferred to his human side. He stayed rational, saw what was happening, and reported it to get help. Vanderman killed him for insubordination."

"That was my feeling," Shumacher said. "I'm glad to have the validation."

I shook my head. "These guys had no independence under Gordon's leadership. Without him, they don't have a clue. They're running on pure instinct—especially if Vanderman killed Crane for going outside the pack. That shut down any chance of sanity they had. I've seen this kind of thing before—do you realize how dangerous those men are?"

Stafford looked even more uncomfortable, if that was possible. Holy crap, we weren't done with the story yet?

"We thought we could work with them, rehabilitate them, maybe even return them to the field," the colonel said. "From a training and tactical standpoint, these men are incredibly valuable. We had to try something."

"Not to mention the fact that they're too dangerous to release on a medical discharge," Shumacher said more softly. "We had to either find a way to retrain them or find a way to heal them."

Neither of them mentioned a third option, but I could see it in their expressions, in the way their gazes kept dropping, in the tang of anxiety touching them. Oh, God, they hadn't already . . . what did I even call it—terminate the experiment? I glared at them, my hands resting in front of me, my shoulders tense. Aggressive body language, daring them to stand up to me. A stalking wolf. Stafford's eyes widened—he recognized the stance. He'd probably seen in it his rogue army wolves.

"It's time for you to tell me why I'm here," I said. "You don't think I can help these guys become happy, well-adjusted werewolves, do you?"

"It's more complicated than that—" Stafford started.

"It's more urgent than that," Shumacher said, leaning forward. "We never had any intention of bringing an unauthorized civilian in on this. If all I needed was advice I'd have just called you. But I needed to warn you, and we need your help. Kitty, Gordon's unit escaped custody. They left Fort Carson this morning. They're on the loose, and they're heading north."

Chapter 4

OKAY. PACK of highly trained Green Beret were-wolves are heading north, toward my territory. My city, my family, my wolves. My pack, which the wolves of Gordon's unit would see either as followers to be recruited, or rivals to be destroyed. They had to be stopped, and Stafford and Shumacher didn't have a clue. Right. I could handle this.

Maybe.

"You're the fucking *army*," I said. "You couldn't stop them?"

"It's not that simple," Stafford said, speaking calmly to hide that he was just a little flustered—sweating, tapping his fingers on the table. He probably didn't even notice he was doing it. "These men have the best escape and evasion training in the world."

"But you know where they are?" I said.

"We lost them in the foothills north of Colorado Springs."

"They're fast," Shumacher said. "They might even be moving as wolves in wilderness."

Stafford said, "We tried microchipping them, but their bodies . . . rejected the microchips."

"It's the superimmunity," Shumacher explained. "Werewolf physiology rejects invasive technologies."

"Really?" I said. "So if I ever wanted to do something like, oh, breast implants?"

Shumacher gazed at me warningly and shook her head. Oh, wow, that was kind of sick. She may not have been up on the psychology, but I was always learning new medical tidbits from the doctor.

"The way Dr. Shumacher is talking," Stafford continued, "this isn't just a matter of getting my people back under control. She says they could pose a threat to the civilian population."

"Yeah, they could, if they're out of control enough to attack people," I said. "Not to mention *my* people. Werewolves are territorial, just like the wild version. They might go looking for my pack to take them out." This was sounding worse all the time.

"That's part of why I called," Shumacher said. "I thought you should be warned."

"For what purpose? So I can worry about it?"

"That wasn't the only reason," Stafford said. "Doctor Shumacher says you have a lot of experience, that you've encountered some similar problems with violent werewolves, and that you might know how to handle this. We wanted to ask for your advice." Stafford tightened his jaw; he probably didn't ask people for advice very often.

Resisting an urge to rant, I leaned my head on my hand and considered. If these guys couldn't figure out how to stop the rogues, I had to do it. Or face an even bigger problem in, oh, a day or so. I had to call Ben and the rest of the pack, to warn them. I could even call Cormac—he knew more about hunting werewolves than anyone I knew. Stafford and Shumacher ought to be talking to him.

I tried to get at the problem step by step. We had a group of out-of-control werewolves. What did they want? What were they after? If they were operating mainly on instinct, which they seemed to be, they'd be looking to set up a territory. Maybe even looking to join an existing pack—if they were between Colorado Springs and Denver they'd probably get a whiff of mine. The thing was, they were big, aggressive, dominant werewolves—they wouldn't just want to join—they'd want to take it over. That was what we were trying to prevent. I had to work with Stafford to head these guys off, to protect my pack. And then what? What did wild wolves want after they set up a territory?

Oh. I had an idea. A crazy idea. But not any crazier than the rest of this situation.

"Let me make a couple of phone calls," I said to them.

* * *

WHILE I was making my calls, Stafford heard from
his guys in the field. They'd tracked the rogue pack
into the mountains of the Front Range, then north.
And how had they tracked them? They'd found a
body: one of the remaining pack members, Sergeant
Estevan, mauled to death, head torn from shoulders.
More squabbling within the pack. They were
arguing, and Vanderman dealt ruthlessly with
dissenters. We only had three werewolves to capture
now, but they were tough, angry, and homicidal. My
plan seemed even flimsier, but the news made trying
to stop them even more important.

Three hours later, a group of us stood in the forest
off Highway 285, south of Mount Evans, west of
Denver. We were going to try to intercept them. The
group included me, Shumacher, and Stafford. I'd
brought Ben along because I always brought him
when I could. It didn't hurt that he was a lawyer. I
also had my secret weapons.

Becky, dressed in a tank top and yoga pants
despite the cold, paced nearby, her arms crossed,
looking out into the woods as if searching. A few
years older than me, she was willowy, with auburn
hair. I'd known her for years, for as long as I'd been
a werewolf. She'd been one for even longer, part of
the pack that took me in at the start, and now she
paced, an unhappy predator. Stafford watched Becky

warily. Shumacher looked like she wanted to take notes.

Then there was Cormac in his tough-guy gear: jeans, T-shirt, biker boots, leather jacket, and opaque shades. He stood apart, in the other direction. He didn't pace; he just watched. I kept glancing over, expecting a shotgun loaded with silver filings to magically appear in his hands, because the guns were part of the tough-guy gear. But he wasn't carrying any weapons. Ben and I both checked.

Now that I'd brought this plan together, I supposed I had to go through with it.

"Explain this to me again," Ben said.

I shrugged. "I'm guessing these guys have never met a female werewolf. Maybe meeting one will stop them in their tracks." I was doing a lot of guessing here.

Ben looked at me sideways. "Isn't that kind of sexist?"

"Yeah, it is," I said, answering his smile. "And werewolves running on instinct are some of the most sexist bastards I know."

"What makes you think they won't rip our throats out?" Becky said, still pacing.

"That's what the backup is for."

We were going to set a trap. Stafford's guys were supposed to have some heavy-duty gear to capture the rogue wolves. Shumacher had a pair of tranquilizer guns, those big rifles like you see in the National Geographic specials.

"I wasn't sure tranquilizers would work on werewolves," I said to her.

"You have to use enough tranquilizer to take down an elephant, but it works," Shumacher said.

I wasn't sure I wanted to know that.

"Are you ready to kill these guys?" Cormac said. "If you can't talk sense into them, if you can't rehabilitate them, are you willing to shoot them?"

That was Cormac, always the realist. Everyone looked at him for a long, silent moment.

"I'm hoping it won't come to that," Shumacher said finally.

Colonel Stafford looked at her, then at Cormac. "My men have been issued silver bullets."

"Just make sure they don't shoot at any of us," I muttered. I wandered to where Cormac was standing, speaking low so the others wouldn't hear. Stafford had been giving him wary looks since I introduced them, and when Cormac asked to look over the gear they were using—nets threaded with silver wire, cages, Tasers—Stafford had argued. I'd explained that Cormac was the real werewolf-hunting expert here. But that only made Stafford look at him even more oddly.

Stafford's men set the traps—cages placed in ravines, since the ground around here was too rocky to dig proper tiger traps; nets to snare them if they avoided the cages. We limited the number of people who'd tromped around the immediate area of the traps, since the werewolves would be able to smell them. But Stafford and Shumacher would be there, with the tranquilizer guns.

It was the best we could do in a matter of hours.

"You don't think it's possible to catch were-wolves," I said to Cormac.

"Oh, sure it's possible," he said. "You've been caught before. But these aren't just werewolves, are they?"

"I can't not do anything. I have to try *something*."

"For what it's worth, I think you're right. If these guys are really looking to set up a pack, I don't think they'll try to kill you and your friend there. But they may try to rape you." That wasn't comforting. "Just be careful. Keep your head on straight; you'll be fine," he said.

"Thanks."

It was getting close to time. Becky and I were both barefoot. The chill didn't bother us—our wolf sides loved it. Good weather for running. We'd head out on foot, crossing back and forth along the were-wolves' projected path, marking as we went. Becky would shift; I'd stay human. Whichever form our wayward soldiers were in, one of us should be able to "talk" to them. If we couldn't talk to them, we were going to run—just run, in a panic, encouraging them to follow us. And we'd lead them to the traps.

The two of us had been over the immediate area, had memorized the way it smelled. All we had to do was remember. Stafford and Shumacher would be there to spring the traps. I also had a radio with me. Theoretically, I could call for help.

"Ms. Norville? It's time." Colonel Stafford lowered a radio—his men had cleared the area.

Ben came to me, held my hands, and kissed me. "Any sign of trouble, I'm coming after you."

"With guns or claws?" I didn't want Ben turning wolf and going after these guys. The whole point of this exercise was to keep my wolves and the rogues from attacking each other.

"The Glock's loaded and in the car," he said, grinning.

Cormac may have had his concealed-weapons permit revoked, but Ben sure hadn't.

"I'll be fine. Everything'll work out," I said, too cheerfully. Ben looked skeptical; he recognized my nervous tone. I grabbed my backpack, which held the radio, a couple of bottles of water, and my own gun, loaded with silver. I hadn't wanted to bring it, but Ben insisted.

I headed out; Becky moved in beside me, and we paced together until the others were out of sight.

"You okay?" I asked.

"Yeah. I'm actually kind of curious about these guys," she said. She was worried—I couldn't blame her for that. But she walked with confidence, her chin up, looking out with clear eyes. That was why I'd picked her—she wouldn't cower. She'd been one of the first wolves to desert the old pack to follow me.

"They're not bad guys," I said. "I think they're just lost."

"I guess we'll find out."

I stopped myself from nagging Becky too much about her anxiety. I was having to work to clamp down on my own. Being in the woods like this—just the two of us, none of the other pack around, aware of the danger we were potentially heading toward—brought back memories of being hunted by very bad people. I kept looking over my shoulder, wondering what else was out here. Places like this were perfect for ambushes. But I was a hunter, too.

We did not move with stealth. We touched trees, broke twigs, scuffed our bare feet through pine needles and dirt. I checked for landmarks—trees, mountain peaks, the sun moving low in the west. I didn't want to get too far from the traps, but we had to get far enough out that the rogues would have a chance of catching our scent. So we wandered aimlessly in a fan pattern, between the trap and where the body of Estevan had been found. If we didn't catch up with them soon, they might solve our problem by killing off each other. That wouldn't feel much like a victory.

An hour later, the sun was starting to set, the woods turning shadowy in the dusk. I wasn't worried about nightfall. We could handle ourselves fine in the dark. But this would be so much easier in daylight.

"Come on, guys," I muttered.

Then a stray breeze shuddered through the pines, carrying a taint with it. Sour, musky, male—urine. Something that didn't belong here had been marking. We'd smelled all sorts of things: rabbits, squirrels, deer, foxes, a bear, and all the other creatures that normally stomped through the woods. But this was different, thick and alien, and it made my muscles clench and my hindbrain scream: foreign werewolves.

Becky looked at me, and we both shivered.

"That's it," I said. Becky undressed, quickly shoving down her pants and panties and pulling off her shirt. She handed the clothing to me, and I stuffed them in the pack. She started shifting without a word. Just a soft grunt as her back arched and her limbs flexed, dropping her to her knees. She looked up, pointing a wolf's snout to the sky. The Change poured over her like water, flowing from one form to the next. She made it look easy, painless. But that was only because she'd been doing this a long time. The Change was never painless. Not fighting it only made it less so.

My own inner Wolf called to me, struggling, wanting to join her. I breathed in and held her still.

In moments, the human Becky was gone and a large wolf shook out her gray and tawny fur, stretched her sleek body, and looked at me. Still the alpha, even if I had only two legs.

I sighed. "Here we go."

She ran ahead, pausing a moment to urinate. Now if we could get upwind of them, let them get a whiff of that, they'd be on us in seconds. And wouldn't that be fun?

Becky loped on, and I ran after her.

Chapter 5

WE FOLLOWED the slope of a hill until it crossed into a narrow valley, where we lost the scent, so we doubled back. Becky covered more ground, crisscrossing ahead of me, nose low, tail out like a rudder. I was more cautious, looking around, searching stands of trees and gaps in the forest for flashes of movement, testing the air with every breath. Becky continued marking our presence.

We found them again, traces on the air, strange fur and musk. Becky sat back on her haunches, tipped her nose to the sky, and howled. The thin, piercing sound echoed, filling the woods, seeping into the stones of the mountain itself. Anyone within miles could hear it. The others standing watch at the trap would be able to hear it. The other wolves had to know we were here.

She howled again, another somber, falling note. *Here we are, this is our land, we're here!* the howl said. Howls marked territory, helped members of the

pack find each other, and warned other packs away—
or offered a challenge. It was an existential declara-
tion, as well as being primeval, mysterious, and
maybe overly romanticized. But I could understand
why people were entranced by wolf howls. I wanted
to join her, but my human lungs and voice wouldn't
do justice to the call.

Her howls might also be like waving a red flag.
The hairs on my neck were tingling, my shoulders
bunching. Becky had started pacing again, nose to
ground.

Then the answer came, a clear howl in a voice I
didn't recognize, waving a flag of its own. It was
close.

I nodded back the way we'd come and called,
"Hey, let's get going." I wanted to be heading toward
the trap instead of away from it when the army boys
started following us.

She raised her head, glanced at me as I jogged
back up the hill, and set off, trotting in graceful wolf
strides. She quickly passed me and moved out ahead,
and I followed. Testing the air, I could smell the
rogues even more strongly. We'd found them, but I
couldn't see them, couldn't guess where they might
come from, and that made me nervous. More nervous. I glanced around, not wanting to get caught in
tunnel vision, even as I tried to move quickly.

Becky spotted them first, or at least one of them.
She stopped and swung to our right, standing tall,

her ears pricked forward and her hackles stiff, all the hair on her back standing up. When I looked, I saw a shape dodging trees—a shadow in the growing dusk, with four legs, a furred outline, taking huge, loping strides. Maybe a hundred yards away, but it was hard to tell distance because the creature was massive. It might have been the biggest wolf I'd ever seen. As a human, he'd be over six feet tall, well over two hundred pounds.

He might have been even bigger, and even closer.

Becky was still staring. Not that I could blame her—I'm sure he was very handsome. I ran past her, slapped her shoulder, and yelled, "Come on!"

They were flanking us. I looked left and found the second one, this one silver, running alongside us, not racing, just keeping us in view. One was still missing. He'd be either right behind us or right in front us, waiting to ambush.

Shit, we might be in trouble.

"Go, Becky, go!" Our job now was to run for the trap and hope it sprang according to plan. Ben would recognize Becky and tell Stafford and Shumacher not to shoot her. We could do this.

By running, we were only encouraging them. But since they were wolves and not human, my plan to stop and talk reasonably with them was out the window. In the wild, a pack of wolves would work in shifts to run their prey to exhaustion, then strike. If that was their plan, we could outrun them and hope they didn't smell the trap. But that depended on whether or not they were looking at us as prey.

They might have had something else in mind.

I could run fast—I had some of my Wolf's speed and stamina. But I couldn't run as fast as I could as a wolf, as Becky was running now. She pulled ahead of me, and my own Wolf growled and leapt, wanting a chance at that power, to shift and escape. No, not yet, I couldn't let go, I couldn't drop the backpack.

The two wolves angled in, closing in on us. They were both huge, especially next to lithe Becky. This wasn't going to be much of a fight. But we were faster.

Then they shut the pincher. One of them, the silvery one to the left, sprang and tackled Becky. The two of them rolled, a tangle of fur and snarling, wolfish lips pulled back from fierce teeth.

I yelled, my voice loud and grating, "Get away from her!"

The first wolf—the darker, shadowy one whose color I couldn't quite determine—swerved, dodging between Becky and me, separating us. I stopped. He planted himself in front of me and stared, and there it was, the other mark of a werewolf: not just his great size, but the shine of human intelligence, the way I could almost hear him say, "Gotcha." His wolf body language showed he didn't think much of my ability to take him. I bared my teeth at him—showing I didn't think much of him at all.

In the middle of their tangle, Becky slipped away and ran—she remembered the plan and rocketed toward the trap. I dodged out from the shadowy wolf's gaze and cut around him. The two wolves only stayed surprised at our slipperiness for a moment. Becky's pursuer shook himself and kept going, and mine launched likewise. There was only so much ducking and dodging Becky and I could do to keep away from these guys. We had ourselves a regular showdown. I didn't want to have to pull out that gun.

I had stopped looking for the third wolf. I didn't expect the hulking human figure to dash out from behind a tree and grab hold of me. I screamed a shocked burst of sound.

He held on to my shoulders, and we glared at each other, eye to eye, challenging. He had dark brown skin, with a broad face and square jaw, dark eyes, head shaved bald. His muscles strained against a gray T-shirt, and he wore camouflage pants. He also went barefoot. He wasn't linebacker big—he was only a couple of inches taller than I was—but he had weight to him, a solidness that wouldn't budge. Sergeant Joseph Tyler, according to Stafford's dossier.

"Who are you?" he said through a snarling mouth. His nostrils flared with his hard breathing.

"My name's Kitty, I want to help you." I hoped my voice stayed steady and confident. I didn't want to seem weak, I didn't want him to think I was challenging him. We were just two wolves having a chat, right?

Becky, bless her, stopped when Tyler caught me. She was maybe fifty feet away, and holding off the two wolves with pure force of attitude. She was snarling at them, bouncing stiff legged every time they approached. The two of them circled, as if trying to figure out how to get through a prickly thicket. She couldn't keep them off forever.

Tyler studied me, brow furrowed, confused, as if he was trying to figure something out. Human brain arguing with wolf instincts. His hands on my arms were firm—his grip didn't hurt, but he wasn't going to let me go. He leaned forward, bringing his nose close to my neck, smelling me. He was careful, even gentle. Uncertain, he turned my scent over in his nose, considering it, cataloguing it. I was betting I was right—he'd never smelled a female werewolf before.

I kept talking, hoping to nudge him more toward human. "Colonel Stafford told me about you. They're looking for you. Now I don't want anyone to get hurt, but you're heading into my territory and I have to look after my people, so I'd really appreciate if you'd back off, tell your buddies to back off, and we can talk about this. There's no reason we can't talk about this."

He smelled of sweat and exhaustion, and anxiety

strained his face. He didn't seem afraid, but he did seem like a guy at the end of his rope. He didn't know what to do. He looked over to the shadowy wolf.

This wolf was huge, and he was also tense, all his hackles up, his fur standing on end—furious. But he hesitated, braced between me and Becky, trying to decide which way to jump. When Tyler looked at him, the wolf drew back his lip to show teeth and flattened his ears.

Tyler quickly looked away and stared at the ground. He wasn't the alpha. Because he managed to stay in human form, I'd assumed he had the most control. But the shadowy one was Vanderman, who'd murdered his squad-mates when they challenged him. He was the one I had to watch out for. He could bite my head off without thinking about it.

Tyler moved behind me and presented me, prisonerlike, to the dominant wolf. *That's right, boss, it's all her fault*. Great.

Would I seem like a complete dork talking to a big, fanged, angry-looking wolf? Probably.

"I just want to talk," I said calmly. "But I'm not going to show you my belly. We talk as people, we work this out, and nobody gets hurt. Nobody else gets hurt."

I didn't know if the wolf even understood me, or if he only heard my voice as alien buzzing. But Tyler's grip on me relaxed. He was listening to me, and he let me go. I stood my ground.

During the lull, Becky took the opportunity to slouch, tail and ears drooping, limbs buckling, bringing her closer to the ground, in the hopes that the other wolves would read the submissive cues and leave her alone. That was just fine—I wanted them to leave her alone, so she'd get out of this in one piece and with no more emotional scars than absolutely necessary.

I wanted them all to pay attention to me. I was the alpha, I had to act like it. And I had to completely ignore how terrified I was, staring down the three biggest, meanest werewolves I'd ever encountered.

"I know you're looking for a safe place. You're looking for your own territory, and you found this one. Mine. Maybe you even think you can take over and have a pack of your own. But you can't. This is my territory, my people. If you want to stay here, you have to do it on my terms." My stare was a challenge. We both knew it. The shadow wolf's lip curled, showing teeth—no way could I intimidate this guy. I tried anyway.

"Colonel Stafford is here. He's coming after you one way or another. I say we do this the easy way. You all settle down, and we talk." I couldn't turn away from the alpha to look at the others, but I sensed them. Becky occupied the other wolf's attention, and the human one, Tyler, was behind me, lurking just a couple of feet away, his muscles tense, heart rate and breathing fast. He was anxious, but he was listening. I was talking to him as much as I was talking to the alpha. Maybe Tyler could talk Vanderman down if I couldn't.

"No one here's out to get you. You're safe, now."

The wolf gathered himself, and the look in his eyes turned murderous.

"Van, no." Tyler said it low, like a growl.

The wolf jumped at me. I fought instinct, which told me to either run or cower, to curl my back, roll over, and show my belly or get the hell out. I didn't. I lunged right back at him, knowing I was going to get hurt. But if I backed down, we were all screwed.

We crashed into each other, and I grabbed at him, digging my fingers into his fur and shoving, twisting out of the way, using his momentum to get him away from me. His jaws were open, saliva gleaming on long, bared fangs ready to bite and tear, but he swung out. His claws reached for purchase and scraped down my arm, which I had raised to protect myself. I lost more skin that way . . .

I clenched my jaw to keep from screaming.

It was chaos. The silver-gray wolf had taken his leader's cue and attacked Becky; the knot of wolf bodies and fur writhed a few feet away from me. The alpha was gathering himself for another jump, and I turned to face him, because what else could I do? Nearby, Tyler had doubled over, fists pressed to his temples. He was fighting the Change, groaning through clenched teeth.

Before leaping again, the alpha hesitated, looking outward, ears perked up. I smelled it before I heard or saw it: newcomers, human scents on the breeze. Machinery and gun oil. Then I heard the voices, and people crunching through the forest.

"Kitty!" It was Ben. He came running over the ridge and braced against the trunk of a pine.

The alpha wolf swung toward him, teeth bared. No, not Ben, stay away from him—

I was about to hiss and pounce on the alpha when a whip-crack stabbed through the air, and the wolf in front of me yelped.

Stafford and Shumacher were on the ridge, bracing air rifles. And so was Cormac. They'd given him a third tranquilizer gun.

"Not that one, she's ours!" I heard Ben say.

A second shot whined out, and a third. Tyler got the next one, and the alpha got another. Tyler arced his back and fell, and that last shock sent him over the edge. He screamed, and the teeth he bared were wolf fangs. He tore his shirt, struggling to get out of it, and kicked at his pants. The tranquilizer didn't seem to be slowing him down any.

Didn't the military have a few choice technical terms for situations like this?

I was bleeding, panicked, and desperate. Wolf scraped her claws down the inside of my body. Stabs of pain seared my gut, but I had to ignore it, I couldn't shift, I couldn't. I looked around, assessing.

The alpha had slowed; he looked like he wanted to attack, but his limbs kept slipping out from under him. Good.

Becky and her opponent didn't seem to notice the commotion. She kept extricating herself from his grip, and he kept attacking her, pouncing, trying to get his teeth over her neck. He'd get his body over her, and she'd slip away. I couldn't tell if he was trying to rip her up or rape her. I wanted to jump in and tear at the guy myself. That would only make the situation worse; they couldn't hit the male with the tranquilizer while the two wolves were tangled up.

"Becky, back off! Get away from him!" I shouted.

Twisting, she bit at his face, kicked away from him, and ran. He got up to chase her, but more darts followed. He flinched and yelped as they struck his haunch. He tried a few more steps. Then he fell.

It seemed to take a long time for calm to settle over this corner of the forest. We all paused, waiting for something to happen. We only started moving when nothing did.

Tyler had turned before the tranquilizer took hold. He was a reddish-tawny wolf, huge like the others, half tangled in his clothes, slumped to his side, tongue lolling. I stood in the middle of a group of drugged-out wolves.

Across the carnage, Becky looked at me, her back

and tail low, panic in her eyes. Blood marred her snout. I couldn't tell if it was hers or his. I nodded at her and whispered, "Go. We'll find you."

She ran. Running for a few miles—or ten or twenty—would calm her down. We were close to home; she'd find our den and settle down. And I didn't want Stafford and Shumacher getting their hands on her.

"Wait a minute—" Stafford called, pointing at her.

"She's mine, you can't have her!" I shouted at him, baring my teeth.

Everybody froze. I took it all in, each person: Dr. Shumacher, wide-eyed and frightened; Stafford, tense and uncertain, along with a pair of accompanying soldiers; and Cormac, holding the rifle loosely in both hands. Classified each as predator or prey, ones I had to worry about and ones I didn't. Wolfish thinking. Shumacher: prey. Stafford: wasn't worried about him, which struck me as ironic. But Cormac—I could imagine him raising the weapon and firing in a heartbeat. Despite the set, unflinching expression on his face, I could see him deciding whether or not to fire.

Then came Ben, sauntering down the slope toward me, gaze down, ready to circle me, all of his signals calming. "Kitty. It's okay. Pull it together," he said gently. Mate to mate, he spoke to me, and I listened. I stood for a moment just breathing, pulling myself back into myself.

I could look around and see past the chaos. This had probably gone as reasonably well as I could have expected. But I had secretly hoped the rogues would actually listen to me.

If it had just been Tyler, we'd have walked out of here without a scratch. As it was, my right arm was covered in blood.

Ben reached me, and we stood face to face. The look on him was wry, full of worry and exasperation. "Are you okay?"

I tried to scrape off some of the blood and more welled up. "Yeah."

"He got your face, too." He rubbed a thumb across my jawline; it stung. Ben's hand came away bloody. The alpha must have nicked me there when he side-swiped my cheek. I kept telling myself it could have been worse. I leaned my face on Ben's shoulder and let him pull me into a hug.

"Mr. O'Farrell," Shumacher said, her voice panicked. "Be careful, her blood's contagious!"

I hadn't told her about Ben. She hadn't spotted him as a werewolf. I giggled into Ben's shoulder.

"It's okay, Doctor," Ben called to her over his shoulder. "I'm not worried."

"But—"

"I think you should be worried about them." He nodded at the unconscious wolves, bulky shadows in the fading daylight.

Shumacher had to leave us alone. In Ben's arms, I came back to myself.

When I was finally ready to stand on my own, I pulled away. But I kept hold of Ben's hand.

"Was all this worth it?" he said.

"I don't know. Tyler—he actually listened to me. He was almost lucid. But the other two . . ." I shook my head. I wouldn't know until I saw them as people. I wanted to hear their side of it.

Shumacher and Stafford oversaw the next part of the proceedings. This involved Stafford's soldiers bringing out their nets and ropes, laced with strands of silver, to "secure" the wolves. That was the term they used. This basically involved bundling them up until they couldn't move. I didn't want to watch.

Instead, Ben and I joined Cormac, who remained on the fringes of the proceedings.

"I thought you weren't supposed to have any guns," I said, nodding at the rifle in his hands.

"It's technically not a gun," Cormac said.

"Why do I even argue with you?" I said.

"Somebody has to, I suppose," Cormac said, calm as ever. I couldn't tell if he was joking.

Ben held out his hand. "Why don't you give that to me, just in case your parole officer happens to wander by." Cormac handed him the gun without arguing.

"Were you really going to shoot me?" I said.

"What makes you think that?"

"You looked like you were going to shoot me."

His frown was long suffering. "I didn't shoot you. Why are we even talking about this?"

I didn't know, so I turned away, still in a huff, still on edge. Ben was watching us, looking amused.

"We need to find Becky," I said to him.

"Don't you think you should clean up first?" He looked me over.

I was still drenched in blood. The wounds had clotted and itched now rather than hurt; they were already healing. But yeah, I should probably change clothes.

"Kitty, are you all right?" Shumacher marched toward us, away from where Stafford and his men were checking over the knots securing the wolves.

"Do they have enough room to shift back?" I said, looking past her to the captured wolves. "Now that they're asleep they're going to start shifting back."

"We'll have them out of the nets before then," Shumacher assured me. "What about you?"

Yeah, the covered-in-blood thing, right. "I'm fine," I muttered.

She seemed doubtful, wincing in sympathy but also curious. She wasn't looking at me, but was studying the wounds, the rows of claw marks streaking my arm. If she watched long enough she'd see the skin close over as the wounds healed.

I self-consciously tucked my arm in and held it protectively.

Shumacher said, "Kitty, what happened here? What's your assessment of them?"

I didn't want to say. I was worried. I'd dealt with some pretty messed-up werewolves before, but never ones this strong and this far gone. I wasn't sure they'd be much more likely to talk once they were human. I wasn't sure they wanted to be human. If they didn't want to be human, but they couldn't control their wolf sides, where did they belong?

Finally I said, "I want to talk to them as people. See how much they really want help."

"Would you do that? Would you come to talk to them?"

I couldn't say no.

A rhythmic thumping sounded in the distance. Ben and I heard it first and looked up and around.

"Is that a helicopter?" Ben said.

"Colonel Stafford called it in to carry the squad back to Fort Carson."

They really had this worked out, didn't they?

"Kitty, thank you," Shumacher said, before the craft's pounding engine made talking too difficult. "This has been a huge help. I'll call you." She went to join Stafford to help with the prisoner transport. I kept thinking of them as prisoners.

Ben, Cormac, and I started the hike back to our

car. I was glum and scratching at the blood on my arm. I'd have to stop off somewhere to get cleaned up. I thought I had a change of clothes in the car. That would help.

"These are the kinds of werewolves I went after," Cormac said. "They can't control themselves. They're monsters. You can't argue with that."

I couldn't. "You'd advocate just putting silver bullets in them and being done with it. That seems like a crappy homecoming after everything they've been through."

We walked a dozen more yards, picking our way through the woods.

"I bet you Flemming knew," Cormac said finally. "I bet you could look through his notes and find out that he expected this to happen. That you could use werewolves as soldiers and maybe they'd be great, invincible, bloodthirsty, whatever. But you'd ruin them for anything else. They'd never be human again. I'm guessing Flemming knew that and that getting rid of those soldiers was part of his plan."

And again, I couldn't argue. Not just because I'd met Flemming and knew that his plans never took individual fates into account. But because the whole government bureaucracy was like that and Flemming had been, if nothing else, a government bureaucrat. "Well, Flemming sucks."

Back at the car, we didn't talk much. I found a roll of paper towels and a bottle of water to wash off the worst of the mess. I made sure I had the backpack with Becky's clothes, then we went in search of Becky.

As I'd hoped, she was at our usual den, tucked into a hillside in the mountains west of Denver. She was still a wolf, curled up and asleep. She must have just gotten here. She didn't seem to be hurt. I made Ben and Cormac wait back in the car.

Approaching her from upwind, I moved slowly. She'd catch my scent, maybe even hear me, and I hoped she wouldn't be startled. She'd stay asleep and slip back to her human form. Then we could all go home.

When I was still a dozen feet away, she started awake, bracing on four legs like she was ready to run.

"Shh, shh, it's okay. It's just me. I'm just going to hang out and keep watch, okay?" I said, staying low, staying calm. Becky eased, tension leaving her spine, the fur on her back flattening. She crept forward until she was next to me and nuzzled my shoulder, and I breathed into the fur of her neck. She smelled scared and tired. I couldn't blame her. "It's okay, we're all okay," I murmured.

She circled once then curled up again, nose to tail, and went to sleep. I sat with her, my hand resting on her back, and waited.

After a time, maybe half an hour or so, the flesh and muscle under my hand began to shift. I drew away, and almost couldn't watch as her body seemed to melt, her bones losing shape, molding into something else. Bit by bit, fur vanished and skin emerged. This happened to me every month; I'd watched it happen to others often enough, but I still had a disconnect: I still had trouble imagining this happening to me. I didn't like to picture it.

At last, Becky was back, a human shape, naked and tucked into a fetal position. I looked her over—any wounds she had were already healed. She seemed to be sleeping peacefully enough.

I let her sleep for another half hour before gently squeezing her shoulder. "Hey, Becky."

She moaned a little, then sat up all at once, fully alert, looking around as if she expected an attack.

"It's okay, we're alone out here, everything's fine," I said, trying to sound calm.

The memory must have come back to her, because she groaned in annoyance and ran hands through her hair. After looking around a moment, squinting sleepily into the trees above, she rubbed her arms and legs, and hugged herself. Feeling the shape of her own body, bringing herself to the here and now.

"Are you okay?"

"Don't ever ask me to do something like that again," she said, glaring. "Those guys were—" She shuddered, then just shook her head. "I've never seen anything like it. Carl wasn't even that bad."

"Carl didn't do tours of duty in Iraq and Afghanistan on top of being a pissed-off werewolf," I said.

Carl was the old alpha male of our pack. He'd had something of a temper.

"So what's going to happen to them?"

"I don't know. I'm afraid Colonel Stafford may just lock them up and throw away the key."

"You don't think maybe that would be for the best?"

It might end up being the best of a bunch of really bad solutions. But it didn't seem fair. This wasn't what they'd signed up for when Gordon recruited them for his little independent project. I kept forgetting that life wasn't fair. I kept trying to make it fair. I said, "I guess I'd like them to at least have a chance." A chance to decide, a chance to get their lives back, if they wanted them.

That alpha. Vanderman. I wanted to look him in the eyes as a human—see if there was anything human left in there.

"Do you have my clothes?" Becky said after a moment.

I handed her my backpack, and she sighed gratefully.

We didn't say much on the drive back. Ben drove, Cormac sat in the passenger seat, and from the backseat Becky kept giving him furtive glances. When we reached her apartment in Littleton, she fled the car quickly, barely saying good-bye.

We drove on, and I leaned forward. "Do all the girls run from you like that?"

Cormac just glared.

"Is she okay?" Ben said, giving both me and Cormac long-suffering glances.

"I think so," I said. "She's a little shaken up."

"And what about you?"

I had to think about it a minute, which said something right there. I put on a good face. "It takes a little more than a couple of insane werewolves to scare me these days."

"So they're insane," Ben said.

"Not really," I said, at the same time Cormac said, "Yeah." We glanced at each other.

"But we're done now, right? You did what they asked, our territory's not being invaded anymore, and we don't have to deal with those guys, right?" Ben said.

That would be too easy. I looked out the window and grimaced.

"You're not agreeing with me," Ben said.

"I want to talk to them."

"Talking fixes everything," Cormac grumbled.

"Kitty," Ben said, "this isn't somebody calling in to your show because they have a hangnail. This, it's too . . . too—"

"Too big?" I said. "Think I can't handle it?"

"That's not what I said," he muttered. We looked at each other in the rearview mirror. "I just don't want you to get hurt."

I didn't want me to get hurt, either. "I have to try."

"I know." His thin smile said, *look, see, I'm trying to be supportive*. Even though I was afraid that he was right, and that I'd be better off walking away and not worrying about the fates of the three men. But then I'd always wonder.

Chapter 6

THE NEXT morning I called Dr. Shumacher to set up an appointment to talk to her patients. That afternoon, I returned to the hospital at Fort Carson.

Shumacher, clipboard in hand, led me to the elevator, and we descended to a basement level, all concrete and fluorescent lights. Flemming's basement office and laboratory at the NIH in Washington, D.C. had looked a little like this, tucked away and secretive, promising dark secrets I'd rather not discover. The hospital smell, antiseptic and haunted, was pervasive and inspired anxiety. Intellectually, I could rationalize that hospitals were good places where people got better. But on a gut level, hospitals meant people were hurt. I braced for horrors.

Several doors along the hallway were open, showing infirmaries, hospital beds, storage closets, laboratories. It was a little comforting; this was all normal, nothing to be frightened of here. Then we came to the closed door at the end of the hall. Shumacher put her hand on the knob and gave me a grim look. Maybe a look of warning. Or a look of despair—she was at the end of her options.

She opened the door, and I followed her inside.

The room was large, all off-white walls and tile, sterile government issue. The lights in the ceiling were dimmed. A few chairs were placed facing a Plexiglas wall that divided the room. The back of the space, maybe fifteen by twenty feet, was a specialized prison. I recognized the Flemming-designed werewolf holding cell: silver shavings embedded in the paint on the walls, giving them a dull patina. A silver-lined door was cut into the Plexiglas, along with a silver-lined slot to shove food through. Theoretically, a werewolf was strong enough to break down the walls, given time and patience. But most werewolves would stay as far away from the silver boundary as possible.

The three men in the cell had, in fact, positioned themselves away from the walls. They'd been given clothes, fortunately. I was afraid they hadn't been, that their keepers had entirely given up on thinking of them as human. More encouragingly, the men were bothering to wear the clothes. On the other hand, they had beards started, and their military crew cuts had turned shaggy.

I recognized Joseph Tyler, who sat on the floor,

hunched over, his back to the door, apparently asleep. Or maybe just indifferent. He wore fatigue pants and a T-shirt, like when I'd seen him before.

In the middle of the cell, a smaller white guy lay on his side, curled up, definitely asleep. I recognized Sergeant Ethan Walters from his picture. I was used to seeing werewolves wake up after shifting looking just like that, in a shape that recalled a sleeping wolf, fetal, limbs tucked in. But he was wearing pants. So maybe he just slept like that all the time. I'd pegged him as the weakest of the three, at least as far as the pecking order went. It may have been that he was just the most vulnerable, the farthest gone, the one needing the most help. I tried to be sympathetic, even though he'd been the one to attack Becky. I still wanted to beat him up for that.

The third soldier paced the window in front of me, back and forth. He kept his gaze outward, to the door, even as he changed direction. Back and forth, about five steps one way and five steps the other. The neurotic habit of a caged predator. He'd worn a clean streak on the tile floor with his pacing. I'd never seen him in this form, but I knew him by his movements, by the rage in his eyes, a focused burning. I could feel the force of it almost as soon as I entered the room. This was the alpha male, the huge shadow wolf. Sergeant Luke Vanderman. He was in his late twenties, over six feet tall and more than solid. Forged and tempered. He went shirtless, showing off a sculpted chest, shadowed with brown hair.

He was more than a little impressive. I didn't know whether to tremble in fear or in awe. *Now there's an alpha* . . . Down, girl.

When Dr. Shumacher moved aside and I came into sight, Vanderman lunged forward. He all but pressed himself to the glass, his teeth bared. His right hand slapped against the partition, his fingers bent into claws.

If I had flinched, if I had stepped back, it would have been all over. I'd never have been able to talk to him. But somehow I held my ground. My heart was racing, and Vanderman would be able to hear it, be able to smell the anxiety in the sweat breaking out on me, the ventilation system drawing my scent into his cell. But I didn't look away, I didn't slouch, didn't cringe. My tail, only imaginary at the moment, stayed up.

I just kept thinking that I had faced worse than this. And there was that wall between us.

When he hit the window, Tyler looked. Walters sat up, his gaze wary. Tyler turned to face me and his eyes widened. I gave him a thin smile. He seemed shocked to see me.

"I know you," the alpha sergeant said. His voice was low, threatening, as if he was talking through clenched teeth.

"Yeah. We met." I tried to stick to my soothing

talk-radio-host voice. My NPR voice. "It's nice to finally talk to you."

"What do you want?"

"To help," I said, but it sounded kind of vague and lame. Help how?

"Maybe she's a bribe," said Walters. He crouched now, balanced on his fingertips, ready to spring. He watched me, his lips parted, and I'd have sworn he was drooling. "We get some ass, calm us down—"

"Grow up, Walters," Tyler said.

"Is that why you're here?" Vanderman said. Growled. He looked like he was going to burst out of his skin any minute.

"Nobody is touching my ass," I said.

"Sounds like a dare," he said, lips parting in a hungry smile. He leaned right up to the wall, his breath fogging the glass.

"I'm just here to talk. Werewolf to werewolf."

"Bitch."

"Yeah," I said.

He snarled and returned to pacing. Back and forth, glaring at me the whole time.

"Sergeant, we can't release you until we're sure you're not going to be a threat to yourself and others," Shumacher said, entirely scientific and rational.

Vanderman slammed against the Plexiglas, pounding it with hands bent like claws, as if he could scratch his way through and get to her.

Startled, she stepped back, fear rattling through her. Vanderman was the boss here and everyone knew it. He'd kill Shumacher if the wall wasn't there.

Calmly, I stepped between Shumacher and Vanderman, blocking his view of her. Protecting her, showing that he'd have to go through me to get her. He was a bully, and I'd dealt with bullies before.

"Could you leave us alone for a few minutes?" I said over my shoulder to Shumacher.

"Are you sure?" She clung to her clipboard like it was a shield.

"I'll be fine, and I'm sure you have a million closed-circuit cameras in here, so you're not going to miss anything, right?"

"Call if you need anything," she said. She pressed her lips in a frown and left, heels clicking on tile.

The door closed behind her, and the air went out of the room, as if we were now vacuum sealed.

For a second I panicked. What the hell did I say to these guys? What could I possibly say that they'd take seriously? But they weren't just badass Green Berets who'd been through a hell I couldn't imagine. They were baby wolves without their alpha. They'd been floundering since Gordon was killed.

Tyler faced me now. "Captain Gordon didn't tell us there were any female werewolves."

Vanderman pointed at him. "Don't talk to her."

"I imagine Gordon didn't tell you a lot of things,"

I said. They were just babies. I'd talked down baby wolves before. That was how I'd have to approach them. "Sergeant Vanderman, what do you want?"

"I want to rip out your throat after I fuck you hard," he said.

"Okay, that's helpful," I said, sarcastic. "Now I want to hear from your human side. Ignore your wolf for a minute and tell me what you really want."

"Maybe that is my human side," he said, baring teeth. And yeah, maybe he was right. He wouldn't be the world's first misogynistic homicidal bastard. I couldn't forget, he'd already killed three of his own teammates.

I smiled. "Then I get to tell Colonel Stafford to pull the trigger on you guys."

They cringed. All of them. Even Vanderman, and I thought I knew why—at some level, their human sides were still observing the army chain of command. Stafford had power over them and they knew it.

"Let's back up a minute," I said. "You guys are in serious trouble. Unless you start pulling yourselves together, you're going to be locked up for a very long time. Shumacher and Stafford are the ones who get to decide whether you're safe enough to be let out of here. I may be the only one who thinks there's a chance you might ever be safe enough to go free. You need to start talking to me."

For a long time, none of them spoke. I kept my gaze on Vanderman—the dangerous one—but could see the others in the corners of my vision. They watched Vanderman as well—looking for cues, waiting to see what he would do before they reacted. Maybe I should have talked to them separately.

"What is there to talk about?" Vanderman said finally. And off to the side, Tyler relaxed. He wanted Vanderman to talk.

"Yarrow. Crane. Estevan," I said. "What happened?"

Vanderman grimaced. "They wouldn't listen to me. They put us all in danger."

"You lost control," I said.

"*I'm* the alpha, they had to *listen*—"

"The alpha is supposed to keep his pack safe," I said.

"I'm *trying*," he said, voice low, snarling.

And I believed him. He really did think he was leading, being the alpha, by smacking down the lesser wolves who dared to challenge him. He was doing what his wolf told him to, and his wolf was angry and afraid.

"I know."

"I didn't want to hurt them," he said.

"You're going to keep hurting people until you can learn to control your wolf. Before you can take care of anyone else, you have to get yourself under control. So let's talk about you for a minute. What do you want? What do you want to do next?"

"I want to go back. Finish the job."

"Back—to Afghanistan?" The answer baffled me. Why would anyone want to go back there? But Vanderman nodded, and I saw the determination in him. It was the first time he hadn't looked murderous. He was focused on his job. "Then you have to get this thing under control. You know that, don't you?"

"Who are you to tell me that? What do you know about it, you bitch, you fucking bitch—" He threw himself against the glass. I would have flinched if I hadn't seen it coming, in his bared teeth and bloodshot eyes. He really did seem more animal than human. He must have known he couldn't hurt me, but he kept driving at me, trying to scare me.

And okay, I was scared. For him as much as of him. But I was the one in control here, which made me the alpha, which was a little gratifying. He hadn't figured that out yet. He thought beating people up made him the alpha.

I turned away, showing him that he wasn't worth my time, and studied Tyler and Walters.

"What about you guys?" I said to the other two. "What do you want?"

Vanderman moved in between them and me. "We're a pack. We have to stick together."

"That doesn't mean anything here," I said. "You're human beings with free will. I want to hear them talk."

Walters looked back and forth between Vanderman and me, shivering almost, trying to decide whom he was more terrified of. I wanted to yell at him to straighten up, to grow a spine, to stop cowering. But he was scared. Screaming at him wouldn't change that.

"I want to go home," Tyler said, frowning, sad. "I want to be normal."

"Sergeant, what the fuck are you doing?" Vanderman said around gritted teeth.

"Van, we can't keep going like this," Tyler said. "They're going to keep us locked up here forever if we don't figure something out."

"Shut up!"

"This isn't how it's supposed to be. Gordon wouldn't even recognize us with how messed up we are."

"Shut the fuck up!"

"Van—"

Vanderman sprang, bowling into Tyler, driving him across the room and shoving him against the far wall. Tyler clawed at him, digging his hands into the skin of the man's back looking for purchase. Twisting his body, he wrenched out of the sergeant's grip. They fought, grappling at each other, locking arms around shoulders and trying to get the other to show belly. I was glad to be on this side of the glass.

I hoped Shumacher was taking notes, because from a behavior standpoint, this was fascinating. When Tyler answered my question, he essentially transferred authority to me—he decided he was going to listen to and obey me rather than Vanderman. And boy, did that piss Vanderman off. But it felt like progress. Sort of.

"Stop it!" I said. Of course they didn't listen. So maybe I didn't have all that much authority. "Vanderman, Tyler! Back off! Back down!" This was how the other men had died. Any minute now, they'd shift and start tearing each other to bits.

A keening, high-pitched electric siren blared through the room, rattling the concrete walls, vibrating up through my feet. I doubled over, hands to my ears to block the noise. Not that it worked, because the noise streaked along the inside of my skull and made my nerve endings shrivel up.

In a couple of seconds, it was over. Though it had seemed to drag on and linger in the way my teeth suddenly felt like Jell-O, it had probably only been a short blast. And it had been effective. When I looked in the cell, Tyler and Vanderman had separated, and were slowly unfolding themselves from protective crouches, hands over their ears, much as I was.

Huh. Dog whistle. Werewolf siren. Whatever.

The room's door opened behind me and Shumacher entered.

"That totally sucked ass," I said. My voice was kind of shaky. I tried to glare aggressively, not sure if I pulled it off.

"I'm sorry, I didn't think there was a choice."

"What was that?" I demanded, trying to regain my

composure—steadying my breathing and putting my heart back into my chest.

"It's the fastest way to get their attention," she said, nodding into the cage where the wolves had, in fact, calmed down. At least they weren't fighting anymore. Vanderman started pacing again, a half dozen steps back and forth along the glass. Walters retreated to a corner where he sat, hunched in on himself, and Tyler settled into a crouch and glared out at us.

We were right back where we started.

"Kitty?" Shumacher said softly, indicating that I should come back outside with her.

In silence, we went back to the conference room from my first visit. Colonel Stafford had arrived in the meantime, and I was betting he'd witnessed the whole exchange between me and the others via video monitor. So much for convincing them I could be successful.

"That's what we're dealing with," Stafford said. "Any bright ideas?"

Frowning, I sat next to Shumacher. What could I say? "Vanderman's setting the tone. A really negative tone. You might try separating them, dealing with them one-on-one to get away from the pack mentality."

"Or I could just court-martial them all on murder charges," Stafford said.

That probably seemed logical to him. But it hardly seemed fair, at least not for Tyler and Walters.

"They'll plead insanity because of the lycanthropy," Shumacher said, as though they'd had this conversation before.

"They'd still be locked up. That may be as good as they're going to get."

In Vanderman's case, it was maybe even the right thing to do. I remembered the look in his eyes, his single-mindedness. He was a fighter and he couldn't shut it off.

"But the others?" I said. "Is there any evidence that they directly participated in the murders? Tyler and Walters may not have had anything to do with it. The pack dynamics mean they're submissive to Vanderman, deferring to him."

"Evidence says it was all Vanderman. I'm willing to consider that the others were coerced. But as much as I'd love to put Tyler and Walters back in the field, if you can't help them, they'll have to stay where they are."

"There has to be a way," I said, but of course it wasn't that easy. "They've never seen functional werewolves living in society. They're like those wild children living on their own in the woods—"

"Raised by wolves?" Shumacher said wryly.

Except wolves were more civilized than they were. "If we could show them, give them an example to follow . . ." They needed to be taught. I wondered if it was as simple as that. If they could be taught, if they would just listen . . .

Shumacher leaned forward. "Could you arrange that? If we moved them to Denver? Exposed them to your pack, acclimated them."

I wanted a moment to consider the implications. I didn't particularly want to bring my people into this any more than I already had. They weren't therapists or guinea pigs. But then neither was I.

"Kitty?" Shumacher prompted.

"Tyler and Walters, maybe," I said finally. "Tyler is listening to me, and Walters is submissive. He'll follow my lead if we get him away from Vander-man." Vanderman was the killer. He was the one we had to worry about. If we got the others away from him, maybe we could influence them.

"Colonel?" Shumacher asked.

He thought a moment, tapping fingers on the table-top. The easy thing to do would be for him to throw away the key. But maybe he would take a chance.

"All right," he said. "Let's try it."

Shumacher sighed, relieved. "Then it's settled. I'll find facilities for them and we can get started as soon as we can."

"And Vanderman?" I said.

"I think Vanderman's finished," Stafford said.

So they were giving up on him. And I couldn't honestly say I was sorry to hear it.

Chapter 7

I CALLED BEN to let him know I was on the way home, and an hour or so later stumbled through the door around suppertime. I felt mostly numb—zombieish, even. Like someone else was guiding my body via remote control. What exactly had I agreed to again?

Ben was in the kitchen, making something that smelled like food. My nerves started to melt, which was both a good and a bad thing. I wasn't sure I was ready for self-reflection quite yet.

"You look terrible," he said. Not the best greeting ever, but it was nice that he noticed.

"I had a rough afternoon." I wandered over, wanting to investigate the scents my nose was taking in. Fresh meat. He was doing something with steak and red wine. I wanted to tear into it.

"How's the werewolf Dirty Dozen? Quarter dozen, I suppose." he said, meeting me halfway and gathering me into his arms. I leaned against him, pressing my face to his shoulder, wrapping myself in his embrace—the good, solid, protective weight of his arms across my back. I turned my nose to his hairline and took in his scent, mildly sweaty, musky, the hint of fur, of his wolf under the skin.

I was definitely home. I took his face in my hands and kissed him to seal the deal. Ben enthusiastically reciprocated, which helped banish lingering tension. I was eager to continue the trend. My hands crawled down his sides, tugging at the hem of his shirt until they found access, then slipped up his back, pressing against his warm skin. He made a sound and pulled me closer, so that I had to hitch a leg around his. His heart was pounding against my chest. We fit together snugly.

Then he said, murmuring into my cheek, "Um. I have to go check the steaks."

"Not really."

"'Fraid so. Unless you want them overdone."

We both liked our steaks rare. Reluctantly, I let him go. Flushed and smiling, I stayed in the kitchen, leaning against the wall and watching him work.

"What's going to happen to them?" he asked.

"They're giving up on Vanderman. Court-martial and locked up for life, probably."

"Rough."

"Yeah, but I don't know what else to do. He isn't stable. He'd barely talk to me. And he is guilty of murder."

"It's not like you to give up on anyone."

"I'm going to try to help Tyler and Walters. They'll be transferred to a VA hospital up here and I'm going to help . . . socialize them, I guess."

"You think it'll work?"

"I know Cormac would say it's too late. But I guess I want to prove someone can come back from that." My same old line: I wanted to believe our human sides were stronger. Or at least just as strong.

Ben turned a wry smile. "It's not your job, you know. You don't have to try to save everyone."

I frowned and looked away. I couldn't save everyone; I'd had that demonstrated to me all too clearly. But if you didn't try, you might end up not saving anyone. I had to try.

"Who else is going to do it?" I said. "Besides, I don't think of it as a job so much as a . . . a vocation."

"Sometimes you can't fix everything. You can argue your best case in front of the most sympathetic judge and jury in the world—and sometimes you still won't win."

"I'm not sure this is about winning," I said. "It's about proving that we're human. That we deserve a chance."

"The life you save may be your own?" he said.

I gave him a grim smile.

THE NEXT day at work, I waited for Dr. Shumacher's call. I wanted to hear that Tyler and Walters had arrived safely and happily in Denver, and that they were eager to embark on bright, happy, well-adjusted lives. I was afraid I would find out there'd been another breakout, and that the trio was again rampaging across the countryside. I was afraid Shumacher would tell me that Colonel Stafford had decided a few silver bullets were the only solution after all.

My phone kept ringing, as usual, but none of the calls came from Dr. Shumacher. It was making me cranky.

I answered yet another call from my desk phone to hear Lisa at reception say, "Hi . . . um, Kitty?"

"What?" I just about snarled that time.

Lisa sounded a little shaky. "There's someone here to see you. He doesn't have an appointment, says his name is Harold Franklin.

Harold Franklin, president of Speedy Mart. Here? "Really?"

"He says he wants to talk to you. Should I send him up?"

"No, that's okay, I'll meet him downstairs," I said, scrambling to gather my thoughts. Why would he be here? He ought to be talking to me through our lawyers. That was the whole point of having lawyers, so you didn't have to talk to people you were officially mad at. My paranoia got the better of me and I decided I wanted to meet him in the open, with people watching, in case he'd decided on more direct and nefarious action.

I was supposed to be a big, scary monster, so why

did I spend so much time worrying about people killing me?

I ran down the stairs and emerged into the KNOB lobby.

He was alone, standing near the reception desk and gazing around the lobby with the abstract interest of someone killing time. He was tall, older—in his early sixties, maybe—his short cropped hair gone to white. He wore a gray suit and overcoat that were probably expensive, and held himself with a lifetime's worth of confidence and authority. Here was a man used to running empires—corporate empires. The only kind that mattered these days.

"Ah, Ms. Norville," he said, turning his attention to me.

And why did he make me think of vampires? He wasn't one. He had a living, beating heart, not to mention it was full daylight outside. It was probably the "I could own you all" attitude.

"Mr. Franklin," I said, and approached him with my hand politely offered for shaking, which he did in standard corporate fashion. Nothing suspicious here. "Would it be a cliché to say that this is a surprise?"

He chuckled politely. "I won't tell if you won't."

There was really no nice way to make the next conversational gambit. "Um . . . why exactly are you here?" Here in Denver, here in my building, talking to me . . .

"Is there someplace we can talk privately?" he

said, glancing around to indicate the public nature of the lobby, including Lisa, who was failing to pretend to ignore us.

I winced in false apology. "Actually, you know what? I think we'd better talk right here."

He smiled as if he'd scored a point. Like he'd proven that I was too insecure to talk in private, that I was actually worried, or something. Oh yeah? Well, I scored a point by not caring about that. He shouldn't even be here while he was suing me. Not without our lawyers. I wanted witnesses.

"All right, then," he said. "I want to make you an offer."

"Maybe you should have made me an offer before filing a lawsuit."

"You might not have taken me seriously, then."

We'd expected some kind of offer—but certainly not delivered in person. I almost pulled my cell phone out of my pocket and called Ben right there. This guy was playing a game that I didn't have a copy of the rules for.

"You want to make me an offer, why not call my lawyer? Aren't you jeopardizing your suit just by being here?" I asked the question knowing he'd have a rehearsed answer, that he probably had an answer for everything.

"Lawyers have their place, but I like to take the measure of my opponents in person. Look them in the eye."

This smacked of corporate backroom dealing. So not my milieu. Maybe I should have taken him to KNOB's college-chic conference room to throw him off his game. Not that anything would throw this guy off his game.

His left hand hung at his side, closed in a fist, as if he was holding something. A cell phone maybe. Whatever it was was hidden, and my gaze kept dropping to his hand, hoping for a glimpse. I had to mentally shake myself, bringing my focus back to him.

I crossed my arms and stared him down. "All right. I may regret this, but what's your offer?"

"I'll drop the case. All I need is a public apology during your show."

I was almost surprised that the offer wasn't more . . . surprising. "Oh, is that all?"

"It's reasonable. Neither of us shells out for a court case, neither of us wastes the time, and no harm's done."

Except maybe to my reputation. I couldn't remember—had I ever apologized to anyone on my show, ever?

"But for me to apologize—that would assume I was wrong. So. Am I wrong?"

He chuckled again, sounding even more condescending. "Ms. Norville, is anything you say on your show the truth? When you tell everyone you're a werewolf, are you telling the truth?"

"Come on, I went over all that years ago. I'm on

film, for crying out loud." This was starting to piss me off. "Here's the thing, Mr. Franklin. Everything I talked about on my show regarding you and Speedy Mart was pure speculation. I can't prove if it's the truth or not. I said that. But your overreaction to the whole thing makes me wonder if I'm on to something. Well? Am I on to something?"

He studied me a moment; I couldn't guess what he was thinking. Then he smiled broadly. "It doesn't matter what I believe. My difficulty is that a lot of people out there believe. They're your bread and butter. They listen to you, whether or not you're telling the truth."

I bet he practiced that speech. I bet he worked real hard to make it sound ominous. I glared. "Did you really think you could come here and make threats and that I'd just roll over and show you my belly?"

His eyes narrowed, a hint of anger. Like he really had expected that to happen.

"I'm not making any threats. I'll be in touch, Ms. Norville." He left, his Italian leather shoes squeaking on the tile.

What a jerk.

"Who the heck was that?" Lisa asked.

I had a feeling there were a couple of answers to that. Harold Franklin, corporate bigwig. Confident businessman. Supernatural conspirator? "That," I said, "was a giant headache."

* * *

I CALLED the lawyer who was handling the lawsuit, to let her know what had happened. She seemed to think the visit might be a basis for throwing out the case, which made Franklin's visit even stranger. It made me think, again, that the lawsuit was a smoke screen for something else entirely. Which begged the obvious question—smoke screen for what? Then I called Ben and told him what had happened, and he responded with a detached-sounding, "Huh." And then he said, again, how his specialty was criminal defense rather than civil law and he couldn't give a professional opinion, but it was a fascinating case all the same. So nice that someone was enjoying this.

I MADE another call. Digging through the log for the last show, I found the phone number for Charles from Shreveport, the guy who claimed that Franklin caused Hurricane Katrina, and who seemed to have a personal grudge against the guy.

The phone rang, until someone answered—a man, but not Charles's voice. "Hello?"

"Hi, I'm looking for Charles?" I said, scribbling on the margins of my notebook paper. I was hoping to have some notes to take.

"Charles Beauregard?" the voice said.

"I think so."

"You're not a friend or relative?"

I stopped doodling and straightened. That didn't sound good. "No—has something happened?"

"May I ask who you are and why you're calling?" The formal, official tone to the voice made sense now—this wasn't a roommate or friend. This was someone with authority who just happened to pick up the phone.

Since I couldn't come up with a slick and plausible story fast enough, I had only one alternative. "My name is Kitty Norville, and I host a talk radio show. Charles called in to the show last week with a pretty wild story and I wanted to follow up."

"Ms. Norville, I'm a medical examiner here. Charles Beauregard was killed at his home over the weekend."

Coincidence, right? Because if you ruled out coincidence, the world became a tangled web of conspiracy. I spoke carefully. "I'm really sorry to hear that. May I ask how he died?"

"He was struck by lightning."

That seemed pretty clear cut. Weird, but clear cut. Except for the panic tapping in the back of my brain.

"Is there anything else I can help you with?" the medical examiner asked.

"No. I guess not. Thanks for your help."

So much for Charles from Shreveport. I wondered if I should add a mark to my map—this would have fit right in with the story he'd told me.

Next I called Cormac. It might have been to simply revel in the fact that I could call him, to get his advice when something weird happened. For the last couple of years, if I wanted to get his advice I had to drive a hundred-plus miles to Cañon City, sit in a sparse, stinking concrete visiting room, and talk to him through glass.

His phone rang and rang, which was normal. Or at least, had been normal. At last, he answered.

"Hey," he said, sounding rushed, like he'd just come in from outside or had been boiling water on the stove.

"Hey," I said. "Is this a bad time?"

"No. What's going on?"

"I've got some new info on the Speedy Mart case—Harold Franklin's in town."

"What's he doing here?"

"Coming to see me and offer a deal to drop the lawsuit."

He made a noise of surprise. "Can he do that? What kind of deal?"

"He wants me to apologize on the air," I said. "I didn't go for it; lawsuit's still on. He may have been trying to bait me."

"Look you in the eye, laugh in your face, that kind of thing?" he said.

"Almost his exact words."

"Classy," he said with a grunt. "We gotta be able to find something on this guy. There's more to this than a libel suit."

"That's what I keep thinking. There's something else—I tried to call the guy who called in to the show. The one who blamed Katrina on Franklin? To find out where he got his info."

"What did he say?"

"Nothing—he was struck by lightning and killed over the weekend."

"That's a hell of a coincidence."

"Either that or Franklin can summon lightning strikes to kill people."

"Don't get ahead of yourself," he said. "I've got a lot more stones to turn before we start admitting that this guy can control the weather."

"So Charles from Shreveport was *right*?" I said, a little too shrilly.

"I didn't say that," Cormac said.

"And what does he want with *me*? I'd probably never have mentioned him on the show again if he hadn't sued me."

"That's the real question, isn't it?" Cormac said. He sounded so calm, like this was the plot of a movie we were discussing, rather than my very-real legal troubles. If he'd been standing in front of me, I'd want to shake him. And he'd stand there and take it, calmly.

He continued, "Any idea where Franklin is staying?"

"No. He came to the KNOB offices."

"Okay. I'll track him down."

"Thanks. And don't get in any trouble, okay?"

He'd already hung up. But Cormac didn't need me to tell him not to get in trouble, right?

Chapter 8

AT LEAST this time I was in the same room with the rogue wolves. It felt like progress, except that only Tyler and Walters faced me. Vanderman was still in custody at Fort Carson and was pretty much skunked. Now we just had to move past that.

The room had been transformed into what I was coming to think of as the NIH special: a cell with silver-flecked paint and probably lots of special features I didn't know about—like that siren. A cell for werewolves, cut off from the rest of the hospital. They didn't even have a window. Instead of watching them through Plexiglas, Shumacher monitored them on a closed-circuit TV system. These guys probably wondered if they were ever going to get to live in a house again. At least they had furniture now: a pair of cots, one plain plastic table and a set of plain plastic chairs, and even a TV mounted on the wall.

I wanted to sit. I wanted us all to sit around the table, but that wasn't going to happen. Tyler was pacing along the back wall; Walters was crouched on the cot, gaze darting between us. Trying to decide which of us was the alpha. I stood so I could stay at their level; sitting would have put myself lower than Tyler at least, and would have called my dominance into question. Werewolf pack bullshit. But it mattered and I couldn't ignore it. Hands on the back of a chair, staying as relaxed as I could manage, I watched them.

They smelled wild and terrible; the room stank with the scent. All werewolves, even in human form, smelled a little wild, a hint of fur and musk touching their otherwise human bodies. These two smelled more wolf than human. More than that, though, they smelled frightened, thick with adrenaline and uncertainty.

What did I tell them? That they should at least try to overcome the instincts to fight and run? That life—a human life—was worth living? They needed therapy, and I was vastly unqualified to be a therapist. Especially when Ben was right and I ought to be getting a little therapy myself. But who else was going to help them? Who else could begin to understand?

"Tyler, sit down," I said. "Please. You're driving me crazy."

He looked at me, shot me a skin-searing glare—then ducked his gaze and slouched into one of the chairs across the table. I was amazed; I tried not to show it. Happy with that little victory, I let Walters continue hunkering. I didn't want to press the cornered wolf, as it were.

"Well," I said. "What's next?" Thinking out loud more than anything. I didn't have to do anything but listen to them talk. That's what therapists did, right? If only.

"Van should be here," Tyler said.

"He's not. I'm sorry," I said curtly.

"We're a pack. We should be together," Tyler said.

"That's your wolf talking. You have to take care of yourselves right now. Vanderman hasn't done a very good job looking after you, has he? He hasn't been a very good alpha. That's what got you all into this mess in the first place."

"What do you expect us to do?"

"Talking's a good start."

Tyler's body language was nearly human. He was slouching unhappily, but his attention was on me. He was leaning on the table, his fingers laced together. Not clenched like claws. Walters, on the other hand, was almost cowering. I could see the ghosts of ears pinned back and a tail clamped close to his body. There was the kind of deference a canine showed because he was offering respect to a leader. Then there was the kind of deference he showed because he thought he was going to get smacked down. Because he didn't know what was going on, and he was afraid. Walters hadn't said a word, yet. He just kept staring at me. If I could break that stare, I might be able to shake him.

"I respect your loyalty to Sergeant Vanderman. But if you want to go home, if you don't want to end up locked in a cell for the rest of your lives, you're going to have to let him go and move on."

"It's not right," Tyler said. "It feels like abandoning him."

"Is this some army 'leave no man behind' thing?" I said, trying to keep my temper—and sarcasm—in check. The last thing the room needed was more aggression.

"You don't understand."

"What Vanderman did to Yarrow, Crane, Estevan—how does that fall into the philosophy? Isn't that leaving someone behind?"

Walters got up and started pacing, just a few feet along the back wall. I ignored him. Let him work off the nervous energy; I could only keep these guys calm by staying calm myself.

I continued. "Captain Gordon seems like he was a good guy. It sounds like he really took care of you. Vanderman shows all the signs of only caring about the power, without any of the responsibility. Now, I don't know how much you really know about werewolves, how much Gordon really taught you. But it's not just supposed to be about the power and playing follow-the-leader. You still have to at least try to be human, if you want to keep living with people."

"We're not people," Tyler said in a rough voice.

That made my stomach sink. I held on to my sanity by clinging to the belief that I was human—maybe a different kind of human with some wacky supernatural problems going on, but human all the same, with a husband, a job, a mortgage, a family, and all the other good stuff.

If Tyler didn't believe he was human and a part of human society, what chance did he have?

"Did Gordon warn you?" I said. "Did he tell you what it was like before he did this to you?"

Tyler winced, as if he was trying to remember something he'd forgotten—or that the remembering was difficult. "It seems like such a long time ago now. But he didn't talk about this. He said he would always be there, he said he'd look after us. We'd always be a pack."

Nobody should ever make that kind of promise.

"What did he say to you guys to recruit you into this? How did he convince you that this was a good idea?"

"We had a job to do in Afghanistan. An impossible job. We didn't have the tools, the resources. But Gordon—he had a way. Of course it wasn't easy, but if you have the chance to get the job done—if you have the ability—you take it. He promised to make us strong—unbeatable. And he did." Tyler raised his gaze and set his jaw, determined.

I wondered if part of the problem with Vanderman was that the pack never accepted him as a replacement for Gordon. They—or at least Tyler—still saw Gordon as their alpha. Their captain. Vanderman couldn't take over, but he was too strong for the others to dominate.

Walters slouched now, arms crossed, still hunched in on himself. But I got the feeling he was listening to me.

I leaned on the back of the chair. "I had to ask, because I didn't want to become a werewolf. I didn't get a choice. I have a hard time understanding why anyone would ask for this." The only situations I'd seen where I could even begin to understand involved life-threatening illnesses—if the alternative was dying, why not become a werewolf?

After a moment, Tyler said, "That's rough. I'm sorry."

"Yeah. Thanks. But you know, moving on."

"You think it's that easy? Just move on?" Tyler said, with a harsh chuckle.

I shrugged. "I didn't say it was easy. Look, you have a lot to think about. I'd like to come back and talk some more. Maybe bring a friend. Figure out what we have to do to spring you guys. Is that okay?"

"Why are you even asking?" Tyler said. "You can do whatever you want. You're the alpha here, right?"

I smiled. "Thanks. I wasn't sure you'd admit it."

"You—you're more like Captain Gordon than Van," Walters said. His voice seemed like an intrusion—startling, unexpected. He was still slouching.

"I'll take that as a compliment," I said. "I'll see you guys in a day or two."

"It's not Van's fault," Walters said. I stopped, my hand almost to the door to knock for Shumacher. "It's mental illness, isn't it? We're all crazy. It's not Van's fault."

Frowning, I nodded. Maybe they'd decide for sure at his court-martial.

Shumacher, her ever-present clipboard tucked under her arm, let me out of the cell. I felt Tyler and Walters watching me until the door closed behind us. We walked to the office she'd taken over.

"It's hard judging any progress with just talking," Shumacher said, sighing as she set down her clipboard and leaned on the desk.

I shrugged. I tended to get a lot out of talking. "I'm going on instinct here. I'm just trying to get a feel for them. Whether there's . . . I don't know."

"Whether there's any hope for them?" she said.

"Yeah. That."

"And?"

"I don't know. I want to get a second opinion. Tyler—I think he's actually doing well. But Walters isn't engaged. They're a long way from being well. But I'd like to talk to them again."

Shumacher looked for a moment as if she was

going to say something, but then pursed her lips, holding back words. When she smiled, it was a mask. "Let's make our next appointment, then. I look forward to it."

She didn't think they could be rehabilitated. She'd given up on them. That gave me a burning desire to prove her wrong.

I MADE a different sort of appointment for that night, at Psalm 23.

The nightclub always made me anxious. I preferred meeting Rick, the Master vampire of Denver, at my place, New Moon. But he'd said this was more convenient tonight. I wondered what problems he was dealing with. At least he was almost always willing to talk to me when I asked. I could brave the club every now and then.

I went straight to the bouncer at the front door, bypassing the line—a line, even on a weeknight. I wasn't dressed nearly well enough to gain admittance—at least I wasn't wearing a T-shirt with my jeans—which meant I was going to have to pull rank. The bouncer tonight was one of the vampires, an unassuming Secret Service–looking guy. Stronger than someone with linebacker muscles, but he didn't look it. And he wore dark sunglasses at night, natch.

He watched my approach all the way up the block. I watched the rim of his sunglasses and put my hands on my hips.

"What do *you* want?" he said.

"I'm here to see Rick."

"What right do you have to demand this?"

I glared. Alpha werewolf, Master vampire, need to talk, blah blah. I went through this bullshit every time I dealt with the vampire minions.

"He's expecting me."

"He didn't tell me."

"That's because I'm pretty sure he considers me to be on a 'come on in' basis. He shouldn't *have* to tell you. But, you know, if you want me to check on that for you . . ." I pulled out my cell phone. I had Rick on speed dial.

His lips twitched—a frustrated frown. "He's too indulgent with you wolves."

"Yeah, yeah, heathen animals, whatever."

He stepped aside just as I was about to push past him, or rather, try to push past him. We both got to look surly.

Psalm 23 was the kind of place that provided the seed of truth to countless vampire stereotypes. The place was beyond posh, all chrome, blue plush carpets, and black leather booths, where the beautiful people standing at the bar and draping themselves over railings by the dance floor seemed like accessories, part of the decor rather than patrons. The club attracted a young, eager, suggestible clientele. A lot of Rick's vampires came here for drinks just as eagerly. An experienced eye could spot them—the pale, appraising gazes, surveying the interior like they were picking out their lobster from the tank at a high-end seafood restaurant.

I found Rick inside, sitting at one of the bars near the wall, surveying his domain, the crowd on the dance floor, couples at tables sipping glowing neon drinks in martini glasses, impervious to the thumping beat of techno music.

"Your minions are very aggravating in their self-importance," I said to him.

Rick was handsome, unassuming, with fine old-world features, dark hair swept back, and an often-amused smile. He wore a blue silk shirt, dark trousers—simple and elegant. He was urbane without being pompous, confident without being arrogant.

He said, "You know how prejudices become entrenched in older generations, how it usually takes younger generations to grow up with new outlooks to establish new attitudes? Imagine how entrenched some prejudices can get after hundreds of years."

Damn kids, get off my lawn, covered a very large lawn then, didn't it?

"You're pretty laid back for being five hundred years old. What's your excuse?"

"I've always had something of an antiauthoritarian streak. Pretty good trick for someone born under a monarchy, isn't it?"

More stories, more stories . . . I almost forgot my own issues, hoping he would say more about his history in Spanish colonial America. He'd claimed once that he'd known Coronado. I still hadn't gotten that whole history.

And I wouldn't get it this time.

"Can I get you a drink?" he asked.

I requested something sweet and glowing in a martini glass. With a raised hand, Rick summoned the bartender and made the request, and in a moment I had a pink and fruity drink to cling to.

"Now, what do you need?" Rick said.

I always needed something from him, it seemed, even if it was just advice. It was silly not to take advantage of the advice of someone with five hundred years of experience.

"I've got a situation," I said, and tried to explain. "It turns out the army's had a unit of werewolves operating in Afghanistan. It's kind of a long story. They worked as a pack, but then their captain— their alpha—was killed. The unit fell apart, the soldiers lost control. The survivors were brought back home. One of them is being court-martialed on murder charges—he killed three other men in the unit. I've been asked to help rehabilitate the other two. I've met them. They're . . . I have no idea what to do with them. I've never seen anything like it. Every little thing triggers a reaction from them. They're always right on the edge of shifting. I wouldn't be surprised if there's some post-traumatic stress going on, and couple that with the lycan-thropy—they're a mess."

Rick rubbed his chin as he listened, looking into a middle distance before bringing his gaze to me. "This isn't the first time werewolves have been used as soldiers," Rick said. "There's a long history of it, in fact. Werewolves tend to be fierce, indestructible."

"So how do I help them? How do I get them to be people again, and not berserker monsters?"

"The problem is not too many people worry about making werewolf soldiers human again. They're disposable troops."

"Excuse me? Disposable?"

"To be unleashed when needed—if you'll forgive the pun—and shunted aside when not. It explains a lot about certain attitudes toward them, though, doesn't it? As well as how the culture of bounty hunters got started."

I could only stare, appalled. At the same time, it made sense. Cultivate that instinct to kill, then set it loose. Everything else was extraneous.

"But . . . but I know a werewolf in D.C., Ahmed, who takes in and helps out-of-control wolves. And there are other safe havens, wolf packs that help—"

"New werewolves, Kitty. Young wolves, cubs who don't know what they're doing but can be taught. These are hardened warriors."

"Then you're saying there's nothing I can do."

"If anyone could find a way, it'll be you."

"What's that supposed to mean?"

"You are a very hopeful person. Those were-wolves are in good hands. Or paws."

I was glad someone thought so. I stared into my glowy martini. *It's never been done before* was not the kind of advice I'd been hoping for.

Rick broke my depressed musings. "So. Have you heard from Anastasia lately?"

Anastasia. One of the baddest-assed vampires I'd ever met, the kind you didn't want to meet in a brightly lit room, never mind a dark alley. She was a schemer, too. And not one of the bad guys. But I didn't know I'd go so far as to say she was one of the good guys, either. She'd recently recruited me to be on the lookout for the actual bad guys, who were trying to take over the world, or something so equally awful that it didn't make a difference. I kept saying I wanted to be left alone. Then I contradicted myself by taking on *projects*. Like Tyler and Walters.

"Not since Montana," I said.

"Probably for the best."

"Yes, probably. I expect when I do hear from her it'll be because the world is ending."

"I wouldn't joke about that," he said, and he wasn't smiling.

I leaned forward. "Why not? You know something I don't?"

"The end of the world is all some vampires have to look forward to."

I hated that. Every vampire I'd ever met loved blithely throwing out these portentous proclamations of superiority and doom and they expected to have me shaking in my booties. I rolled my eyes.

"Are you one of those?"

"No. It's not all that healthy to believe the world was put here for my entertainment."

"Well. Kudos to you." I raised my martini glass to him.

"Back to your soldiers. Are you planning on setting them loose anytime soon?"

It was a leading question—the full moon was coming up in a week. Were Tyler and Walters going to spend it indoors or out? I shrugged. "Depends. Do you want me to let you know if I do? Warn you?"

"That's all right. I trust you to make the right decision."

"Well. Miracles never cease."

"Amen to that."

Which, upon reflection, was a very strange thing to hear a vampire say.

Chapter 9

I BROUGHT FOOD to my next meeting with the soldiers. A bundle of take-out lamb kabobs from a
Greek place, juicy meat and not much else. I hoped
they'd go over well. Food always made things better,
right? Tyler and Walters perked up when I set the
Styrofoam boxes on the table, their noses working as
the room filled with the smell of warm cooked meat.
I wondered when was the last time they'd had a real
meal.

Their expressions and stances changed when Ben
followed me into the cell. Tyler at the table, Walters
from his usual place hunched up on the cot, glowered at him, lips parted, like they were thinking of
growling. Their noses wrinkled, as if they smelled
something bad. Tyler flexed his hands, and his shoulders bunched up. When I introduced him, they
looked up him and down, judging. While they recognized him from the scuffle in the woods, they hadn't
gotten a good look at him then. Now they were

deciding whether they could take him down. Who was bigger, tougher, and all that. I wanted to cling to Ben, to say, *You can't have him, he's mine, I'm his, hands off.* Like Ben couldn't stand up for himself.

This was where Ben's human background served him well. As a werewolf, he didn't look that tough: lean, wiry, unassuming. Not as built and hardcore as someone like Tyler. But as a criminal defense lawyer, he had that stare. That smirk. He'd spent a lot of time in jails and courtrooms dealing with not-very-nice people, and not a lot phased him. He projected that image now, and it made the tough guys look at him twice.

They didn't shake hands or go through any of the *Hey, what's up, how's it going* greeting rituals that normally accompanied a meeting of total strangers. Instead, they exchanged a subtle acknowledgment of politeness: no one was going to get offended, no one was going to start a fight, no one was going to try to assert dominance over anyone else. Tyler nodded and glanced away, acknowledging Ben's presence, not offering a challenge. Walters studied us while not engaging. He'd throw occasional glances—trying not to stare, which would have looked like a challenge. I couldn't figure him out. I couldn't tell if he was scared or just stubborn and refusing to play nice.

Ben and I sat at the table, opened packages of food, and started eating. This was one of the things that made my human side twitch—the human side wanted to offer food to Tyler and Walters first, out of politeness. But to the Wolf, that would have meant handing over authority—alpha wolf ate first. So Ben and I started eating, and the others watched, which meant they were still willing to give me the authority.

"You two should come eat something," I said after the first minute. I pushed one of the boxes to Tyler, who ducked his gaze and took up a skewer of meat. Walters gathered himself, hesitating and drawn to the meal at the same time. I left one of the skewers in front of the empty chair and didn't look at him again.

Soon, all four of us were sitting around the table, having what from the outside looked like a normal meal. Success. Then, we talked. Just talked. I asked about favorite foods, bad restaurant experiences, hometowns, and families. Got them to open up a little—got them to ask questions. I wanted to show them that werewolves could have lives. I passed around cans of soda. Maybe next time we'd bring beer. I didn't really trust them with beer just yet.

Eventually, the conversation came around to the elephant in the room: the supernatural, being a werewolf, and what else was out there.

"Vampires? There really are vampires?" Tyler said.

I forgot how little experience they had.

"Yup, there really are," I said.

"I guess I figured they were real," he said. "You

turn into a werewolf and figure a lot of things must be real, right? But it's weird. I never thought I'd actually meet one."

"I can arrange that, if you want," I said.

"I don't know that I do," Tyler said.

"They smell funny," Ben said. "Kind of dead but not really."

"You'd like Rick. He's very easygoing, for a vampire," I said.

"I still wouldn't want to piss him off," Ben said.

"No," I agreed wryly.

"Do you run into a lot of this kind of thing? Vampires, rogue werewolves, whatever?" Tyler asked.

"Yeah, I kind of do," I said.

"How?" he said. "I know you said you were attacked, but how? You don't exactly look like the creepy supernatural type. Either one of you. You look like a typical yuppie couple. No offense."

None taken. In fact, I was sort of flattered. Ben and I looked at each other, exchanging one of those familiar glances, all our history passing between us. Neither one of us had chosen this life. But we'd done pretty well with it, together.

"My cousin's a hunter," Ben said. "I was helping him out when I was attacked."

"I had a really bad date back in college." I shrugged. That statement covered so much that a detailed explanation just couldn't.

Tyler looked as if he wanted to ask questions, to

get elaboration, but he only shook his head. "I volunteered for this. But Captain Gordon—he didn't tell us everything. Like how to deal with people. What to do when you don't have anyplace to run."

"I think he expected us all to come home together," Walters said into his food. He'd raised his head to look at us, his expression mournful. Wounded, I decided. He was wounded. "He expected us to still be a pack. That he would still be taking care of us."

I wanted to tell him everything was going to be okay, as if he were a little kid. So strange to see someone that tough and capable look that lost.

"Bad planning on Gordon's part," I said. "He should have spent a little more time teaching you to take care of yourselves. The whole pack thing . . . it can be a lifesaver. It can be supportive and amazing. But it can also be codependent as hell."

"We were a family," Tyler said. "That's part of why the captain picked us. None of us have wives or kids. It was just us."

"Thank goodness for small favors," I muttered, not quite under my breath. These guys having kids would have added a whole other level of tragedy to the situation.

"It didn't matter how much the captain explained, we still wouldn't have known what to expect. Like this," Tyler said. He wiped his hands on a paper napkin and pushed up his left sleeve. "What do you see?"

A really buff arm, with a rounded shoulder and well-defined biceps. The dark skin was smooth, unblemished even by goose bumps. I shrugged and said, "Your arm?"

"I had a tattoo here. Really nice, tribal—covered half my arm. We all had tattoos—names, unit badges, good-luck charms, usual army shit. Then Gordon turned me. When I woke up, there was a big ink stain on the sheet and no tattoo. That happened to all of us."

"It healed," I said. "Werewolf superimmunity—your body rejected the ink as a foreign object." Good thing I hadn't been thinking of getting one of my own.

"It was like being erased," Tyler said. "Starting over with a clean slate. But it also felt like losing something. I lost something I thought was going to be part of me forever."

I knew how he felt. Saying so would sound trite and probably not help much.

"Have you heard anything about Van?" Walters asked suddenly. "The doctor won't tell us anything."

I didn't imagine Shumacher talked to them much, if ever.

"Vanderman you mean?" I said. "No. Not apart from his being charged with murder."

Walters slumped. "It wasn't him. I mean, not just him. He wasn't in his right mind."

"He still has to stay in custody."

"He's taking the fall for us," Tyler said.

"I don't think you should feel guilty," I said.

"You're so keen on helping us, you ought to be helping all of us," Tyler said.

"We're a pack," Walters said, as if it was a mantra.

I started thinking this would have been easier with Vanderman included. If I could rehabilitate him, the others would follow. Then I remembered the look in his eyes, that killer instinct. If Tyler and Walters were going to function on their own, they had to do it without the alpha.

They *were* making progress here. They were talking. They weren't panicking or raging or about to shape-shift. They were acting almost normally. I had to give them goals, keep them motivated. Distracted. We had to make progress.

"Do you guys want to get out, maybe see a little of Denver?" I said. Ben glanced at me, questioning.

Tyler and Walters looked at each other, and Tyler said, "Could we really do that?"

"Why not? You can sit here and have a conversation. The next step is to sit out there and have a conversation." I nodded in the direction of the door. "Discipline. It's all discipline and self-control."

"The army way," Tyler said, quirking a smile.

My phone rang with "The Good, the Bad and the Ugly." The soldiers jumped, and I glanced around the table apologetically.

"Cormac," I told Ben as I clicked the phone on. I'd finally given him his own ringtone so I'd have some warning.

"*That's* your custom ringtone for Cormac?" he said.

I smirked back at him as I went to the corner for some privacy. Into the phone I said, "Yeah?"

"Your guy, Franklin? I found something," Cormac said.

Life could never be simple, could it? I couldn't deal with just one problem at a time, could I?

"What is it?" I pressed a hand to my other ear and listened.

"Your friend was right," Cormac said. I almost corrected him, that Charles wasn't my friend—but when he needed to talk, he'd called me. What did that make me? Cormac continued, "Harold Franklin was traveling in all those locations on those dates. I'm not sure it means anything—the *post hoc ergo propter hoc* fallacy—"

"Whoa—what was that you just said?"

He paused before saying, "Never mind."

"But—"

"Maybe Franklin had something to do with those storms, maybe he didn't. But it's interesting that he's never been present for major earthquakes, mudslides, wildfires—just storms."

So Franklin coincidentally shows up for major, historically significant storms, but not other natural disasters. It wasn't much to base a defense on. "Like you said, that doesn't necessarily mean anything. And I don't think it's admissible in court."

"Probably not. But it's a start. I've got some more checking to do."

"Great. Cool. Whatever you can find. Do you need help?"

"You know—I might," he said. "Let me talk to Ben a minute."

Sure, he could connive with Ben but not with me . . . I held the phone out to Ben and raised my eyebrows at his curious expression. "I may not be guilty of libel after all."

"Not about Speedy Mart, anyway," he said.

"Hey!" I pouted.

Grinning, he took the phone and replaced me in the corner. I tried to listen in, but Ben's side of the conversation mostly involved him saying, "Yeah . . . okay . . . okay . . ." Cormac was speaking low enough that I couldn't hear his side.

"What's that all about?" Tyler asked.

I sighed. How did I explain this in as few words as possible? "I spent part of my show last week talking about whether or not something supernatural is going on with Speedy Mart—the 24-hour convenience store chain, right?"

"Something supernatural—like vampires and werewolves?" he said.

"Kind of. Anything, really. Magical, supernatural—weird. Anyway, the president of Speedy Mart is suing me for libel. So now we want to prove that there really is something going on with him because then it isn't libel."

Tyler leaned forward a little. "If someone's giving you trouble, Walters and I could maybe take care of it—"

"No," I said. "That will definitely not be necessary. We've got it under control."

Not that siccing a couple of Green Beret werewolves on Franklin wouldn't be fun to watch . . .

Ben returned to the table, folding my phone and handing it back to me.

"Well?" I said.

"Later," he said.

"You two lead interesting lives, don't you?" Tyler said.

I shrugged. "For certain values of interesting."

We finished the meal. The sodas were drunk, the skewers lay empty and bloody. I was feeling quite pleased with myself.

"Thanks," Tyler said. "Been awhile since I've eaten that well." Walters made a sound of agreement. Was he actually smiling?

"You're welcome," I said. "Think about that next step, okay? I'll see if I can't arrange a field trip." I tried to sound encouraging.

Tyler's responding smile was grim, but it was a smile. Walters looked up, then away. But tension in the room was less than it had been when we entered.

Ben and I left shoulder to shoulder, and Shumacher led us back to her office for the debriefing. She kept looking at Ben—who had, of course, blown his cover by coming here and talking werewolf with the soldiers. Ben looked back at her, unconcerned and amused. We'd discussed this—and if he hadn't been okay with her knowing, he wouldn't have come.

"I assumed you'd guessed when I didn't mind getting Kitty's blood all over me," he said finally.

She blushed and ducked her gaze. "I didn't spot it. I thought I was getting good at identifying werewolves on sight. But you hide it well."

"I'd appreciate it if you kept it quiet," Ben said. "I'm not the publicity hound Kitty is."

"Publicity hound? Is that a joke?" I said, and he kissed my cheek in response.

"Of course," Shumacher said. "Of course." She was nervous around us—her body tense, her gaze darting, her smell sharp. I'd have thought she'd gotten used to being around werewolves by now. Maybe she didn't like being outnumbered. "Are you sure taking them outside is a good idea?" She set her clipboard on her desk.

Ben and I took chairs across from her.

I shrugged. "They'll be supervised. We have to start somewhere."

"I'm not sure they're ready," Shumacher said.

"Have you even talked to them? Found out what they want?"

"I'm not sure they're in a position to be making those kinds of decisions, after what they've been through."

"They're not children," I said. "Sure, they need help. But they deserve to have a say in what happens to them. The only way they're going to get better is if they have a *reason* to get better. It's the carrot approach." I sat back and tried not to frown.

"Is she always so optimistic?" Shumacher said to Ben.

"Yes. I usually just stand out of her way and let her go. It's easier than arguing," Ben said.

Shumacher studied her clipboard a moment. It held what looked like a stack of charts, computer printouts of some kind. I couldn't tell what information she derived from them.

"They did well today, didn't they?" she said finally.

"I think so," I said. "They're listening to me. I think they'll listen to me if we go outside."

"Maybe I can allow a short trip. An hour or two."

"That's all I'm asking for," I said. "Baby steps."

"I'll need to get authorization from Colonel Stafford," she said.

Which was touch and go at best, but I couldn't complain.

We said our farewells, left the building, and emerged into an increasingly overcast winter afternoon. The air smelled wet.

"That went well," Ben said as we crossed the parking lot, and he didn't even sound sarcastic.

"Really?" I said hopefully.

"Yeah. Those guys deserve a break. I hope we can help them."

I wrapped my arm around his middle and hugged him. "So what's up with Cormac?" I said.

"Oh, you'll like this." Ben wore a shit-eating grin. It was his courtroom attorney "I will bury you" expression.

"What? What does he want?"

He just kept grinning, stringing me along.

"Come on. Just tell me."

We reached our car before he said anything.

"We're going on a stakeout."

Chapter 10

"JESUS, THIS is just like old times," Ben muttered. He leaned back in the driver's seat and tapped the top of the steering wheel.

"Old times" meant the days when Cormac loaded his Jeep with rifles and silver bullets and called Ben for backup when things got rough. I remembered Ben saying something about how he mostly drove the car on those treks. Kind of like he was doing now.

That thought didn't soothe my nerves. I sat on the passenger side, watching through the windshield, ready for anything. We were parked in downtown Denver, waiting for Cormac's phone call. He was on foot, staking out the Brown Palace Hotel, where Franklin was staying. The Brown Palace was the posh, fancy local hotel, and had been for the last hundred years or so. It was the stylish place to stay, and that he had a room there told us that Franklin cared about appearances.

Cormac wouldn't tell us anything more of what he'd learned about Franklin. Just that my crazy caller, Charles, might have been on to something. But we needed evidence that it wasn't all a big coincidence. Hence the stakeout.

"Has Cormac ever done this before?" I asked.

"Sure, he's tailed lots of guys before."

"No, I mean has he ever been so . . . vague? Tossing off Latin phrases, buying into conspiracy theories. Ever since he got out of prison he's just seemed a little out of it."

"You don't think just getting out of prison might have something to do with that?"

"I suppose. But sometimes, he doesn't even smell right."

After a few silent moments, Ben said, "Yeah, I noticed that."

"What's happening to him?"

"I don't know. As long as he keeps his nose clean and stays away from his guns, I'm not sure it matters."

My phone rang—Cormac's tone. I jumped and rushed to answer. "Yeah?"

"He's on the move. I'm at the corner of Seventeenth and Glenarm."

I relayed the info to Ben, who started the car and pulled into the street. We turned to the next block and found Cormac, who opened the back passenger side door before the car slowed completely to a stop, and Ben had pulled away from the curb before the door was finished closing. Real getaway pros, they were.

"He's heading south on Broadway," Cormac said.

"Got it. What are we looking for?"

"Black Hummer, you can't miss it," Cormac said.

"That's excessive," Ben said with a huff. "Help me keep an eye out, Kitty. And don't be so obvious."

I had started craning forward and twisting in my seat to look at the lanes of traffic on either side of us.

"I'm not very good at this cloak-and-dagger thing, you know."

"You're fine," Cormac said from the backseat, sounding amused.

I glanced back. He'd put on his sunglasses, and I couldn't tell where he was looking—out the windshield, I assumed, searching for Franklin's black car. He seemed relaxed, and smelled like clean, cotton T-shirt and skin. He'd donned his familiar leather jacket, like a piece of armor.

"What exactly are we doing?" I said.

"We're going to see where he goes and what he does when he gets there," Cormac said.

"What if he's just going to the liquor store for a six-pack?"

"Guys like Franklin have people to do that for them. No, he's up to something." He was wearing his sardonic smile. The one that suggested he was outside the world and just watching it go by.

"I'm so not cut out for this," I grumbled. "I shouldn't even be here."

"This is to save your ass, remember," Ben said.

"Not my ass so much as my bacon," I said.

"What does that even mean?" Cormac scooted up so he was looking between the front seats.

"Bacon," Ben said. "As in bringing home the."

"Ah." Cormac still looked like he was secretly laughing at me.

"I'm glad you're so amused," I said, turning to sit straight, looking for the Hummer, which surely had gotten away from us by now. A Hummer shouldn't be able to hide.

"Just happy to be alive," Cormac said.

I was about to twist around to look at him again and ask him what he was talking about when Ben said, "Is that our guy?"

"That's him," Cormac said.

Ben had nodded to the urban tank, three cars ahead of us and to the right, looking like a black hole in the middle of traffic. Ben cruised along like nothing was different, but we all got quiet.

Broadway was one of the main drags through Denver. The Hummer—not exactly subtle—could continue for a long time without turning. We followed, never closer than three or four cars, often as much as two blocks away from it. Those moments, my heart would start pounding faster, I'd start tapping the armrest, sure that Franklin was getting away from us. Ben and Cormac never even twitched. I wondered how many times they'd done this sort of thing.

We went on like this for miles, into the suburb of Englewood.

"There," Cormac said, without urgency. "Is he turning?"

And he was. The Hummer signaled, slid over a lane, kept signaling, and turned into the parking lot of a Speedy Mart.

"Maybe he's just here to check on the local branches," Ben said. We rolled on past the Speedy Mart and turned at the next block.

"Fair enough," Cormac said.

"We're still going back, right?" I said.

Ben turned again, and again, bringing us back to the block with the Speedy Mart. He pulled the car over and shut down the engine.

From here, we could see part of the store's front parking lot and most of the back. The Hummer parked at the side, and Franklin, looking spiffy in his suit, was putting something into a box out back. It looked like a breaker box, attached to the brick wall of the building, painted gunmetal gray, but no cables or pipes or anything led into it. It was just a box stuck to the wall. Franklin opened the door, and whatever he set inside was no bigger than his hand. At this point I totally knew what the plan was: wait for Franklin to drive away, then check out what he'd put into the mysterious box. Maybe it was nothing more nefarious than money. Maybe he was being blackmailed and this was the drop. Maybe he had some weird smuggling scheme going. The possibilities were endless even without considering the supernatural. Maybe it was just a four-leaf clover to bring luck. Maybe that was the secret to the chain's success.

Franklin started back to his car, but paused, and looked at us. We'd been quiet, sneaky, but maybe the pressure of three gazes made him look over and see the car. We weren't even parked all that conspicuously—several other cars were parked on both sides of the street around us. But he looked, saw us staring back at him, and he certainly recognized me.

The man raised his hand, like he was saying hello. I started to slide down the seat, though it was too late to hide. Then I passed out.

The world seemed to vanish for a moment—pure blackout. Missing time. I was staring wide-eyed at Franklin, then I was slumped to the side, my face pressed against the window, my mind awash in vertigo, wondering where my memory went. Inside me, Wolf howled.

"Whoa, shit, what was that?" Ben had one hand on the dash, pushing himself away from the steering wheel, where he'd apparently slumped over. He blinked and shook his head. "What happened?"

I had a headache pounding in the middle of my skull. I couldn't seem to focus. By instinct, I reached and put my hand on Ben's arm, hoping to steady myself and my speeding heart. His hand went to mine, squeezing. His skin was clammy.

"You blacked out, too?" I said, my voice sounding tinny. I squeezed my eyes shut, and they came a little more into focus when I opened them again.

Franklin and the black Hummer were gone. Figured.

I opened the door to get some fresh air and clear my head.

Cormac was already outside, standing by the open passenger door of the car, his right hand raised as if preparing to throw something at the spot where Franklin had been standing. I just stared at him dumbly.

Ben got out and called across the roof of the car. "Cormac?"

He didn't respond.

The object he held in his hand was small, metallic—wire twisted into a knot-work pattern. An amulet, maybe. The expression on his face was set, determined, as if he was sure of himself, the situation, and what to do about it. A soldier preparing for battle. But he had a gleam in his eyes as well, an eagerness that I'd never seen before. I'd always thought of him as a cold killer, who would shoot his target—kill another human being—without emotion, without reflection, treating it like a job, like taking out the trash. It was what made him scary. But now he seemed excited about a coming battle. He even smelled different—adrenaline and endorphins. The scent of a chase. For half a heartbeat, I almost didn't recognize him.

Then it was gone. I might have imagined it all.

"Cormac!" Ben shouted it this time.

Cormac blinked and took a deep, recovering breath. The set expression faded into a frown, and his gaze turned studious, distant. He lowered his arm. The metallic charm went into his jeans pocket.

The bounty hunter looked at Ben and me and seemed to need a moment to collect himself to speak. When he did, his voice was way too calm. "You two okay?"

"What was that?" Ben demanded.

"Bastard's a wizard," he said.

That wasn't even the wackiest thing I'd ever heard. I'd met a wizard before. And he was one of the strangest, scariest guys I knew—so what did that make Franklin?

"Okay, but what's he up to?" I asked.

"You took that a lot better than I would have expected."

"You tell me he's a wizard, okay, I believe you. Me bitching isn't going to change that."

Cormac started walking toward the lockbox on the wall.

Ben called after him, "As the lawyer present I'd

like to point out that actually interfering puts us on shaky legal ground."

"We can't even look?" I said.

"Legally, we just need proof that he's up to something; we don't have to know what," Ben said.

"You aren't curious?" I said.

"That's got nothing to do with it. Cormac? Anything even remotely resembling trespassing or breaking and entering is going to look bad to a parole officer."

Cormac stopped, then turned and sauntered back to the car. "I hate that."

I thought a minute—I wasn't on parole. I started for the box.

"Kitty," Ben said, admonishing. I waved a hand.

"Don't touch anything you find," Cormac said as we passed each other.

The box seemed to be bolted to the brick wall, and it didn't seem to be locked, which was odd. I looked all around it, searching for wires, arcane symbols, anything. Holding my breath, bracing for the inevitable lightning strike, I opened the door.

At the floor of the box lay an amulet, a couple of inches long, made of pewter or tarnished silver and shaped like a fat, stylized "T." The top part of it was curved inward—like the whole thing was a miniature, double-headed ax.

I didn't touch it, but closed the door and backed away slowly. Back at the car, Ben and Cormac were standing, leaning on their respective doors, watching. They must have seen the quizzical look on my face.

"Well?" Ben said.

"There's some kind of amulet or charm. Looks like a silver double-headed ax."

"Can you draw it?" Cormac asked.

"Yeah," I said, looking around for some paper. The nearest thing at hand was the dust on the outside of Ben's car, so I used that. Cormac studied it, rubbing his chin, then looked up. I followed his gaze to the big Speedy Mart sign on its post out front: the words of the store spelled out in a leaning, speedy font, on a red backdrop shaped like an oval with bites taken out of the top and bottom—like a double-headed ax.

"Huh," Ben said.

"So what's it mean?" I asked.

Cormac was shaking his head. "That's what I want to figure out."

AFTER OUR little episode playing *Mission Impossible*, I was sure I'd get another visit from Franklin. At the very least he'd serve me with a restraining order. I wouldn't even be able to blame him for it. But nothing happened that day, or the next. Nobody got struck by lightning. The lawsuit was proceeding apace; KNOB's lawyer was working on an argument to get the case thrown out on the basis that no one actually took my show seriously. I wasn't quite sure how I felt about that.

Cormac said he was going to work on figuring out what Franklin was doing with the amulets and symbols. I called the next day for an update, and his phone rolled to voice mail. He hadn't bothered putting on a personal message; it was just an automated voice reading back his number. I had to wait for more information, but it was hard not to sit by the phone hoping for someone—Cormac, lawyers, Franklin, anyone—to call and tell me my fate.

Fortunately, I had distractions. I was determined to get Tyler and Walters to New Moon.

First, I called the members of the pack who frequented the bar, both to warn them and to recruit help. Shaun would be at New Moon. A few others who I considered heavy hitters in the pack would be there. I'd asked Becky to be there, which might have been flirting with disaster. But I wanted to see what would happen, if Walters would remember her and what he'd done to her. I promised her she could walk out the door the second she wanted to. She said she definitely would—after she looked Walters in the eye as a human being and saw how he reacted.

If worst came to worst and Walters flipped out, we'd lock the doors and keep the army guys there until Shumacher and her tranquilizer guns came to the rescue.

Shumacher really wanted to come along. She

wanted to be right there with her clipboard, taking notes, observing. We talked about it on the phone.

"I'm not sure that's such a good idea," I argued, trying to sound nice about it. "I think you make them nervous. They might be a little more comfortable in a more relaxed situation."

She hesitated, no doubt forming her argument. I could almost hear the unspoken "but" floating on the signal. "They're my responsibility," she said finally. "Colonel Stafford expects them to be supervised by someone with authority."

The safe haven of the government bureaucracy. How could I argue against that?

"If something goes wrong you can court-martial me," I said, realizing that I probably shouldn't. I imagined myself fighting two court cases simultaneously. Ben would have conniptions.

"You're a civilian, you can't be court-martialed," Shumacher said.

"Well, thank goodness for that. Doctor, these are people, not a science experiment. Can't we try and let them be people? Just for a couple of hours?"

"How about a compromise: I'll go with them, but I'll wait outside. You get a more normal situation, and I'll be there if anything goes wrong."

She was so convinced that something was going to go wrong. "Deal," I said.

"And I want to record the session," she said quickly.

"Doctor—"

"Videotaping therapy sessions is a widely accepted practice," she argued. And what did I know? I let her come to the restaurant early and set up a pair of remote cameras over the bar.

Ben and I went together to spring the guys from the VA hospital.

Chapter 11

THE GUYS didn't much like being in the enclosed space of the car. We opened all the windows to let in air. I half expected one of them to stick his head out, nose into the wind, blissful expression on his face. I'd have understood the impulse. Even if they were tense and watchful, being out of the stuffy hospital had to feel good. But they just slumped in their seats and looked surly.

"This is Denver?" Tyler asked at one point. We followed I-25 to downtown, which presented a vista of skyscrapers, the sports arenas, Elitch's amusement park, and the Broncos stadium.

"Yup," I said. "Ever been here?"

"No," he said. "Never have."

"What about you, Walters?" He shook his head.

Just a mile or so later, we pulled off the freeway at Colfax and entered the grid of side streets. A few minutes after that, we were at New Moon. Tyler saw the funky neon sign and smirked.

"That some kind of joke?" he said.

"Not really," I said. "It's kind of a philosophy."

Ben pulled around back and parked.

Inside, late afternoon, the place was pretty empty, which was also part of the plan. The soldiers looked around carefully—at the tables, brick walls, into the ductwork along the high ceiling, across the bar, studying every inch. I wondered how long it had been since they'd been in a restaurant.

Behind the counter, Shaun noticed us, straightened, and frowned. He was strong, but more than that he was decisive—he could take a stand. I counted on him to back up me and Ben in the pack. If he ever decided he wanted to take over, we'd be in trouble. So we got him firmly on our side by hiring him to manage New Moon. We were a team.

Others of the pack were here as well. Two of them, Dan and Jared, tough but sensible, sat at a table in the corner munching on what looked like buffalo wings. Becky was sitting at the bar, talking to Shaun. They all glanced at Ben and me. I nodded at them, and they quickly looked away—showing deference, acknowledging that I was the boss. But they stared hard at Tyler and Walters, who in their camouflage pants and gray T-shirts stood out. Tyler, closest to me, stiffened. Walters had parted his lips, showing teeth.

The whole scene was like something out of a spaghetti Western. Everyone was still, silent, sizing each other up. Waiting for someone else to flinch first. I could almost hear the Morricone soundtrack.

I touched Tyler's arm, half expecting him to jump away and snarl, the first step to starting a fight. He just looked at me, at my hand on his arm, as if he was trying to figure out a code.

"It's okay. They're my pack. They're friends," I said.

He relaxed a notch, and so did Walters. I kept contact with Tyler for a moment—contact meant comfort within the pack. I didn't know if he was quite pack yet. I didn't know if that was what we were doing here—bringing them into the pack. Maybe we were. Tyler and Walters still watched the other wolves warily, and wouldn't look at anything else.

"Let's sit down," I said, and steered them toward a table in back.

At the table, a weird kind of dance ensued. I just grabbed the first chair I came to. Ben stood back a little, as if he knew what was going to happen. Tyler and Walters slinked around me, looking over their shoulders, sidling along until they reached the chairs closest to the wall, which they pulled back and arranged so they were looking out. They weren't quite sitting at the table, but they could keep everyone in the place, as well as all the exits, in view. It wasn't quite natural, even for werewolves. I blinked at them, confused.

Ben leaned over and whispered, "Backs to the

wall. It's a soldier thing. Haven't you seen Cormac do that?"

I'd only recently seen Cormac in a setting like this to be able to judge. Before then, it was all shadowy nighttime battles, and then the prison visiting room. But Ben was right. I suddenly felt like I was baby-sitting dynamite.

Tyler and Walters perched on their seats and glared out at the world. I settled in across from them, attempting to send out all the soothing vibes I could. Be calm, we're all friends here.

Then Shaun came over.

This was a perfectly normal human situation: we were customers in his restaurant, he needed to take our orders. But he looked like a wolf on the prowl.

He reached the table, and Tyler and Walters stood, leaning forward, bracing. Ben and I stood along with them, out of pure instinct. We had to be tallest. And even if I wasn't I had to act like it. But we all stood as part of a dominance display and our heart rates rose right along with us.

I took a calming breath. "Everyone settle down. Nobody's getting into any kind of a fight."

I sat first, glaring, making it clear I was lowering myself to show a good example, and they shouldn't read anything into it. Tyler kept watching me closely, as if he was waiting for me to slip. The two soldiers slowly returned to their seats; only then did Ben sit.

"I'm Shaun," he said, offering his hand for shaking.

Tyler took a moment to figure out what to do with it. Shaun waited patiently until Tyler finally shook it, and Walters followed his lead. "What can I get for you?"

"What are you doing working here?" Tyler asked, accusing, maybe even confused.

Shaun chuckled nervously, equally confused. "Kitty hired me to manage the place. Is there something wrong with that?"

"But you're a werewolf," Tyler said.

"And what am I supposed to do, live in the woods and eat rabbits for the rest of my life? I still have to pay the rent."

Tyler looked sullen. "This just doesn't seem like the best job for a werewolf."

Shaun glanced at me for a cue, or maybe even to take over the conversation. For my part, my heart kind of broke a little, at the thought that Tyler believed that as a werewolf he could only be a warrior.

"That's kind of the point of coming here. There's such a thing as a nonmilitarized werewolf," I said. "I run a talk radio show. Ben's a lawyer."

Tyler and Walters seemed to ponder, but they also seemed to not quite believe us. They just stared as though they expected the whole setting to turn into a joke.

"Do you all want anything to drink?" Shaun tried again.

"My treat," I said. "Go crazy."

Walters looked at Tyler, almost asking permission. "I could really use a beer," he said.

"Yeah, tell me about it." Tyler actually chuckled.

"When was the last time you guys had a beer?" I said.

"When we deployed. No alcohol in the field, and since then . . ." He trailed off, shrugging.

"Maybe you'd better hold off," I said. "Not until we know you're not going to sprout claws and go bonkers."

"Cokes all around then?" Shaun said. He probably liked the idea of not having a couple of military werewolves going bonkers in the restaurant.

Tyler and Walters acquiesced. Tyler wore a smile, a bit thin, a bit wry, as though he'd thought of a joke. Even with half the smile his face lit. "Is this all some big ploy to show us that werewolves are real people, too?"

"You haven't actually listened to Kitty's show ever, have you?" Ben said.

Neither one showed any sign that he had.

"That's okay," I said. "I don't think I'm broadcast in Afghanistan."

"Kitty's the supernatural self-help guru," Ben said. Tyler raised a disbelieving brow. I couldn't blame him; it did sound a bit ridiculous.

"Why do you think Shumacher called me? I've faked knowing what I'm talking about for so long I've become an expert."

"Sounds like the army to me," Tyler said.

Shaun arrived with a tray of sodas, and the others managed not to flinch at his approach. I nodded, and Shaun left us alone; but he lingered behind the bar, glancing back at us, keeping an eye on us.

Walters didn't pay much attention to the drink in front of him; he seemed distracted. I looked to where he was staring: to Becky. She was staring right back at him, and frowning.

"Walters," I said. I had to say it again before he looked at me. "Stop staring."

"I know her," Walters said, nodding at Becky, quickly glancing away. "She was in the woods the other day. With you. The other wolf."

"Yeah," I said. "You kind of beat her up."

He flinched, cringing. But his gaze inevitably crept back to her. "What's she doing here?"

"I think she was hoping for an apology."

Walters blushed and looked into his glass. But he glanced at her a couple of times in the space of a few seconds, with a longing, hungry gaze, looking for all the world like an awkward teenager. I couldn't tell what he was thinking, and I was afraid to ask. Ben wore a smirk, leading me to think that he understood what was going on in the guy's brain. Now, was that because he was a guy and this was a guy thing, or because Ben was a criminal law attorney and he understood the dynamic? I'd have to ask him about that later. I wondered if I should move to block Walters's view of Becky.

So. Here we were. Having drinks. Like normal grown-up people. What came next, again? Conversation? Oy.

We managed a half hour of small talk—a very human activity. I was pleased. By the end the two soldiers had even stopped looking around like they expected an attack.

Then Walters said, "I wish Van was here. If we could get him here, you could help him. Show him that we can be normal—"

"Ethan, you have to let Vanderman go," I said.

He appeared so forlorn, looking at me with a lost gaze. He had both hands wrapped around his glass, clinging to it.

By then, we'd nearly finished our sodas, which meant it was probably time to quit while we were ahead, or cut our losses, whichever metaphor seemed more appropriate. I waved at Shaun, put the drinks on my tab, and herded the pack toward the door.

On our way, Walters stopped by the bar near Becky, who stood, uncertain, one hand clenching the edge of her seat. She didn't back up, but I could sense her quivering, as if she wanted to. Shaun looked like he might leap over the bar at him. We all watched, astonished.

Walters kept a space between them, wide enough

that he couldn't reach out to touch her. Ducking his gaze, deferential, he took a moment to gather himself, his lips moving, working to say something. Probably struggling at the wolf roiling inside him. The smells, the wolfishness and hormones they'd sensed in the forest, were still apparent. However faint, our wolves could sense them.

Finally, Walters said, "I'm sorry."

He slouched, rounding his back, shoving his hands in his pockets, and stomped away.

Becky and I looked at each other. She was wide-eyed, a little baffled. I shook my head, unable to explain, beyond the fact that Walters was socially awkward but trying. I waved a farewell to her and Shaun, and followed the others outside.

I was surprised to find the world overcast but brightly lit—still afternoon. I felt like we should have been at about two in the morning. I'd exhausted myself, just from sitting there. We all looked that way. Ben was glancing up and down the street, as if expecting trouble. Tyler and Walters remained sullen, turned in on themselves.

Shumacher waited near her car. "Well? What happened?"

I stepped with her away from the others to discuss. "I think it went fine. You can tell me after you take a look at the footage." She was no doubt on her way to retrieve her cameras.

"No problems? Everything was normal?"

"I wouldn't call it normal," I said. "Not with this crowd. But we're all alive, aren't we? Hey—can we talk about this later? They're tired and probably ought to get home."

She looked like she had more questions, but relented. I urged my pack into the car, and we rolled away. I had to admit, I let out a sigh of relief when they were once again safely behind their locked door at the VA hospital.

The field trip had been a success, and there was hope for Tyler and Walters.

Chapter 12

A COUPLE OF days had passed since we'd followed
Franklin and he put the whammy on us. I hadn't
heard from him since.

I'd distracted myself by worrying about the werewolf soldiers. And I had a show to get ready for. I
wanted to bring on Tyler and Walters for an interview—real-live werewolves in the army, what did
that mean, and so on. It was topical, newsworthy,
interesting, and I didn't believe for a minute that
Colonel Stafford or Dr. Shumacher would agree to let
it happen. I was working on compromise ideas, like
maybe conducting a prerecorded interview that the
powers that be could approve. I fantasized about possible interview questions, and how I could be sympathetic, yet incisive and hard-hitting at the same.

Ben and I talked about Cormac not answering his
phone. He insisted he wasn't worried, that Cormac
was fine, that he often went for weeks without com-
municating with anyone. He didn't want to annoy

Cormac by babying him. But he spoke as if he was trying to convince himself.

I didn't have that problem, so I stopped by his place on my way home from work. Just to check, for my own peace of mind. And to make sure Franklin hadn't gone after him.

Cormac had an apartment at the north end of town, in a run-down building in a run-down neighborhood off I-25 and the Boulder Turnpike. One in thousands. He could melt into the city, not stand out, not get in trouble. That was the idea.

I parked next to his familiar Jeep in the parking lot. So, his Jeep was here. He hadn't fled anywhere, and nothing about it looked like he had gotten in trouble. Maybe he'd been home the whole time and just ignoring us. Maybe he forgot to charge his phone. I was just being paranoid. Maybe that was it.

I climbed the stairs to the second floor and knocked on his door. There wasn't a window in front for me to peer through. I drew a couple of slow, careful breaths through my nose, taking in smells. I caught his scent, the soap, leather, and ruggedness of him. He'd been here recently. I didn't sense anything that set my hair on end—like, say, blood. But I did smell a tang of burning sage, like incense. It tickled my nose and touched a memory—a ritual, a magic spell.

Confused, uneasy, I knocked again.

The door opened and Cormac stood there, staring

a moment, blinking in surprise. He gripped the door-knob. His light brown hair was tousled and his eyes were shadowed, sleepless. He wore a white T-shirt and jeans. Socks, no shoes.

"Hi," I said, raising my hand in a stupid little wave. "We haven't heard from you in a few days and I wanted to . . . I guess see if you'd found anything out. And . . . are you okay?"

"I'm *fine*," he said.

"Can I come in?" The smell of smoke and burned sage grew stronger when he opened the door. My first thought had been that someone—Franklin—had cast a spell on his place. But the burning had happened inside. Cormac had never struck me as the incense-burning type.

Frowning, he stood aside to let me enter.

I hadn't been here since we helped him move in—a process that took about an hour and involved two pieces of furniture and a cardboard box—and he'd scowled at my suggestion of a housewarming party. The apartment wasn't much. It aspired to be a studio, in fact. They called these efficiencies. A square room, part of a block of square rooms, it had a tiny bathroom with a shower stall, a window in back, a kitchenette of sorts with a small, dorm-sized fridge, a sink, and a hot plate. It all seemed terribly grim. But then, I had no idea how Cormac had lived before he went to prison. His home then might have been just like this.

Ben and I had offered to give him—or loan him, if he preferred to call it a loan—a down payment on a nicer place. His aunt—Ben's mother—offered to let him stay with her in Longmont, a town about thirty miles north of Denver. But he'd refused. He said wanted to be independent. He said he wanted his own space, after spending two years locked in a building with hundreds of other guys, under constant supervision. So, here he was, living on savings and working part time, scraping by.

He'd done some decorating since we moved him in here. He had a futon with a plain gray comforter against one wall. Near it was a nightstand with a fifteen-inch TV on it. Near the kitchenette, in pretty much the only other open space available, stood a kitchen table—small, round, retro, with a pair of worn chairs.

The table was covered with books. More were scattered across the bed and stacked on the floor by the bed. Many of them were open, or had sticky notes bristling out of them.

Cormac had also never struck me as the academic type. I'd sent him books in prison—one of the few things you could send to someone in prison—as something of a joke. But near as I could tell he'd read everything I'd given him. And he was still going.

"What did you do, rob a library?" I said. I didn't mean to, it just came out.

Cormac's expression didn't change. "I used a library card, like a normal person."

I peeked at titles, peering sideways so I could read the spines, hoping to figure out what he was researching. But I only grew more confused. The titles were mostly nonfiction: history books, art books, photography, military history, science, and politics. Most of the titles had some variation of "twentieth century" or "last hundred years" in them. The course of study was simultaneously broad and strangely focused.

"What are you doing?" I asked.

"Catching up," he said. He sat in one of the kitchen chairs, leaned back, crossed his arms, and glared.

"On what? You were only in prison for two years."

"Kitty, what do you want?"

The next step would be to rifle through his fridge and cupboards to make sure he had food and was eating. I refrained from going that far. Ben was right, we were treating Cormac with kid gloves, and that couldn't have been going over very well with him.

"Have you found out anything else about Franklin?" I stood near the table, trying to look interested, but was actually sneaking looks at more book titles. *The Sacred and the Profane: The Nature of Religion* by Mircea Eliade? *The Larousse Encyclopedia of Mythology?*

"I've been trailing him," he said. "Been keeping my phone off. Sorry about that."

"It's okay. So what's the story on him?"

"He's visiting Speedy Marts all over town. He does the same thing at each one—puts a charm in a box and leaves. I haven't checked all the boxes. I thought I ought to keep my distance after that last encounter."

"He has to be doing this for a reason."

"The signs are he's prepping some kind of spell. I just don't know what kind—protection spell, get-rich spell, whatever."

"Or summoning hurricanes?" I said.

He gave me an annoyed look. "Or maybe he visits all his stores to recharge the magic, like a cycle. He has a regular travel schedule to visit various franchises, and it doesn't usually coincide with hurricanes."

"That could just as easily be explained as regular business. President of the company inspecting his franchises and all that."

"Best kind of magic hides in plain sight," he said. "Like working a ritual symbol into the store's logo. This could be a little more underhanded. He's planning something, getting ready for something."

"Like what?"

"Sabotaging his own buildings for the insurance money? I don't know. It may just be good-luck charms."

"He just happened to have his Denver trip scheduled right after he sues me."

"That's the kicker," Cormac said. "He could have harassed you over the phone, but he came to do it in person. No, he's up to something. We just have to figure out what. And maybe stay away from thunderclouds in the meantime."

I leaned on a wall and crossed my arms. "Have you always known so much about magic?"

He looked away. "I might have picked up some things here and there."

"In prison?"

"It doesn't matter."

"This"—I gestured to the library around me—"can't all be about Franklin. What else are you researching?"

"Nothing." He leaned forward, gathering together the books, shutting them, arranging them in piles, out of my reach and easy view.

"And have you been burning sage?" I said. Books, incense—I could even claim I smelled a faint whiff of magic, though I was sure it was my imagination. I had no idea what magic smelled like. No guns, no weapons, and even the smell of Cormac's leather jacket was buried. "Seriously—are you okay?"

"I'd forgotten how damn nosy you are."

I tamped down a flush of anger at that. Instead of rounding on him with the witty comeback no doubt sitting on the tip of my tongue, I started for the door.

"I have to get going. I told Ben I'd be home soon."

"You two seem happy," he said to my back. "I'm glad."

There, just stab me through the heart . . . Which wouldn't necessarily kill a werewolf. But it still hurt.

My hand on the doorknob, I hesitated, looking back at him and mustering a smile. "Thanks. And what about you? Are you happy or just coping?"

"Ask me again in a year."

"That's actually encouraging. You're still planning on being around in a year."

He shrugged. "I told you; I've got a lot of catching up to do."

"I'll see you later," I said, and he nodded.

BEN WAS at work at his desk in the corner of the living room and turned when I came in, his look inquiring. "Rough day?"

"I stopped by Cormac's place," I said, propping myself on a nearby wall.

He leaned back in his chair. "You thought he needed checking up on?"

"I got worried," I said, shrugging. I suddenly felt like I'd done something wrong.

"So how is he?"

"He's alive. Making progress on the case. But—

have you noticed anything odd about him? Anything different?"

"Like what? You mean something other than what's usually wrong with him?"

Like the surliness, the borderline sociopathy . . . "I don't know. He had piles of books everywhere on some of the weirdest topics, and I think he's been burning incense. You've known him your whole life. Has he always been this . . . I don't know . . . studious? Obsessive?"

"Kind of, yeah. Obsessive, at least. All about getting the job done, especially with the hunting. Especially since his father was killed."

"And now it's like if he can't do it with weapons he'll do it some other way? Books and research?"

"Maybe. You didn't expect him to have some kind of epiphany in prison and turn into Little Mary Sunshine, did you?"

"I don't know. I didn't expect anything, I guess." Honestly, I hadn't known Cormac all that well before he went to prison. He'd been this shadowy vigilante figure who slipped in and out of my life. He wasn't much different now, I supposed. But all those books were just weird. Maybe I felt like he had changed, but I couldn't figure out how. "But he *smells* different. Just a little."

"And if we weren't lycanthropes we wouldn't notice it." Ben turned thoughtful. "There is something else. He gets distracted. Staring off into space, like he sees something or is listening to something. When I shake him out of it he pretends that it didn't happen. I haven't really asked him about it. I figure he's just adjusting to being on the outside again."

"When have you ever known Cormac to get distracted? When has he ever not been completely focused on the world around him?" I said.

"I don't know," he said. "But I do know the more we pester him the more annoyed he's going to get. We just have to leave him alone."

Cormac was a grown-up. He didn't need us to worry about him.

"We're acting like a couple of alpha wolves carrying on about a wayward pup," I said, smiling.

"When you say you want kids I didn't think you meant one like Cormac."

Was that what it was? Displaced maternal instinct? I wrinkled my nose and thought about it. Ben stood, joined me at the wall, and leaned in to kiss me on the forehead.

"What was that for?" I said.

"You're cute."

Well, that was something, anyway.

I leaned into him for a hug. He wrapped his arms around me. A few inches taller than me, he put his nose to my hair and inhaled, taking in my scent, sending a pleasant flush along my scalp. I sighed, and he shifted, breathing in along my ear, my neck, and bending to breathe along my shoulder. Something wolfish showed through in his movements, which in turn brought out more of my own animal instincts, and lowered my inhibitions. I ran my fingers through his hair and brought my face close to his so I could return the gesture, breathing in the scent of him. His arms squeezed me, and he moved to smell my other shoulder.

Then I realized he really was smelling me, taking in my scent. Checking me over.

I pulled away and cupped my hands around his face to make him look at me. I didn't even have to explain my confusion; he looked sheepish. Guilty.

"What exactly are you looking for?" I said.

I expected him to pull away and get surly, to deny that he was looking for anything—suspicious of anything. Instead, he reached around my arm and brushed hair out of my eyes.

"I was just thinking about you and Cormac alone together."

"So you had to check?" To see if I smelled like Cormac. To see if Cormac and I had gotten together. "And?"

"You smell like his apartment," he said and shook his head. "But you don't smell like him."

"Of course not, I didn't even touch him," I said, exasperated. "Did you really think I'd cheat on you? With your cousin?"

He shrugged. "I don't think I expected to smell anything."

"But you had to check anyway."

"You two did have a thing."

Yeah. A still undefined "thing." Whatever it was. "That was awhile ago. A lot of water under the bridge."

He sighed with what sounded like relief. Maybe he had to hear me say it. Maybe it was his human side that needed reassuring, not the wolf side. We were still touching, my hands resting on his chest, his hands on my shoulders.

I pulled myself closer to him, and he leaned in to kiss me, his mouth against mine, working and eager. My mind fuzzed over as the taste of him became my whole focus. I didn't think I could get any closer to him, but he ran a hand down my backside and pulled me more firmly against him. Claiming his territory, which was just fine with me.

Chapter 13

I ASKED FOR that live interview with Tyler and Walters for the show, but Shumacher and Stafford refused outright. I wasn't surprised, and I had a compromise lined up: a taped interview, and they could approve the questions. Reluctantly, they agreed—as long as they could screen and vet the resulting recording. Otherwise, no deal. I had misgivings about letting them have that much control—but it was that or nothing. So I brought the recording equipment to the hospital and conducted the interview, which ended up being mostly with Tyler, since Walters didn't do very much talking. Once Tyler settled down and got used to the microphone, he seemed to get into it, like he was eager to tell his story. Then I had to hand the recording over.

What Shumacher gave back to me was milquetoast. The military had excised anything that mentioned that Tyler and Walters were, in fact, werewolves. Which was most of the interview, of course. They prohibited me from saying anything that indicated that the army had fielded lycanthropes in Afghanistan or Iraq. They didn't want people to know it had ever happened. When I argued, I read between the lines and figured out it wasn't even that it was a military secret they were trying to protect— they were worried about the political fallout. A chunk of the public—and Congress—didn't trust the supernatural. They thought we were trying to take over, and every now and then some wing nut came up with a theory about how the White House was controlled by vampires. Something like this would only add fuel to the fire.

They had a point.

I considered laying it all out anyway. But I imagined Stafford could do worse than serve me with a libel suit. And I worried that he would take it out on Tyler and Walters. So I played nice. I really wanted to run the interview because it had some good stuff in it. Not only about lycanthropy and coping with being a werewolf under awful circumstances, but about the experience of being a soldier and trying to come home.

Tyler explained, "Everybody tells you coming home is tough—you don't expect it to be easy. But you're still not ready for it. You think you can handle it. But it's like your mind is still back there. Your body is here, but you can't stop thinking about what happened there, the things you saw, what you did. And nobody here really gets it. You try to fit in, but you get this feeling you're never going to fit in again. So why bother trying? You put being a werewolf on top of that—it's like I'm living in a different world. How am I supposed to deal with that? You keep asking me what I want to do—but I can't imagine what I'm going to do next week much less any kind of future."

Even though I couldn't run the edited interview, Tyler and Walters gave me the idea to anchor the rest of the show. The opening and theme song—CCR's "Bad Moon Rising"—ran, and I dove right in.

"Tonight, it's the werewolf help line: if you're a werewolf, or know a werewolf, what's your story? Any problems you want to talk about, advice you want to share, tonight's your night. You see, I met a couple of folks this week, werewolves who need help and who are trying to find their feet, and I want them to hear how we do it in these parts, and that it is possible to survive. They may not be listening, but just in case they are, this show's for them." I hoped they were listening. I asked Shumacher to give them a radio, Internet access for the streaming version, anything.

"First caller, you're on the air."

"Hi, Kitty, thanks so much for taking my call, I've been listening to you since forever."

"Thank you. What's your question?" The monitor said this was Mark from Los Angeles. Nothing in his voice sounded funky.

"Okay, so, I'm a werewolf. And I'm not really part of a pack, but I know some other werewolves in the area and we try to look out for each other, you know?"

"That's great," I said. "The world would be a better place if we looked out for each other a little more. Go on."

"I wanted to ask you about a problem—well, it's not really a problem yet, but I always worry about it. It makes me crazy sometimes, worrying about it. Like, what if it's a full moon night and I can't get out of the city to shape-shift and hunt? So far I've managed it, but what if I can't someday? I have nightmares about getting stuck in a traffic jam, and shifting in my car. Or just losing it before I can get to open space. Am I worrying for nothing? Is there something I can do to keep this from happening? What if it does happen?"

I could hear his anxiety, and an undertone of embarrassment, as if he thought no one else worried about this kind of thing. I tried to reassure him. "It's a legitimate concern. Especially living in a big urban area—you never know what's going to happen. But you can take precautions, like giving yourself plenty of time to get out of town."

"But what if you get stuck? People must get stuck sometimes. What do you do? Have you ever gotten stuck?"

I had, but only because of events totally outside

my control. I wasn't going to bring up those messes. "I've never been in a situation I couldn't handle. The problem with getting stuck is, our wolf sides really want to get out and run. So while you *could* lock yourself in your house, werewolves are pretty good about breaking out, even scratching through doors and breaking windows. You need a really solid room or cage to prevent that from happening. I know that some werewolves have built cages in their houses for just such emergencies, if they're close to shifting and don't have time to get into the wild. Another thing that helps is having fresh meat on hand. If the werewolf has a big juicy rump roast to gnaw on, he calms down and stays put. Does any of this advice sound useful, Mark?"

"Yeah . . . yeah. It makes sense."

"Having coping strategies in place can reduce a lot of anxiety."

"Yeah, I can see that. I may never use a cage in the basement, but just knowing it's there would help. Thanks, Kitty."

"And thanks for your call. If any of my listeners out there have other good coping strategies, I'd love to hear about it. Next caller, please." I shifted in my swivel chair and leaned toward the mic.

"Hello, yes. Oh my gosh, am I really on?"

"Yes, you're really on," I said, amused. "What's your question?"

"Um, well. Do you have any advice about telling

your family that you're a werewolf? It's not something that ever comes up in regular conversation. And, well, I just don't know how to bring it up with my parents."

"I get this question pretty often. There isn't a good, right answer because everyone's situation is different. Have you been a werewolf for a while, or is this a recent thing?"

"Oh, it's been a couple of years. But that's just it. I'm finally comfortable with it, I think. And it feels awful keeping this big secret from my family. It's eating me up. But I'm scared to tell them, I don't know how they'll react."

"Here's the advice I usually give: truth isn't always the best policy in cases like this, if it's likely to upset your family and they wouldn't understand. But you might consider that they've already guessed that something's going on, and they might be worried about you. If that's the situation, it might actually be a relief for them to hear the truth."

"That's it!" she said. "That's it exactly. My mom's been asking all these questions, and I have to keep dodging. She must think I'm on drugs or something."

"And next to that how bad is being a werewolf? If you do decide to tell your family, you might also give them as much information as you can, like copies of magazine articles, or even my own book, *Underneath the Skin*." Shameless plugs never hurt anyone . . .

"Okay. I'll have to think about it. But cool. That helps."

"Good luck to you. Now, moving on." I was trying to pick relevant calls, questions that would help Tyler and Walters with situations they might run into, answers that would help them cope. So far so good. I hoped they were listening.

"Hi, I have a question about getting along with other werewolves and things?"

"All right, bring it on."

"I've got this situation, I've never heard of anything like it. It must be kind of strange, but it seems to be working out." He was male, young sounding. Either inexperienced or embarrassed—a true-confessions kind of call.

"What's going on?" I said.

"Okay, so I'm a werewolf. And I met this girl—she's a were-tiger. How cool is that?"

"That's pretty cool."

"We decided to move in with this other couple—they're were-leopards."

"What was that line about dogs and cats, living together? Sounds a little wild, literally. You all get along?"

"Yeah, we seem to. We all go out on full-moon nights together. And I bring along my friends—a couple of werewolves. We're not a pack or anything, it just works out."

"Well, that's just great," I said, wondering what

the real story was, because I didn't get happy stories like this too often. "So what's your question?"

"Is there a name for something like this? You know—werewolves have packs. Were-lions have prides. But what are we? My girlfriend wants to call us a collective, but that doesn't sound cool enough."

"Collective or a zoo?" I said.

"Come on, there's got to be some kind of technical term."

"How about 'roommates.' Why make it any more complicated? Let's take another call."

I clicked the line on as I greeted the next caller. Instead of the usual enthusiastic answer, I got a deep sigh, and I braced for the heavy-duty confession that would inevitably follow. People only sighed like that when they had real problems and no one else to talk to. It was difficult, but it was also the reason I'd started the show in the first place—so people like this would have someone to talk to.

"Hi, Kitty," he said. "I'm not even sure why I called. I just . . . I just have to tell someone what happened."

"That's what I'm here for. Just take your time." I tried to sound comforting and authoritative. It was all an act, but it seemed to fool people—they kept asking me for advice. One of these days, everyone was going to see right through it.

"I want to talk about my brother," he said, speaking quickly, as though he wanted to get it out before he changed his mind. "He was a park ranger and was attacked by a werewolf while working in the back country. He killed himself a few months later. He couldn't live with it, he couldn't stand it, so he found a silver bullet and shot himself."

I closed my eyes and rubbed my forehead against a sudden headache. I hated this. I wanted to reach out and hug him, but I also wanted to scream. At least radio—the microphone—gave me a shield. A mask to hide behind.

"I'm so sorry," I said. "That's very difficult." I sounded so trite.

"I keep wondering—could he have gotten help? Is there anything I could have done to help him? Did he have an alternative?"

I tried to sound professional, as if I had the ability—or even the right—to serve as someone's therapist. "I'm guessing that since he was attacked in the wild, he was never brought into a pack. He didn't have anyone to tell him what had happened to him or help him adjust. In my experience, it's difficult for someone like that to recover and achieve any kind of stability. Sometimes they do, or sometimes they run away. I don't know if anyone could have helped your brother. There isn't a standard procedure for this. He must have felt very alone." That was what happened—you felt alone, lost, paranoid, helpless. The rage and violence followed.

My caller said, "I'm the only person he ever told

about what had happened. And I'm glad he told me, because at least I know why. At least it makes a little bit of sense. I try to tell myself it's better this way. He was so afraid of hurting someone. Isn't this better than him hurting someone?"

It must have seemed like the responsible thing to do. He must have thought he was saving more than he was losing. I imagined all that despair. It made me think of Tyler and Walters, lurking in their hospital room.

"I don't know," I said. "I like to think there's always a choice. I can't put myself in your brother's shoes. But you're right, he probably didn't see any other way out."

"I wish . . . I just want anyone who's listening to your show, anyone who's thinking they don't have another way out, who thinks that's a solution—try to get help. Try to find someone, anyone, to help. Don't give up. Because me—my family—we'll never be the same. I don't know that he thought about that." I didn't know how he could say all this without sobbing.

"Thank you very much for calling. And again, I'm so sorry. Good luck to you and your family."

He clicked off without saying good-bye. I wasn't surprised. I hoped he'd gotten some comfort out of sharing the story and his grief.

"All right, let's take a break for station ID, and I'll take more calls when we get back to *The Midnight Hour*." I looked at Matt through the booth window.

He nodded—he'd already cued up the announcements. He must have known what was going through my mind. I pulled off my headphones and scratched my scalp. I still had half the show to get through, and I had to get back to being positive.

Somehow, I managed.

Chapter 14

TWO DAYS before the next full moon, I met with Dr. Shumacher to discuss her patients. She sat behind her desk, looking harried, her hair slipping from its bun, gray shadows under her eyes. She kept glancing at the pages on her clipboard as if they would start speaking, telling her what to do.

"Tuesday's full-moon night," I said. I sat across from her, staring her down, playing a dominance game and putting her on edge. "I'd like to give them the chance to get out, with my pack."

She blinked at me. "Do you really think they're ready for that?"

The truth was, I wasn't sure. The safest thing would be to keep them locked up, but that wasn't the goal, ultimately. "If they're going to move on, either to go back to civilian life or to active duty, they'll have to do this eventually. My pack can keep an eye on them. We ought to be able to keep them safe." As well as surrounding civilization . . .

"I suppose they deserve to have that opportunity." She was reluctant. I wondered what she wasn't telling me.

"I'd like to ask them. See if they feel up to it."

"Yes, of course," she said. I got the feeling Shumacher wasn't used to giving her lab rats a choice. "But Kitty—do you really think they'll ever be able to lead normal lives? Don't you think they'd be safer—better off—staying under supervision?"

"What? For the rest of their lives?" I almost laughed. But Shumacher just looked at me, matter-of-factly, as though the suggestion wasn't outlandish.

Then I realized that maybe she wanted to keep them locked up for the rest of their lives. Not for their own good, but for hers.

"Do you even see them as people? As patients? Or just as an experiment?" I said.

"That's not fair—I'm trying to do good work here."

"You can't keep them locked up forever. *They're* not guilty of murder."

She spoke with passion—desperation, almost. "We've never had a chance to study the long-term effects of lycanthropy like this. I've never had subjects I could study this closely. It's too good an opportunity—"

"At the cost of their sanity?" I said calmly. "They're *people*, Doctor."

She looked away.

She'd seemed so different than her predecessor at

the NIH, but maybe there wasn't any difference at all. The only results she wanted were raw data.

"Doctor, you have Vanderman. I'm not going to argue with you about letting him loose. But you have to let the others go. Please."

She leaned forward, resting on her elbows. "I've been to see Vanderman. He hasn't spoken in days. He paces, sleeps. If we try to confront him, he shape-shifts. He throws himself against the walls of his cell. I don't know how to bring him back. My only option is to keep him sedated. That's not a good baseline, even for a werewolf."

Tyler and Walters I could help. Vanderman . . . I didn't even want to see him. "I've heard stories of werewolves going so far that they don't come back. I wondered sometimes if it was just stories. The way shifting feels, the way it gnaws at you—it's easy to believe it could take over."

"Nobody knows how to deal with him," she said, shaking her head.

"This is where the bounty hunters usually come in," I said.

"That's terrible."

"Yes."

She sighed, seeming resigned. "I don't suppose it's that much worse than any other violent, mentally ill patient who has to remain confined."

I said, "Most violent mental illnesses aren't conta-gious." By her frown I could tell that I wasn't helping.

"Can I go ahead and talk to Tyler and Walters? We can help them, I'm sure of it."

She took me down the corridor to their room, opening doors with her pass key. I straightened, readjusting my mood to leave the grimness of the conversation outside. I didn't want them to see me frustrated or upset.

The men actually seemed to perk up when they saw me. Walters was sitting on his bed and looked up, interested. Tyler had been at the table, reading a dog-eared paperback. He set the book aside and stood, almost at attention, when I came through the door.

"Kitty. How are you?"

"I'm fine," I said, smiling. "And you?"

He shrugged, Walters glowered, and I had to smile. Those were perfectly reasonable, human reactions to being locked up in a cell. Another step toward normality achieved. Shumacher left us, but I knew she was watching on her closed-circuit camera. My skin prickled at the scrutiny.

The normal thing to do would have been to pull up a chair to talk. But I remained standing to keep myself taller. And I wanted to let these guys out on the full moon?

"So," I said. "Did you guys get a chance to listen to the show Friday?"

Tyler donned a crooked grin. "Shumacher let us have a radio. You do that every week?"

"Yeah. It's kind of fun."

He shook his head and seemed amused. "It's kind of crazy."

"I didn't know there were so many of us out there," Walters said, from the bed. "So many people called in saying they're werewolves. Are there really that many?"

"They call in from all over," I said. "I don't really know how many of us there are. But they're out there. Most of them lead pretty quiet, normal lives. They keep themselves secret and no one knows they're there." *And you can do the same,* was the conclusion I left unspoken. Walters nodded thoughtfully, which heartened me. Maybe he really had been inspired. "Full moon's in a couple of days. You two feel up to maybe spending it outside?"

They looked at me, eyes wide, like kids who just found out they might get to go to Disneyland.

"Really?" Tyler said, hesitating, obviously not believing it.

"It's a step," I said. "You want to get out of here, you want to go home, you're going to have to deal with the full moon. You can come spend it with my pack. See how real werewolves handle it."

"I'd go for that," Tyler said, glancing briefly at the camera in the upper corner of the room, where Shumacher was watching, before looking back at me. I wouldn't blame him for thinking this was some kind of psychological experiment. Subject them to stress and disappointment, and so on.

"It's not a done deal yet," I said. "You need to be honest about whether you think you can handle it. Because if you screw this up, you may not get another chance. And if you hurt any of my people, I'll finish you off myself."

"You could try," Walters grumbled.

I looked at him. "Yeah. And what would you say if I told you I've done it before?"

"What, stopped a werewolf?" he snickered.

"Killed," I said. "Killed a werewolf."

He frowned and looked away, suddenly uncertain.

Tyler smiled wryly. "I believe you. I don't want to fuck with you."

"Good man," I said. "Walters?"

"I want to get out of here," he said softly.

"Then we have to toe the line," Tyler said to him, leaning in, a private conference. "Follow the rules and we get out. Got it?"

Walters nodded, closing his eyes, gritting his teeth, as if it was an effort.

"I still need to talk it over with Dr. Shumacher and my people. But if you're up for it, we'll come get you on Tuesday."

"Kitty. Thanks," Tyler said.

"I WAS under the impression that werewolf packs were not meant to be run by committee," Ben said as we pulled into the parking lot behind New Moon Monday evening, just before closing time.

"Yeah," I said. "But I don't want to be like all those other werewolves, you know?"

"Says the werewolf named Kitty."

"It's too late to change my name now," I grumbled.

A half an hour later, we stood before our pack of werewolves and explained the situation. Everyone had an opinion.

"I do not like the idea of baby-sitting those guys," Becky said, glaring at me from her seat at the end of the table. "We can't control them. They can't control *themselves*."

Twelve of the pack's seventeen members were here. Word had gone out through Shaun. I'd told him over the phone what I wanted to talk about, he saw others of our pack as they came in and out of the bar, and the grapevine would have continued from there. They came to find out if what they'd heard was true: was I about to let a couple of new wolves join the pack? We clustered around a few tables in the back of the restaurant. Head of the pack, Ben and I sat at our own small table for two, presiding over the gathering.

Becky wasn't wrong. She had every right to be worried, since she'd dealt with them up close. Our outing at the restaurant last week hadn't immediately made everything all sunshine and show tunes.

"I know," I said. "We need a plan. Several of us need to look after each of them. Help keep them in line, keep them grounded."

"You're asking us to keep tabs on a couple of Green Berets here? Are we even up for that?" Jared was in his late thirties, unassuming. Older and more experienced than I, but with no desire to be a leader, so he deferred. Like a lot of us, he just wanted to be left alone to live his life. And like it did for a lot of us, the pack helped keep his wolf side sane.

I couldn't bullshit these guys. They'd only go along with me as long as I kept the pack stable.

"Um, yeah," I said. "But they're motivated. They want to go home. They need our help."

"I understand that," Shaun said. He was leaning on the bar, on the other side of the gathering. "But I don't want us to turn into Kitty's home for wayward werewolves." A few of the others nodded in agreement. I couldn't blame them. We'd been stable for over a year now—no invasions from the outside, no dissention from within—and most of the pack wanted us to stay that way.

"You want me to just turn my back on them?" I said.

"Your own people have to come first," Shaun said.

"I want us to be a little altruistic here. These guys are war vets, they've been through a lot. They need to see what well-adjusted werewolves look like, and I think we can do that."

I looked around at my bunch. *My* pack. It had taken a long time for me to think of them that way. When I'd first met most of them, I'd been a newly minted werewolf, freaked out and constantly on the edge of panic, rolling over to show my belly to keep out of trouble. Now look at me—giving orders. And they were actually listening. I liked to think it was because I made sense, usually. All three of the pack's women, apart from me, were here—Becky, Kris, and Rachel. Rachel was older, quiet and submissive. She didn't want any trouble, and Ben, Shaun, and I tried to keep trouble away from her. She was looking particularly jumpy, her shoulders bunched, her gaze darting. Becky, sitting nearby, put her hand on her shoulder to calm her. The men of the pack weren't the most aggressive werewolves I'd ever met—the previous alpha had rather ruthlessly gotten rid of anyone who posed a threat to his authority—but they weren't pushovers, either. If Ben and I vanished, Shaun, Becky, or Dan could serve as the pack's alphas just as well. But they weren't going to challenge us for the hell of it. We were a stable group, which was why I thought we could handle Tyler and Walters.

"What do you think about this, Ben?" Jared asked. I tried not to bristle, even though this felt as if he was going over my head. I glared at Jared, and he ducked his gaze.

Attitude counted for so much around here.

"I've met 'em," Ben said. "I'm with Kitty. They need a break and I think we can help. Call it our patriotic duty."

A couple of the guys snorted—patriotism didn't count for much when you sometimes felt like a stranger in your own country. Werewolves *were* their own country.

Kris—a thirty-something woman with thick brown hair, and a little bit of wolf always lingering in her brown eyes—sat back, her arms crossed. She was looking at the floor when she spoke. "My little brother's in Iraq right now. If it were him, I'd want someone to help him."

I'd known about her brother. She'd come to me about it, because knowing her brother was in danger and out of her ability to help him set her on edge, and she'd needed help—a friendly ear, a leader to help her keep herself together. But she must not have told everyone, because the others seemed surprised, then looked away, not knowing what to say.

We didn't get any more arguments after that. So, the pack wasn't comfortable helping other were-wolves, but they'd help the soldiers. I'd take what I could get.

Chapter 15

TUESDAY MORNING, it started snowing. The weather had gone from clear and windy the night before to overcast and settled. Times like these, when the sky was gray and full of weight, you hardly noticed when the flakes started falling—just a few at first, then more, until the air was a wall of snow. If I'd been paying attention to the forecast there had probably been great pronouncements of a front moving in. But I'd been a little preoccupied. The weather matched my mood.

Ben slept in and woke to find me sitting on the sofa, staring out the balcony window at the depressed gray day. He was shirtless, dressed only in sweats, and his skin looked warm and touchable.

"Think this'll clear up by tonight?" he said.

It was full-moon night. Even when the sky was overcast, I could feel its power tugging at me, a restlessness turning in my gut that would grow stronger until the night itself, when it would boil over.

I reached up to rub his back, then put my arm around his waist. We'd been out in nastier weather than this. To a wolf, covered in fur, the cold was nothing. Our human forms retained some of that resilience. When we slept, we'd all curl up together, keeping each other warm, even as the snow fell over us. In the morning we'd wake as human, grumbling about coffee and hot showers. But we'd never freeze out in a storm. I mostly worried about the snow keeping us from driving home.

"Yeah. If it's too bad maybe we can go out east," I said. Depending on where a storm hit, either the mountains would get dumped on with snow, or the plains would. We could usually find someplace else to be if the snow got too bad.

Normally, I wouldn't worry about a winter storm impacting the pack's night out. This time, maybe I should be. "Do you think we should give Cormac a call?"

"What—in case Tyler and Walters give us trouble?" His brow furrowed. I knew he didn't want to get Cormac involved—he might be tempted to take action.

"No. To find out if maybe Franklin can start blizzards as well as hurricanes."

"We don't even know that he can start hurricanes."

"Cormac said he was up to something. What if it's this?" I pointed to the falling snow.

It wasn't a blizzard. Not yet. In fact, it might have been slowing down—the gray clouds were only spitting flakes, which melted as soon as they touched down. Wet, messy—but not a blizzard.

"You're—" He stopped.

"What? I'm what?"

"I was about to say paranoid. But sometimes, you're right."

"So I should call Cormac."

"Maybe in just a minute," he said, and wrapped his arms around me, trapping me against his body. I could feel his chest move with his breathing, and time stopped for a moment as we watched the snow fall. If only all mornings could be like this.

CORMAC WANTED to meet and talk, which meant he had something. He came over to the condo midmorning, sheltering a manila folder inside his leather jacket. His brown hair was dark with damp from the falling snow.

Ben and I were dressed and ready for company by then. We gathered around the dining room table over hot coffee.

"What have you got?" Ben said.

"Two things: a lot of speculation, and this." Cormac pulled a page from the folder. It showed a blurry photograph, low resolution, high angle— footage from a security camera, maybe. The setting seemed to be the lobby of an office building, at night—polished granite floors, potted ferns in the corners and at a security desk. Lights flared in reflection off a row of glass doors.

Two figures were shaking hands. One of them was clearly Franklin, much as I'd seen him last week, in his expensive coat and confident bearing. The other was a blur, indistinguishable. As if the person was moving, maybe turning quickly at the sound of a noise.

But that wasn't it. I had seen this before.

"It's surveillance footage," I said.

Cormac nodded. "From the lobby of the building in New York where Franklin has his offices."

"How the hell did you get this?" Ben asked.

"You sure you want to know?" Cormac answered.

"This isn't going to be admissible in court, is it?" Ben said.

"Probably not, but we're past that. Here's the speculation: I think Franklin's a hired gun. But I don't have a clue who he's working for."

"That's a vampire," I said, pointing to the mysterious blurry figure. Vampires didn't always show up on camera—they could when they chose to. But they could also manipulate the way they interacted with light—traveling in shadow, seeming to appear and disappear magically. No reflections. And blurring their recorded images.

Cormac looked at me, his lips pressed in a line.

After a moment he said, "Yeah. Maybe. That's more speculation."

"Franklin's a hit man?" Ben said, leaning over the table, looking confused. "But why? He owns a multimillion-dollar corporation."

"You should know better than anybody, some guys don't get into it for the money," Cormac said. "If I'm right, then Kitty's right, and Speedy Mart's a front that lets Harold Franklin travel all over the country, anchoring his spells to do whatever he needs to do. And it always looks like an accident. A natural disaster. Collateral damage covers up the hit even better."

"Isn't it more likely that Franklin's doing the hiring of whoever this guy is?" Ben's inclination was to argue. To poke holes in arguments. I was grateful for that now, because Cormac's story sounded crazy. Except that it made so much sense. I bet even Charles from Shreveport hadn't considered this explanation.

"Anything's possible," Cormac said, and the phrase had never sounded truer. He nodded at me. "Except you look like you know who this vampire is."

"Roman," I said. Ben rubbed his hand through his hair. His shoulders had gone stiff, like hackles rising, and his body seemed poised to spring.

Cormac noticed it and glanced between us. "That guy you tangled with last year? The two-thousand-year-old vampire?"

"Yeah."

"This sound like something he would do?"

"Yeah," I said. And I wasn't surprised, I couldn't be. I knew Roman would be back, somehow. "So Franklin's trying to kill me—"

"Or punish you. Show that he—and whoever hired him—has power over you. They waited for an opening, and you gave them one when you did your show. Discredit you with the lawsuit, punish you with whatever Franklin has cooking. They might even have planted some stories to encourage you."

So I'd brought this on myself. If I'd just shut up, if I hadn't gone poking the wasp's nest . . . But no. I had every right to question Franklin. Because I was *right*, dammit. I said, "You guessed all this because this is how you would do it. The hit-man mentality."

He nodded. "It's when he came to see you. There are a couple of kinds of hit men. There are the pros, the ones who do the job quick and clean, no fuss, collect the pay and go home. Then you have the thrill seekers. They have to be clever. Look the target in the eye. Put some flash into the job. Taunt. Franklin's a wizard first. He just hires out for the thrill. He wasn't kidding when he said he just wanted to see you face to face."

"So what do we do? How do we stop him?"

Ben and Cormac glanced at each other, then away.

"We don't," Ben said finally. "Because we have no proof."

Cormac said, "All we have is speculation. We can't do anything until he makes a move. Unless we want to take him down ourselves."

Which put us in legal trouble, if we got caught.

I got up and went for my phone, in my bag on the coffee table.

"Who are you calling?" Ben said.

I'd already speed dialed the number; I held my hand up to ask Ben to wait. And the voice mail came up, which I expected. I left a message. "Hi, Rick. It's Kitty. We may have a situation. I'll explain later, when you're awake. If I'm still here, that is." I flipped the phone shut.

"Rick's not going to be up until nightfall," Ben said.

"I know, but at least he'll know there's trouble when he is up." Then I dialed the second number.

Detective Hardin answered on the first ring. "Hardin here."

Detective Jessi Hardin was my ally in the Denver PD, head of and pretty much only officer in the Paranatural Unit. She handled crimes involving the supernatural and had a generally open mind—and a hard nose.

I opened my mouth and realized I had nothing to say. This was what Ben and Cormac meant by not having proof. What did I tell her, that the respected president of a major company was really a wizard hit man out for my blood and that the entire city might be in danger? That was crazy even by my standards. Hardin was usually sympathetic, but this might be pushing my luck.

"Hi, Detective. How are you?" I said instead.

"Kitty, I'm a little swamped here. Do you need something?" I heard the sounds of traffic and yelling in the background.

"I don't know," I said, wincing. "I have some . . . suspicions. I'm afraid something might be up." Was that vague enough?

She sighed. "I'm sure it's very interesting, but unless you have an actual crime for me to investigate, can it wait?"

In other words, until we had something we could arrest Franklin for, she couldn't do anything. "Yeah, sure. Sorry to bother you."

I wasn't sure she heard me—she was shouting at someone about getting a car off the road. "Kitty, I'll talk to you later, okay?" she said into the phone.

"Sure. Hey, take care, it sounds rough out there."

"You have no idea. Later," she said, and hung up.

I closed the phone. Ben and Cormac were both looking at me, smug in their lack of expressions. They didn't even have to say *I told you so.*

"The question still stands," I said. "What are we going to do?"

"It's a full moon tonight," Cormac said. "I assumed you'd both be busy."

Shitty timing, as usual. But if Cormac was right, it was all part of the plan. I returned to my seat; my coffee had gone cold.

"We'll just keep our eyes open, as usual," Ben said, and gave a fatalistic shrug.

"You'll keep an eye on Franklin while we're out?" I said.

"I'm stuck on him like a burr," Cormac said, getting up and grabbing his coat off the back of his chair. He left the photo on the table.

"Be careful," I said. He nodded, and closed the condo door behind him.

Chapter 16

THE SKY hadn't done more than spit snow all after-noon. Meteorologist predictions didn't call for anything worse than that, but I wasn't making any bets. Low cloud cover made for a depressing trip out; the sky seemed darker than it should have been, settling over the city like a lead blanket.

Cormac called once to say he didn't have any more news—Franklin was lying low. He told us to be careful, which indicated that he was, in fact, worried.

Well before sunset, Ben and I picked up Tyler and Walters at the VA hospital. Dr. Shumacher met us at the door. She wore jeans, a sweater, and a heavy down parka and looked like she was getting ready for an Arctic expedition. Fair enough; it was cold out. But it was so incongruous, so unlike her usual prim appearance and bearing. It set me on edge.

"Hello, Doctor," I said. "Are they ready to go?"

"Just about, I think. I've asked them wait inside while we talk."

I glanced at Ben; his expression was neutral. One of his courtroom faces, which made me pretty sure he wasn't going to like what Shumacher was about to say any more than I would. She had a tension to her—tight lips and stiff shoulders.

"What's the problem?" I said.

"I need to know where you'll be tonight,"

Of course she did. I shook my head. "I can't tell you that, Doctor."

"I have to know where you're taking my patients." She straightened, trying to make herself look taller; we were about the same height. She'd probably been working herself up to this conversation all day. She smelled nervous, sweating under her coat.

"I'm sorry, but this isn't just about your patients. It's about my pack. I need to keep them safe and that means no outsiders. As long as Tyler and Walters are with me they're part of my pack."

"But I have to monitor them, I have to record their progress, and if something were to go wrong—"

"So you can have Colonel Stafford there with the tranquilizer guns? Around my wolves? No." And I realized that she'd probably been planning it. Stafford and his soldiers were probably on alert, waiting for Shumacher's call in their van or troop carrier or whatever they used. They'd expected to be able to watch our full-moon adventures. I had to rein in my frustration, my anger. Next to me, Ben's shoulder brushed mine, a brief touch to anchor me: *settle down, now*.

"How can you call them *your* wolves?" she said. She'd probably thought of them as hers.

"Because they're my responsibility. I've promised to protect them."

"Can you even do that?"

I asked myself that every day. How the hell did I end up here? With this responsibility? Who was I to deserve that kind of loyalty? To demand that kind of respect? Because I was the one who was there. Because I could.

"You don't understand, do you? All the research you've done, everything you've learned, and you don't understand. I'm the alpha of this pack. And you'll never find out where we're going."

Her gaze flickered away for a moment. Her authority wasn't working on me.

"I can refuse to release them to your custody," she said. "I don't have to let them go."

I suppressed a growl. I almost exclaimed, shouted a denial in my panic. After all we'd accomplished, she wouldn't do that, would she? She just couldn't. I almost begged. But I stopped myself and took a deep breath.

I said, "Then you're going to have to be the one to tell them that they get to spend the full moon locked up in a concrete cell. You're going to have to deal with them when they go crazy and try to break out."

"We have procedures for that. This wouldn't be their first full moon in custody," she said, but her voice wavered, like she wasn't sure. I wouldn't have wanted to tell Tyler and Walters—I could just about see the looks on their faces. Disappointment, betrayal, rage, and no reason to hold back.

"I don't want to argue with you," I said. "You're the one who asked me to help, and I told you what I think will help—getting them outside and showing them how to control themselves. I promise I'll bring them back in the morning, if that's what you're worried about."

"No, it's not that. It's just—" Instead of finishing the thought, she bowed her head and sighed. "I want to be there. I want to watch."

Ben spoke up. "Has it occurred to you how dangerous that could be?"

"But to see a werewolf pack during the full moon, to record it . . ." Again, she trailed off. Of course she knew how dangerous it could be. That was why she was never going to see it for herself.

"I suppose you could try one of those cages that the guys who study polar bears use, but I'm not sure how much good it would do you," I said.

Ben glared at me. Shumacher's brow furrowed.

Ben and I were wearing our full-moon clothing: old jeans and T-shirts. I went braless; the fewer clothes to keep track of, the better. We went without coats at all—the cold didn't affect us so much. We didn't strike a very intimidating picture. But in our stances, our carriage, our glares, we were so much more than we appeared. Shumacher had worked with werewolves, and she knew what she was seeing: an alpha pair defending their territory.

"Let us take them," Ben said. "Just for the night. If you really have their best interests in mind, if you really want to rehabilitate them and not just study them, it's the right thing to do."

Shumacher nodded, and I suppressed my sigh of relief. Clearly, Tyler and Walters were part of my pack. Maybe just for tonight, maybe not for the foreseeable future. But now, they were mine to care for. Mine and my Wolf's.

The doctor went back inside the building. A growl burred in my throat and I started pacing in front of Ben. "What does she think she's doing? Did she really think I'd just tell her?"

"Settle down," he said. He looked calm, but his back was stiff, his shoulders raised. A little of his wolf showed in his eyes, as I was sure my Wolf showed in mine. It was almost time to run; we could both feel it. I stopped pacing and hugged myself. Ben touched my arm and leaned in to kiss my ear, breathing out as he did so. Wolf language: be calm.

Shumacher returned with Tyler and Walters. They were obviously edgy. They kept looking around—

along the side of the building, out to the edges of the parking lot, even up to the roof. I wondered how much of their apprehension came from being were-wolves on the night of the full moon, or from being soldiers recently come home from a war zone. It was as if they expected grenades to drop.

I stood between them and gave each of their arms a squeeze to anchor them. *Everything was going to be all right*. I felt something, Wolf awakening in my eyes, catching each of their gazes in turn and staring at them, not in challenge but with assurance: *we'll be fine, we're a pack, I'll look after you*. It seemed a ridiculous claim to make; I was half Tyler's size. But they both settled, their shoulders easing, the wolves in their gazes acknowledging me.

"We'll be fine, Doctor," I said to Shumacher with all the confidence I'd just shown to the soldiers. "Come on, guys." Hands on their arms, I steered them toward Ben and the car.

Shumacher looked at me, lips pursed, holding back arguments. I just didn't care anymore and walked away.

We piled into Ben's car, the soldiers in the back-seat, me in front, Ben driving.

"You guys okay?" I said, looking over my shoulder.

"What happened back there?" Tyler said. "Shumacher looked ready to spit, but she was scared."

We'd all smelled her fear. "She wanted to know where we were going, to keep tabs on us. Bring Stafford and his guys along, 'just in case.' I wouldn't let her. She threatened not to let you out for the night." They reacted, jaws clenched, noses flaring— nerves, anger. "Don't worry, I talked her out of it."

"I bet they'll try to follow us," Ben said. "Track us, if they can."

"Can we dodge them? Lose them?" I looked around, out windows, for the imaginary Humvee following us. If Shumacher and Stafford really were following us and they knew what they were doing, I wouldn't see them.

"I can try."

Tyler leaned forward. Neither of them were belted in, but that didn't seem important enough to worry about. It's not as though a car wreck would be likely to kill any of us.

"Don't take the direct route," he said. "Are there any one-way streets around here? Big parking lots or garages with multiple exits? You can double back and get away before they've figured out what you're doing."

"We'd have to go downtown for that," I said.

"I think I have an idea," Ben said. He drove a few blocks then swung east on Colfax. Ten minutes later, he turned again, and a couple more blocks brought us to a familiar wide, grassy lawn. We followed the long, looping drive around Cheesman Park. It wasn't the mazelike parking lot Tyler had asked for, but the road here was twisting and confusing, which amounted to the same thing.

Ben said, "Even if they follow us here, we might fool them into thinking this is where we're stopping.

"They don't really think we'd shape-shift in downtown Denver, do they?" I said.

"I'm guessing they don't know much of anything or they wouldn't have called you," Ben said, giving me a look.

"Gee, thanks," I said.

We'd made half a circuit of the park when Ben turned onto a different street than the one we left. He made a couple more turns, then we were heading north toward I-70.

"You see anything, Walt?" Tyler said.

"No, I do not. Think we're clear."

Maybe Shumacher and Stafford hadn't sent anyone after us. Maybe they had and we really had lost them. I'd never know for sure, but the soldiers were calm, and that counted for something.

Behind heavy clouds, the sun set, and as the light faded, we drove in silence.

Chapter 17

WE HEADED east, into the Great Plains. Usually we spent full moons in the mountains, with sheltered forests and valleys. Close enough to town to be convenient, but far enough away to be isolated. And plenty of hunting: deer, rabbits, and so on.

In the nineteenth century the Great Plains were called the Great American Desert because the region was so desolate. You could travel for hundreds of miles without seeing a tree, or a single living creature apart from the sea of grass rippling in a constant wind. Of course, the impression wasn't the true picture. The place was rich with life. Even in the cold of winter, I could sense a tapestry of smells: dried grass, foraging rodents, the owls and hawks that hunted them, coyotes on the prowl. The rustling of brush and grasses made a constant rhythm. I soaked it all in—my world, my territory. Inside me, Wolf kicked, ready to run. *Soon . . .*

On the prairie, we'd be isolated, and we'd find plenty to eat—pronghorn, rabbits, prairie dogs—but we wouldn't have much shelter. At the same time, Tyler and Walters wouldn't have anywhere to hide. On the flat, wide plains, I could keep an eye on them. We could keep watch over each other. And we'd avoid the snow scheduled to hit the mountains overnight.

A hundred years ago, wild wolves lived out here. We could, too.

We didn't all park in the same place, as we usually did when we went to the mountains, where we had a sheltered turnout on private land to use. Here, the sudden midnight parking lot would have attracted too much attention. Instead, we used state park trailheads, remote dirt roads, and fence lines, a car or two in each place. Then we gathered, down a sloping hill where a creek lined with cottonwoods cut a gully through the land. We'd be safe out here. I made doubly sure we were well away from cattle ranches and any herds of grazing cattle. Fresh steaks might sound great, but I couldn't think of a worse way to draw attention to ourselves.

Ben and I reached the rendezvous spot first with the two soldiers and waited for the others.

Tyler stood on a rise, face turned to the sky, to a silver-lined bank of clouds that hid the rising moon. He pulled off his T-shirt, dropped it. Flexing the powerful muscles of his shoulders, he was like a living shadow. Nearby, the smaller, wirier Walters was pacing.

"We haven't been free on a full moon since Afghanistan," Tyler said.

"How does it feel?"

"I'm excited. I want to run." A faint smile turned on his lips. He was more excited than nervous. His wolf was rising.

"What was it like?" I said, cautious, because I was maybe opening wounds. "In Afghanistan, when Gordon was leading you. What did you do during full moons?"

"We hunted," he said. Walters barked a laugh.

Quiet and thoughtful, Ben watched us. We exchanged a glance. I could almost tell what he was thinking: *we're going to have to be careful. Stick together and watch out for them.* I nodded.

Ben glanced toward the horizon. "They're here."

"Okay," I said. "I want you guys to stay together—stay with the group. That's all I want you to worry about—"

Tyler said, "But we hunt—"

"We hunt as a pack. But don't worry about that, it'll happen. I need you two to stay close. That's more important this time around. Walters?" I called to the other soldier, who was looking over the plains at the spot where Shaun approached with Becky.

"Yeah, yeah," he said.

"Any questions before the party starts?" I said to them.

Shaun wore only sweatpants and went barefoot. Becky had on sweats and a tank top. We looked like we were out here for a picnic, despite the cold nighttime breeze.

Tyler was breathing hard, sweat dripping down his neck. He was trying to keep it together. "I don't know if I can do this," he said. "I don't know if I can get along with the rest of them."

"You'll be fine. Walters, can you please stand still?" I said. And wonder of wonders, he stopped pacing.

Maybe there was a better way to introduce new wolves to a pack. Maybe there was a ceremony or ritual that would have made this easier. These were werewolves, not friends at a cocktail party. I couldn't just ask them to shake hands and tell each other about their jobs.

I moved to stand between the new arrivals and the soldiers. They'd have to cross me to get to each other. I was hoping to keep it that way all night.

"Shaun," I said. "You've met Tyler and Walters. And Becky."

The four of them looked each other up and down. None of them were happy. But they weren't exactly unhappy, either. Hackles were up, but no one was baring teeth.

"Are we going to have trouble?" Shaun asked.

"No, man," Tyler said. "No trouble."

Shaun nodded, satisfied. He went to the first tree in the grove and stripped off his sweatpants. He stood waiting, naked and powerful in the dim, cloud-shrouded moonlight. Becky followed him to the tree, keeping her gaze on Walters—who glanced away.

The other wolves of the pack arrived, stalking cautiously, looking to me for reassurance after glancing at the strangers. Most of them hadn't met Tyler and Walters yet. I made sure to introduce them all, give them names, make them look at each other. I'd touch my pack member on the shoulder or arm, then touch Tyler and Walters. Nostrils flared, heads cocked as they studied each other, smelling each other. The soldiers were starting to smell like pack. Some of the antiseptic, institutional tinge that clung to them because of their time in the hospital was wearing off. They were picking up the scent of other wolves, of the wild wind that blew from the mountains and over the plains.

The biggest problem we'd have was if one of my wolves decided to challenge either of the soldiers for dominance. It was bound to happen—they looked like dominant wolves. They looked like threats. But if I acted as if they weren't a threat, and if they in turn didn't do anything threatening, we ought to be able to get through this. The point was to show Tyler and Walters what a normal, peaceful wolf pack looked like.

Becky grunted and fell to a crouch. Anticipation spiked through the air, and the scent of fur began to overpower the scent of skin. Experienced, she hardly made a sound when she changed, just a gasp of effort, and her body began to melt, a sheen of fur sprouting over her skin, bones sliding into new shapes. Others followed quickly after that, until a dozen wolves were shaking out newly grown fur, stretching limbs, and trotting, jumping, spinning to revel in new muscles, like pups at play. The wolves were free; it was a time of celebration. Some of them came up to me, heads and tails bowed and submissive. They rubbed against me, bumping my hips with their heads. Smiling, I dragged my fingers through their coats. Their bodies were furnaces in the freezing air.

Walters shifted first. Crying out, he fell and ripped his clothing off as if it was burning him. Tyler quickly went to him and put a hand on his shoulder.

"He's never gotten used to this," Tyler said. He kept a hand on Walters, whose body shifted under him, from human to wolf, from skin to fur. "Take it easy, man. It's okay," he murmured. The whole time, Walters's teeth were bared in a pain-wracked grimace. He didn't want to let go; his wolf was raging inside him, clawing at him, tearing its way free, and Walters struggled against it.

It hurt less when you just let it happen.

Then it was over, and Walters's silver-furred wolf

lay panting for a moment. Tyler backed away and quickly shoved off his pants. Breathing deeply, wordlessly, he glanced at me—asking permission. I nodded.

He curved his back, hunched over, and Changed. Unlike Walters, he knew how to let go, to let the Change pour over him like water. When his hands touched the ground, they were furred and clawed. When he turned his face upward, to the moon, he had a long snout and amber eyes. In a handful of heartbeats, he was a wolf, reddish and bristling. And he was huge, broad through the chest and shoulders, with hindquarters that could keep him running across the harshest landscape for days.

Walters looked at him and bared his teeth, and Tyler pounced on him, knocking him over. Walters rolled and showed his belly. Tyler outranked Walters and would keep him in line.

My wolves gave the pair a wide berth, keeping me between them. My own Wolf was howling inside me: *run, hunt, now.* My human side was wondering what I'd gotten myself into. Best to let that go and let Wolf be in charge. My skin tingled, as if the moonlight were tangible, caressing me.

Ben had taken off his clothes. His pale skin shone almost white under the pale moon, which even if we couldn't see it, we could tell was high over head, calling to us, singing to us. *It's time, it's time . . .*

Stepping up to me, he slid my shirt over my head,

kissing me as he dropped it away. I tasted tension in him, anticipation. This was the best of nights. We were mates, this was our pack, our territory. I ran my hands through his hair, imagining a wolf's pelt.

Beyond words now, I stepped away from him, closed my eyes, and let go.

Cold air sparks through her lungs. Moonlight gleams; the world is stark, wide open, waiting for them.

Her mate greets her, bumping her shoulder to shoulder, nipping her ear then licking her face to say he's only teasing. She breathes in his musky scent and gives a yip. He play-bows, chest to the ground and haunches up, and she wants to tackle him. But now isn't the time. She breathes into the ruff at his neck to tell him this is serious, then surveys the others.

Her wolves are milling, tracing the same paths back and forth, panting, whines caught in their throats—nervous, frightened.

The two newcomers, massive and wary, wait apart, legs braced, staring.

Stupid wolves, acting like they want to start a fight.

She runs to her pack and snaps, biting at their haunches, getting them to move. They pin their ears at her but lower their tails and hunch their backs— they don't want trouble, after all. They're scared, though—but she can deal with that. She knows what it's like to be scared. They had to move, all of them, the whole pack, and focus their attention outward to the job at hand, rather than on each other.

Sitting back a moment, she tips her head back and howls, a short clean note, to call them together. Her breath fogs silver.

Her mate dances, then runs to the open plain. The pack follows, a river of fur, brindled, shadowed, edged with white. She brings up the end, herding the two new wolves, snapping to make sure they follow.

At the edges of the pack, wolves put noses to earth, searching for trails. This land may be cold, wind-swept, but it is rich with life, dense with the trails of mice and rabbits. But they'll need more to feed them all this night. So they move on, searching for larger prey.

At no other time does she feel so alive. Her ears are raised, her nose active, her fur on end and quivering. Her senses spread out to join the larger pattern of the world.

Then she finds it, a bright blaze across the trails of scent—large creatures moving slowly, hooved footfalls cutting into the earth. They all catch it and begin circling, agitated, excited. She nips at them, urging calm, patience.

The silver newcomer, the smaller of the two, dawdles. She urges him back, snapping at his haunches to keep him with the pack. He lays his ears back at her, but listens. Several times, though, she has to run after him. The bigger newcomer helps her, when he sees it.

Her mate ranges ahead, then stops and pricks his ears. The rest of the pack crouches, waiting. She sidles up alongside him, and sees it: deer, three of them, young and hesitant, eating a few mouthfuls of dead grass at a time before lifting their heads to keep watch. They're wary, but the pack only has to catch one. She brushes past her mate, body to body, and licks his face.

Crouching, she hides in the brush and waits. They all know their jobs, even the newcomers, who pace forward, huffing, limbs trembling, ready to run.

The pack creeps slowly until her mate, the other alpha, gives the signal by launching forward, leaping from the grasses in a flat run. Several of the others join him. The deer—heads up, snorting—spring away in a panic.

The chase is on.

Over the next half hour, the pack runs the deer down. Some of the wolves race, biting at the creatures' heels, spurring them to greater heights of fear while the deer run hard, eyes rolling, breath steaming in clouds. Then those wolves fall back, and others take their place. The wolves can continue this chase all night; the deer can't. One of them falters— that's the one, the unfortunate victim.

It doesn't fall, but the stumble is enough. A pair

of wolves jump in front of it, cutting it off from its fellows who race on, unconcerned, uncaring. The victim dodges, twisting on thin, graceful legs. But everywhere it turns, there are wolves.

She races on now, leading her newcomers. The deer is exhausted, trembling, mindless. The attack takes seconds. She springs at its haunches, ripping into it with her claws. One of the newcomers, the big one, strikes at the deer's nose, clamping its face with vicious teeth, yanking downward.

The neck twists; the deer falls. She crawls over it and bites into its throat. Its heart still beats, just for a moment, pumping blood into her mouth as she rips apart the veins and arteries. It twitches, then lies still, dead.

A glorious finish to a glorious hunt.

Then the growling and nipping start.

The newcomer—the talented hunter—glares at her, catches her gaze and doesn't break it. His kill, he seems to say. His prize. She matches his stare: pack's prize. Standing on the carcass, she looks down on him and bares her teeth. They've had this conversation already, her bristling hackles remind him. If he wants to run with the pack, he must follow the rules. They will all fight him if he breaks their peace.

He lowers his gaze and turns away.

There is enough meat for them all. She won't let any of them starve, and proves it. Tongue lolling happily, eyes gleaming, her mate joins her, and they get to work, tearing past the tough skin into rich flesh and viscera. After she and her mate choose their pieces, they step away and let the others feed.

It is a good night, filled with the sounds of feasting. Her mate lies next to her and licks blood off her muzzle, which makes her smile, jaw open, ears flat.

Nearby, the newcomers settle, bellies to earth, licking blood from their paws. They're all right, she tells herself. Everything's going to be all right.

After feeding, leaving behind bone and skin for the scavengers, they run. For the fierce joy of it, they run, tails out, streamlined, wind flattening their fur. Even hidden behind clouds, the shining moon blazes a trail for them until it sinks westward. Then weariness pulls at her; the pack slows. Time to lead them home, to their den, to sleep. She and her mate circle back to where they started from.

She moves through them all, touching noses, brushing ears, counting, tracking scents, making sure they're all here, all safe. Even her two new wolves, whose scents are no longer so very strange. In small groups spread throughout the glade, they sleep curled up, pressed against each other, noses on flanks, tails brushing faces, deep in warmth and comfort.

Someone's awake. Calls out a name. The others shift, restless, half awake . . .

I started awake because something was wrong. First, it was snowing. But that was just annoying. We'd woken up in snow before.

Across the grove, Tyler was climbing to his feet, the broad muscles of his back flexing as he turned, looking back and forth. "Walters!" he called again. "Ethan!"

A few yards away from me, frowning, Shaun caught my gaze. Ben's hand closed around mine; his skin felt burning hot in the freezing cold morning.

I'd taken a count the night before, I remembered that—everyone had been here and safe. I quickly did so again, both by sight and by smell, even though I already knew what I'd find. Tyler, hands clenched, paced up to the rise to get a better look at the surrounding landscape. He called his squad-mate's name again, and his voice echoed in the silent, snowy half-light of morning.

"Walters is gone," I said.

Chapter 18

SHARED ANXIETY woke everyone up. Mornings after the full moon should have been relaxed, all of us mellow and smiling because our wolves had had their run, nothing had gone wrong, and the monsters inside us would stay quiet for a couple of more weeks. But this morning, everyone dressed silently in wet clothing, eyes downcast, sneaking glances at Tyler.

Still naked, Tyler moved around the copse of trees, hunched over, nose working, looking for scent.

"Find anything?" I asked. Stupid question. But I was afraid that if I didn't keep talking to him, he'd decide to run off, too.

He shook his head. "The snow's messing up the trail. Washed it clean."

"You have any idea where he's gone?"

"Yeah. I think he's gone after Van."

"He has to know he can't get to him. Vanderman's

locked up, Walters would have to get through an entire city—"

Now that was a terrifying image. And why had I trusted Walters? Why hadn't I seen this coming?

"I should have known," Tyler muttered, echoing my thought. "I should have known, I should have stopped him."

"Think maybe he'd planned this all along?" I said. "That he fooled both of us?" I found my clothes, grimacing as I pulled them on. The jeans were stiff and stuck to my skin, and the T-shirt sagged. Wet T-shirt, no bra—yeah, I was looking classy this morning.

Tyler shook his head. "I'd have known if he was planning something. He couldn't hide it. I think maybe he never went to sleep. That he decided to run when there was no one to stop him, and he just took off." He wrung out his damp T-shirt. "I have to go after him, I have to find him."

"No," I said, putting a hand on his arm. His muscles were taut as piano wire. "I need you upright and able to talk. Get dressed, please."

"It's my fault," he said, his expression drawn, staring out at nothing. But he pulled on the shirt and found his sweats.

"Kitty?" Ben called from the grove. The pack, all dressed now, appearing relatively human, had gathered, everyone looking at me, waiting for instructions. Like I had any clue. I didn't know what to do, but I had to act as if I did.

"Everyone go home," I said. "I'll call if we need help."

"Let us know if you see anything strange," Ben added.

My wolves moved off, leaving in small groups the way they'd come, jogging across the fields back to their cars. As the group dispersed, Becky faced me and stopped.

"Should I be worried?" she said.

I couldn't honestly say no. Any reassurances would sound false, and that wouldn't exactly put her at ease or make her trust my leadership.

But Tyler was confident when he shook his head. "He's not after you. You'll be all right."

She nodded and seemed comforted. I touched her arm. "Shaun will take you home. Stick with him while I take care of this. Shaun?"

He nodded and put his arm across Becky's back. The touch made her relax. They left together.

I felt better, knowing everyone else was on the way home, safe, warming up and drying off.

"What do you think happened? Why take off now?" Ben said. He stood next to me, the skin of our arms pressing together. I shivered. We may have been able to withstand a lot of cold, but we were going to have to get out of this weather soon.

"I think he got scared," Tyler said. "Or mad."

"Where's home for him?" I said. "Do you think he may be trying to reach family?" His original pack, I thought. If he didn't feel safe with us, he'd try to find someplace safer.

Which brought us back to Tyler's original guess: he was going to find Vanderman.

"No. Gordon picked us because we weren't married, didn't have kids or girlfriends, didn't have big families. So we wouldn't have any other loyalties."

I scowled. "If he was so smart why'd he go and get himself blown up?" Tyler ducked his gaze, his shoulders tensing even more. He looked like he wanted to tip his head back and howl. "I'm sorry," I said softly. "That came out wrong."

"Yeah," he said, with a grim chuckle. "I've been asking myself that every day since it happened."

"Let's get out of this mess," I said, and started on the hike back to the car. Ben matched my stride, caught my hand in his, and squeezed. I pressed near to him. Tyler followed closely. He didn't have to, I supposed. But I was relieved that I wouldn't have to fight with him about it.

I didn't want to have to make the call to Dr. Shumacher. I didn't want to listen to her tell me that I was wrong, and she was right. Actually, we were both half right. Tyler seemed to be doing just fine.

"We need a plan," I said as we reached the car. I couldn't wait to start drying off. Maybe then I could think straight.

"I guess we go after him," Ben said, sounding resigned.

"He can't have gone far, right?"

"Except that this is what we *do*," Tyler said. "We spent the last two years running, evading, hunting. If he thinks he's on a mission, I don't know if we can stop him."

If Tyler thought this, what reason did I have for optimism? Because I didn't want to think about the alternatives.

"That's not acceptable," I said. "How long will it take him to get to Fort Carson, if that's where he's going? Two days?"

"If he goes straight there at top speed he'll be there by the end of the day."

A hundred miles in a day. Yeah, that was what we were dealing with.

Inside the car, Ben started the engine and blasted the heater. Cold air came out, and I shivered. It would warm up soon enough. I dug in the glove box for my cell phone and made the dreaded call.

"Yes, what is it?" Shumacher answered on the first ring. She'd probably been waiting by the phone all night—she didn't sound like I'd waken her up.

"We have a problem. Walters went rogue. He ran and Tyler thinks he's headed for Vanderman." I tried to get it all out before she could say anything, ask any questions, or make accusations.

"And Sergeant Tyler, he's still with you? He didn't run?" She sounded surprised.

"He's fine. He's been a big help."

"I'll call Colonel Stafford," Shumacher said, as if she'd been expecting it.

"We'll head to Fort Carson," I said, glancing at Ben and Tyler for confirmation. Their expressions were set in agreement. "Maybe we can intercept him."

"Kitty, I think you should go home. Stafford and his men can find Walters. We'll take care of it."

The others could hear Shumacher's side of the conversation. Tyler frowned, looking as though he wanted to say something.

"I'd really like be there, Doctor." I slowed down my breathing to try and calm myself.

"I appreciate all of your help, I really do. I'm grateful for the attempt."

I could tell when I was being kissed off. "Doctor, I don't think you're listening to me—"

"You'll be bringing Sergeant Tyler back to the VA hospital as soon as you can, I trust."

One strike and that was it? We'd screwed up with Walters and now I was kicked off the team? For once, I couldn't think of anything to say. I couldn't think of what would change Shumacher's mind or convince her to keep me in the loop. I didn't even have a snappy retort.

I slammed the phone shut and dropped it on the floor.

"I'm not going back there," Tyler said. "I think I've earned the right not to be locked up."

"You have," I said. "We're not going back." Tyler

let out a sigh and slumped against the seat. "And we're going to Fort Carson anyway."

"Of course we are," Ben said. "But I feel a professional need to point out that messing around the U.S. Army could get us in a serious amount of trouble."

"You're saying we shouldn't do it?"

"I didn't say that," Ben said with a shrug. "I'm just making an observation."

The snow was falling harder, driving thickly at an angle across the country highway. Visibility was low and the asphalt was wet. The windshield wipers banged, and Ben peered forward, turning all his attention on the road.

Here was the problem: who was the outsider here? We were the werewolves. We ought to be able to take care of our own. We had every right to go after Walters, not them. They were outsiders. They didn't understand. They didn't belong. That was my Wolf's instincts talking, though. Was that rational? Was I assessing the situation by the wrong standards? Should I just let it go?

No, because I still wasn't convinced Shumacher knew what she was doing, and that she and Stafford's gang wouldn't make the situation worse. Like, Walters and Vanderman breaking loose and rampaging in Colorado Springs.

"It should only take us a couple of hours to get there, right?" Tyler said. "We should be able to head him off."

"Usually. But I don't know in this weather," Ben said, shaking his head. "Plus we'll hit the Springs in time for morning rush hour. I can try 83 or one of the back ways."

"Maybe we should go on foot," Tyler said.

"We'd have to go on four feet to cover the same ground," I said. "I'm not sure I want to risk it."

"You're just not used to it," Tyler said. "That's all we did over there."

"And if you could operate a cell phone as a wolf I'd let you go, but you can't. It's not a good idea," I said, twisting to look at him in the backseat.

"I could just go." He gave me a stare. A challenge. Ben glanced at him in the rearview mirror, his hands tightening on the steering wheel.

I so didn't need this right now. "Or I could haul your ass back to Shumacher at the VA hospital."

I was impressed with myself talking back at this big scary Green Beret werewolf, except that for a moment Tyler looked like he wanted to jump me and bite off my face. The only way I kept my gaze locked with his and my back straight was thinking about what would happen if I flinched. If he decided I was weak and he could assert his dominance. That would make our trip real short.

I pushed, taking a gentler tack this time. "Look, I've gotten you this far, haven't I? You'd still be locked up and climbing the walls with Vanderman without me. Trust me, okay?"

And he lowered his gaze. "All right. But what are we going to do when we find Walters?"

The tires sloshed on the wet pavement through several moments of silence.

"I guess that'll depend on what happens when we get there," I said, which was nothing more than waffling.

With false cheer, Ben said, "Best-case scenario, Stafford gets there with his tranquilizer gun first. Then we show up all huffy and defensive."

I snorted in lieu of chuckling. But yeah, that was kind of how I was hoping it would go.

"Worst-case scenario," Ben continued after a moment. "The Glock's in the glove box."

"That isn't going to be necessary," I said, more as a defensive mantra than any solid belief.

"You have a gun?" Tyler said, leaning forward.

"With silver ammo, even," Ben said.

My husband the werewolf kept silver bullets in his glove box. I didn't question it.

I asked Tyler, "You think he's headed back to Vanderman. Can he really get past Fort Carson security, into the building? He can't really break Vanderman out, can he?"

"We broke out easy enough. We waited until they were moving us into the building. Then we knocked them over and ran. As a wolf, he can get onto the base easy. He'll be fast and camouflaged, and Fort Carson is huge. A lot of it is open plains. He'll have to be human to break into the building, though. He'd need his hands."

"Could he do that? Sneak onto the base, sleep off his wolf, then break into the building? Isn't that a little goal-oriented for a werewolf?" I said.

"We trained to remember our targets. Even if we didn't remember anything else, we remembered the mission."

I remembered a story. One of Paul Flemming's informants had been an old man, a German soldier and a veteran of World War II. He'd also been a werewolf, and he told me about being trained by the SS to carry messages across enemy lines. People would stand out, but wolves were part of the landscape. Obviously, there were techniques for training werewolves. I wondered how many secret histories there were, how many wars included units of werewolves fighting for one side or the other. Roman centurions, Norse berserkers, Mongol raiders, Persian infantry . . . It sounded all too plausible. Werewolves were too ideal for the job not to use as soldiers.

The thought sent a chill over me, raising gooseflesh. I shivered and turned up the heater.

"What's the matter?" Ben said gently. Maybe he could smell my unease.

"Implications," I said, then shook my head. "Never mind. Won't there be guards? Won't they be able to stop him?" I looked back at Tyler.

"Not if they're not firing silver," Tyler said. "I think only Stafford's guys have silver. They'd have to do too much explaining if they started issuing silver ammo to the regular MPs."

"FUBAR. Isn't that what you guys call this sort of thing?"

"Yes, ma'am," Tyler said, chuckling.

This could be a public relations nightmare. Werewolves had stayed hidden from public sight, behind folklore, for a very long time. We'd stayed secret by policing ourselves. Then people like me started blowing the whistle. The old system was falling apart. Police started getting involved, and one bad incident hitting the news would ensure that everyone saw werewolves as monsters rather than people. So what now?

We reached a freeway. I-70, it should have been. A string of red taillights flowed like a river before us, distorted by the snow and wet. Rush hour. Bad weather.

My phone rang—"The Good, the Bad, and the Ugly" played. I dived for the floor and grabbed for the phone. The music set my nerves on edge—it couldn't be good. The dash clock said 7 A.M. Too early for normal people.

"What is it?"

Cormac sounded as urgent as I'd ever heard him. He didn't even sound like Cormac. "I think this is it."

"What, this is . . . oh. Franklin."

"This blizzard isn't natural," he said. He sounded like he was in a car, speeding somewhere through traffic.

"So what are we going to do about it?"

"I've got an idea, but I'm still working on that part," he said. "I wanted to make sure you and Ben are home and ready to get socked in."

"Um . . ." I said, trying to figure out how to explain this. "I'm afraid we've had something come up." Could I sound any more vague? Like this wouldn't make him suspicious.

I could almost hear the deep sigh over the line. "What happened?"

"So you know last night was the full moon? Well, the guys from the army came with us, and one of them kind of went rogue—"

"And you're chasing after him? Good luck with that." How did he manage to sound so sarcastic without changing his tone of voice?

I grumbled, "Yeah, thanks."

"You need help?"

"Not yet," I said. I hoped it wouldn't come to that. "I'd rather have you figuring out how to stop Franklin. Don't worry about us, we won't freeze."

"You spend enough time worrying about me, I'm going to return the favor. I'll call you when I have something," he said, and hung up before I could argue.

I stared at my phone a moment.

"Was that Cormac? Was that about Franklin?" Ben said.

"Yes. He's says this is because of him." I gestured to the massive snow.

"Great. Now what do we do?"

"I'm thinking of calling Odysseus Grant." Grant was the other wizard I knew. He always seemed to have an answer for a magical crisis.

"Can I make a suggestion?" Ben said. "Don't pull any more people into this if we don't have to. If you really think Franklin fried your caller in Louisiana with a lightning strike, you could be painting targets on anyone else you call about this."

He was right. I huffed a sigh and stared out the window. "Cormac says he'll call back when he's figured out how to stop him."

"Then we'll wait," Ben said.

I tried not to worry—Cormac could take care of himself.

I-25 was even worse than I-70.

We were well into morning, well after sunrise, not that we could tell with the overcast sky. Everything had a light gray tinge to it rather than a dark gray one. The snow wasn't letting up. Plows were hard at work—ahead, a couple of safety lights flashed and reflected against the fog. They'd already piled a ridge of snow onto the shoulder of the road.

We moved at a crawl, and I wondered how bad it would have to get before the freeway closed. At this rate, even on foot Walters would get to Fort Carson before us.

"I can't sit here," Tyler said. "I have to get out of here. We're wasting time." He was gripping the arm-rest on the door, his hand trembling.

"Keep it together," I said. "If you head out and turn wolf they'll just scoop you up along with Walters."

He breathed low in his throat, making a sound like a growl. I reached back and touched his arm; what-ever calm I could find in myself, I sent to him. As pack alpha, that ought to be part of my job, right? I was playing it all by ear, though; I hadn't had too many role models to draw on. But Tyler's hand relaxed, and he settled back against the seat, staring out the window.

I turned on the radio and found a news report, which was all about the weather and traffic. Which was good, since I was afraid I was going to start hearing about rogue werewolf attacks. According to the news, the storm wasn't behaving according to any predictions. While it was snowing across the Front Range, the storm seemed to be centered on Denver—the system had rolled in from the moun-tains, but didn't get bad until it had hit the plains. The city was getting more snow than the mountains had. The freeways were being closed in some places—but we seemed to have gotten past those spots just in time. If we got stuck, I wouldn't be able to argue with Tyler about setting out on foot.

My phone rang and I answered. It was my mother, with her usual great timing.

"Hi, Kitty. I'm just checking to see if you're okay. I know you went out with your friends last night, and I wanted to make sure you got home all right through all this snow."

My mother knew I was a werewolf. I wasn't sure she entirely understood what that meant. She knew I went with the pack to shape-shift on full-moon nights. Trying her best to be supportive, she called it "going out with my friends." I couldn't complain, but it led to some awkward conversations.

"Um . . . I'm not really at home right now, Mom. Something came up." I winced. It was the conversation with Cormac all over again. And who ever thought my mother and Cormac would have something in common?

"Kitty, do you have any idea what the weather is like right now?"

"Yeah. A pretty good idea." I looked out the car window at the falling snow and near-zero visibility.

"Are you all right?"

"Yeah, I'm fine. I'm going to check on a friend who needs help."

"Couldn't you call the police? Don't you think you should be safe at home?"

I could almost picture her wringing her hands. "Mom, I'm a werewolf, I can't freeze to death. I'll be just fine." I could, however, be torn limb from limb by rogue werewolves. I didn't mention that. "Ben is with me—does that make you feel better?"

"Well, I suppose." The tone of her voice said no.

"Seriously, Mom, I wouldn't be out in this if it weren't really important, and I'll be fine. I'll call you tonight, okay?"

"That would be nice, just so I know you're all right."

"I love you, Mom." She said she loved me, too, and I put the phone away.

Tyler was staring at me, plainly disbelieving. "That was your mom?" I nodded. "And she knows you're a werewolf?" Again, I nodded. "How did you tell her?"

"I lied about it until it blew up in my face and she found out anyway." That was the short version of the story.

"And she's okay with it?" he said, wonderingly.

"I wouldn't say she's okay with it. She doesn't really get it enough to have an opinion. But you know, she's my mom."

Tyler leaned back, looking thoughtful. Maybe wondering how he was going to tell his mom.

It took us an hour to get to Castle Rock, a trip that should have taken twenty minutes. This was ridiculous. I tapped my fingers on the armrest and grit my teeth.

Up ahead, a row of blinking lights—blue police lights, yellow hazard lights—blazed across the freeway, breaking up the gray sheets of falling snow. We couldn't see the road much, so Ben followed the lights. They guided us off the freeway and up the exit to the middle of Castle Rock. This wasn't good.

The car in front of us stopped, and a cop leaned into the driver's side window. After talking a moment, the officer stepped backed and the car continued on in Castle Rock. This didn't look good at all.

The highway patrol officer came to talk to us next. Ben rolled down his window.

The guy was wrapped in a rain slicker and looked like he was having a really bad day. His voice was monotone. "The interstate's closed. I suggest you find a place to stay and wait the storm out."

I could have howled. I wondered if Franklin was manipulating this as well.

"Any idea when it'll open back up?" Ben asked the officer in a maddeningly calm voice. I wanted to shriek.

"Once the snow slows down and we get the road cleared. It's just too much of a mess out there right now," the officer said. "Sorry."

"Thanks."

Ben closed the window and pulled out to cross the overpass behind the previous car.

"You didn't even try to argue with him," I grumbled.

"I've warned you about arguing with the cops before," Ben said.

My angry sigh sounded like a growl. He wouldn't look at me, meet my gaze, or stare. I wanted to pick a fight, but he wasn't cooperating.

From the backseat, Tyler made a sound, half grunt, half growl. He held his hands in fists, braced against his legs, his eyes shut, and was breathing too quickly.

I was angry; he was picking up on my mood. I forced myself to breathe slowly, calmly, and I spoke in a whisper. "Keep it together, Tyler. It's okay." Ben put a hand on my thigh and looked at me, worried.

Tyler sighed, letting out a shuddering breath. He didn't open his eyes, but his hands opened. If he wasn't entirely relaxed, at least he didn't look like he was about to burst out of his skin.

"We'll find a different way to get there," Ben said. His back was stiff, and he was starting to smell angry—a hint of sweat, tangy around the edges. So he wasn't as calm as he let on.

Three werewolves trapped in a little metal box during a snowstorm, going nowhere fast. Wonderful. It was amazing we'd gotten as far as we had. I cracked the window and let a blast of cold air hit us. Driving snowflakes sent a stinging, icy wave across my skin, and it felt good. It woke me up, focused me.

We made a quick stop at a Village Inn to use the restroom, wash up a bit, and get some coffee and food. The deer from last night wasn't stretching too far. In the restroom, I regarded the mirror. I didn't just still smell wolfish, I looked it. I hadn't brushed my hair, just haphazardly tied it back. Strands were coming loose in a tangled halo around my head. My eyes were shadowed, glaring, and my frown was fierce. I was a muscle twitch away from snarling. I was still wearing nothing but a damp T-shirt and jeans. And I had a ways left to go.

The guys didn't look too much better. We left quickly.

Back in the car, Ben picked our way to the state highway east of the interstate. The weather wasn't any better, but traffic was a little easier. Wind blasted eddies of snow across the blacktop.

A massive pileup stopped us north of Colorado Springs. It looked like an SUV braked too quickly at an intersection and momentum carried it, slipping and fishtailing, into the waterlogged intersection, where it hit a sedan and sent it spinning into another car. Two other cars had slammed into the mess when they couldn't stop in time. We waited forty-five minutes before the cops cleared enough of a lane for traffic to pass by.

The weather seemed to be conspiring against us, which was terribly ominous, given recent events. I resisted an urge to call Cormac to see if he'd learned anything new. He would call when he had something to say. Probably.

Chapter 19

I COULDN'T BELIEVE it had taken us most of the day to get here.

We went east before turning south, hoping to avoid most of the city and its traffic. Finally, we turned west, picking our way through the various grids and arteries that passed for the Springs's road network, toward Fort Carson.

After all that—the snow, the traffic, the worry, and arguing with Tyler—we reached Fort Carson and were stopped cold at the gate. When I'd come here last week, the gate was staffed by regular security guards in blue uniforms and safety vests. Now there was a pair of soldiers in army fatigues, bundled up with gloves and parkas, carrying rifles. A siren was wailing in the distance.

"We're here to see a patient at the hospital," Ben told the soldier as he offered his ID.

"I'm sorry, sir. The post is under lockdown. I can't let you through."

On the roundabout ahead of the gate was a lot of activity: trucks and vehicles in desert beige and a bunch of guys holding rifles. A couple of soldiers were stringing razor wire, creating a serious roadblock. Something was happening. I thought of all that tract housing, the quiet residential neighborhoods with the normal-looking schools and nice playgrounds that made up this part of the base—and then I thought of Walters as a werewolf tearing through those neighborhoods. My heart grew sick.

Tyler opened the back door and started to get out.

"Excuse me, sir—" The guard looked panicked for just a moment, as if he thought he was going to have to tackle Tyler and really didn't want to. Who would?

Tyler took charge. "I'm Sergeant Tyler, stationed here. What's happening?"

The guy let his guard down, shaking his head. "They're not telling me anything. There's been some kind of hostage situation. Some guy back from Afghanistan snapping—you know how it is." He glanced over his shoulder at the burgeoning roadblock. That was one hell of a snap, he must have been thinking.

"I know who it is," Tyler said. "He's a friend of mine. I'm here to help. Call Colonel Stafford and tell him I'm here."

The soldier was scared. He didn't know what was happening, he'd only been told not to let anyone through. I wondered what rumors were flying, what he'd heard. And how bad it really was. In the face of that, Tyler's solid presence and determination was a calming influence.

"I'll call. Wait right here," the soldier said, and went inside the booth.

Tyler waited, resting an arm on the roof of the car and looking ahead, as if expecting an attack.

"I don't like this," I said, stating the obvious.

Ben reached over and took my hand. "We can turn around and go home."

"Tyler won't leave," I said. In my gut, Wolf was defiant. This was our mess, we'd clean it up. Protect our own, defend our territory, punish the rogue. I didn't always understand the Wolf's black-and-white worldview. I usually didn't want to. I rubbed my forehead, trying to smooth away the headache I was developing. "How could I have been so wrong about Walters?"

"You want to think the best of people. There's nothing wrong with that."

"But it gets me into so much trouble. My back's been stabbed more times than I can count."

"That just means I ought to do a better job of watching it, right?" His smile was grim.

"It's not your fault when I keep not listening to you."

He raised my hand and kissed it, lingering to let his warm breath brush over my skin. The feel of it tingled and flushed all the way up my arm. I squeezed his hand back.

"We do okay," he said.

The back door opened, and Tyler climbed in. "We're in. Sort of."

The guard had returned to standing at attention and seemed relieved to get us off his hands. Whom had he handed us off to?

A beige army Humvee approached down the straightaway, did a turn, and slid to a stop in front of us. Colonel Stafford, wearing a heavy coat over his uniform, climbed out of the passenger side and marched toward us.

I hurried to get out of the car. I wasn't going to face him sitting down. At least my T-shirt was dry now. Ben and Tyler did likewise, and we moved to intercept him, facing him like a pack: me in front, the two men at my shoulders. Looking very out of place, we were still wearing what we'd gone out in the night before: shirts, sweats, and sneakers. No coats and winter gear. None of us seemed to mind. I was betting it looked pretty impressive, because Colonel Stafford stopped a couple of yards away, well out of reach, when he probably wanted to yell in my face.

"This is your fault!" he said.

"I won't argue with that," I said.

He seemed surprised, as if he'd been bracing for a dress down that he wasn't going to get to give.

"I'll have you all up on charges. Aiding and abetting, negligence—"

"Sir, this was an accident," Tyler said.

Again, Stafford was taken aback, and seemed to need a moment to remember himself. "You're out of line, Sergeant."

"Yes, sir," Tyler said, sounding tired.

"What's going on?" I asked, pointing to the roadblock with its armed guards.

"You think Walters is going to come back here—so do I. When he does, we'll stop him."

I stared. "You think he's going to just come marching through the front gate? That he's going to drive up in a taxi?"

He glared at me, mouth pursed like he was chewing lemons.

I ranted on. "This guy's a trained soldier and a werewolf; he can sneak in here from anywhere and he may not even be human when he does it."

"We'll have plenty of time to track him," Stafford argued. "He started out a hundred miles north of here, without any resources—"

"Sir," Tyler said. "As far as Walters is concerned, he's on a mission. This is the kind of thing we trained for. A hundred miles in a day—we *did* it, over worse terrain than this." He kept his expression cold. Official.

Whatever Stafford thought, I knew we were right: Walters was already here. He would have gone top

speed the whole time. Which meant he'd be exhausted, panicked, even more dangerous.

"We can find him," I said. "We can track him. We
think he's going to the hospital to find Vanderman.
That's where you need to have your people set up."

Stafford shook his head. "I've got men stationed
at every entrance to this base and on patrol at the
borders. He's not here yet, and we'll find him when
he gets here."

This was a man whose job was being right. Or at
least acting like he was right. I wasn't going to
change his mind just by asking him to. And you
know, maybe he even was right. Maybe Walters
wasn't here yet. Maybe he'd gotten stuck in some
pileup outside of Castle Rock.

I still wanted a backup plan.

"Then you won't mind if we head over to the hospital and check on Vanderman," I said. "We won't
get in your way, I promise."

He blinked. He probably wasn't used to people
talking back at him. "Fine. But with an escort. You
step out of line I won't hesitate to shoot," he said
by way of encouragement. He pointed at Tyler.
"And you—you're still active duty and under
orders. Got it?"

"Yes, sir."

Stafford returned to his Humvee, we returned to
Ben's sedan and followed the colonel's vehicle up
the straightaway. After some shouted orders and a

rush of activity at the roundabout, a space was cleared, just wide enough for the car to pull through. Ben did so, very slowly, both hands on the wheel. A different Humvee with a couple of men in fatigues sitting in it followed us. I was betting they had silver bullets in their rifles.

"All this for one guy?" I said in awe.

"I'm guessing they're a little freaked out," Ben said.

Tyler shook his head. "Stafford never understood us. He thought this was just like any other training—that we can turn it on and off, that we can control it, when it's really the other way around, isn't it?"

All the men in Gordon's unit ever wanted to do was their job. Serve their country the army way, and all that. Now look where they'd ended up.

Then we were through and making our way along the road to the hospital. The escort Humvee swerved past us and led the way. Other than that, we didn't see any other cars or people. No sign of life, whether because of the blizzard or the lockdown.

"Sir," Tyler said to Ben, which was kind of odd. "You said you had a weapon?"

"Yeah, in the glove box."

"May I?" Tyler asked.

He would make better use of it than either of us, assuming Walters showed up in a murderous rage and wouldn't listen to us. Which was what everyone was apparently assuming would happen. I handed the weapon, a matte-black semiautomatic pistol, to him grip first, along with the box of ammo.

"Be careful," I said. "Silver bullets."

The box felt warm, as if the silver was burning me through the plastic case. Tyler took the gun, ejected the magazine, and started inserting bullets into it—after wrapping his hand in a corner of his T-shirt. Even encumbered by the shirt, he loaded the gun with expert skill and speed. After he'd finished, he returned the box of remaining bullets to me, tucked the gun into the back of his waistband, and let his T-shirt fall over it. He gave a nod as if saying, *now I'm ready*.

"Can you really shoot your teammate if you have to?" I asked.

Tyler wouldn't look at me. "We take care of our own. Last thing any of us want is to hurt anyone. What did you say at the start of all this—that if we couldn't shape up then you'd pull the trigger on us?"

"That was a metaphor," I said, frowning.

"I'm just taking responsibility," he said, his voice flat.

We arrived at the hospital behind our escort. A dozen or so cars were parked in the lot—people who'd arrived before the lockdown and now were stuck. I was thinking worst-case scenario.

"Any ideas?" Ben said as we climbed out of the car. We had to squint into the wind blowing at us. Driving snow stuck my arms like needles. The two soldiers climbed out of their Humvee and took up positions on the sidewalk outside the hospital's main entrance, looking outward, rifles at the ready. I wondered how much Stafford had really told them about what to expect.

Tyler looked around. "We secure the perimeter— take a walk around the building and figure out if he's been here yet. If he hasn't, we go in and wait for him to show up. And if he has—we go in after him. How does that sound?"

My grin felt wry and stiff. "Sounds like a real military operation, sir."

He glanced at our escorts, who nodded. I wondered if they'd done time overseas, they seemed so wary.

We moved forward at a careful pace—a hunting pace. Our chins up to take in the air, nostrils widening, we breathed. Mostly, the area smelled like exhaust, gun oil, and anxiety. Cold air stung my lungs. A sheen of icy mist covered my face, making my hair stick to my cheeks.

I caught the tang of blood, sharp, incongruous against the clean chill of the winter wind. Rich, heady—a treasure in this landscape, a promise of injured prey in hard times. Or so the Wolf thought. But I smelled a dead body. I bit my tongue to keep my mouth from watering and trotted ahead to the front door of the hospital. Ben and Tyler were right with me.

At some point this morning someone had tried to shovel the walks, leaving snow piled along the path. Since then, the storm had gotten the upper hand, sending drifts of snow sloping along the building. Recently, there had been a fight in front of the front door. Instead of a smooth plane of snow, there were trenches, rifts, snow kicked and swept aside. Not footprints as much as body prints, as though someone had charged through.

We found him a few feet off the sidewalk, facedown in a mound of snow that had been shoveled off the walk. Spatters of blood had sunk into the snow around him. They weren't visible from the surface, which still looked clean, as if he'd just slipped and fallen. The guy couldn't have been more than twenty or so. His black beret had been knocked off; his scalp showed through a pale crew cut.

I could smell that he was dead and quickly cooling. Putting a hand on his shoulder, I intended to turn him to see how he'd died, but I didn't have to. His throat had been torn by something sharp and not very precise. Claws, teeth.

"What the—" one of Stafford's soldiers exclaimed, peering over our shoulders.

Tyler stared down at him, lips pursed. Ben let out a sigh. I looked around. Wind had altered the tracks, making it harder to decipher what had happened. But I didn't smell Vanderman. And the snow was only disturbed in one direction. I could almost see it:

this poor guy had been walking by on some other duty. He spotted a crazed maniac, probably naked in freezing weather, running across the sidewalk. He'd yelled at the guy to stop. Threatened, his target had run at him. The soldier may not even have had time to fire the handgun now lying in its own bed of snow nearby.

Tyler retrieved the pistol, slid back the chamber, then threw the gun away.

"He got shots off," Tyler said. "But the bullets aren't silver."

I crouched in the snow and rested my hand gently on the soldier's body, as if it mattered. Taking a careful, searching breath, I learned what I needed to and quickly moved away.

"It was him?" Tyler said. He must have been hoping for a different outcome.

I nodded. Walters's scent was all over the body.

Chapter 20

WALTERS, TRAILING blood across the snow, had gone inside. No one else had come back out. He and Vanderman were still in the building.

"Where is he? Where is he now?" one of the escorts said swinging his rifle around.

Tyler glared at them. "You two—go back and tell Colonel Stafford that Walters is here, at the hospital."

The pair hesitated. One was searching wildly for the unseen killer. The other was staring at the bloody body. Tyler touched this one on the arm. "Go on. Tell Stafford." He spoke it like an order.

The soldier nodded, grabbed the other, and they ran back to the Humvee.

"Thanks," I said, relieved. I'd started to worry that they would either shoot us—or that we'd have to rescue them.

"They're safer this way," Tyler said.

The three of us went inside the hospital and locked the door behind us.

The building was quiet. The cars in the lot meant that people must have been there, and while I could smell them, none were out and about. I hoped that meant they were safely locked away in rooms and offices. A heater vented somewhere, a distant hissing. We found stairs leading to the basement—I didn't want us getting stuck in an elevator. Ben was at my side, face tight with concentration, looking all around us. He kept flexing his hands, as if feeling claws instead of fingers. Tyler walked behind us, turning to scan all directions, above and below in the stairwell.

Before we reached the downstairs level where Vanderman was being kept, a noise began to echo. The crunch of something metal breaking, the scuffle of a fight. Of a body smacking against tile. Then more quiet.

"Hoo, boy," I muttered.

Slowly, I opened the metal door and emerged into the corridor.

Tyler stepped in front of me—*taking point,* the term was. He and Ben kept me between them, a protective shield, which was sweet, but made me growly because I couldn't see past them very well.

"I don't need bodyguards," I said, stepping away from them to get some breathing room.

A tangy-sweet smell cut sharply through the

chilled air, stabbing from my nose to my brain, and lingering on the back of my tongue as a familiar taste. More blood, freshly spilled. The second time in ten minutes—we were too late.

Part of me wanted to leave—this was army business. Not our territory, not our fight. But it was—I'd promised to protect Walters, and he'd seriously overstepped his bounds. That meant he was also my responsibility. I should have stopped him, I should have stopped *this*.

Ben and I stood back to back, a natural defensive posture, as we scanned the area, looking for the body. Or bodies. Tyler ranged a couple of yards ahead, glancing down the hallway and back at us—scanning for danger, and looking to us for cues about what to do next.

The smell came from an intersection ahead. I approached it slowly, breathing deeply and listening, and turned right to follow the scent of blood.

We found the body a few feet in, hidden around the corner. In a white uniform, he might have been a nurse or an orderly. His blood streaked across the linoleum floor. I knelt beside him, started to turn him over, and got as far as seeing his ruined neck and face before letting him be. The muscles on my back twitched, Wolf growing in my awareness, listening for enemies, waiting for an attack. This time, I smelled both Walters and Vanderman among the blood.

"I assume that's Vanderman," Ben said. "Walters got him out." He looked in the opposite direction I did, and his breathing quickened. The two rogues could be anywhere now.

"I'm assuming," I said.

"I could have stopped this," Tyler said. "I should have kept better track of Walters. I should have made sure none of us got out. We shouldn't have—"

"Stop it," I said. He lowered his gaze. But I knew how he felt—I was the one who argued to let Walters out in the first place.

"Kitty," Ben said, whispering. "Can you really talk them down?"

A couple of Special Forces–trained werewolves on the loose? I had to shake my head. I didn't think I could, not with blood spilled. I remembered Vanderman in his cell, endlessly pacing, glaring out at me, murderous and unrepentant.

"We've got the gun," Tyler said. "We can take them." He sounded bitter, but determined.

That somehow didn't make me feel any better.

"Come on," I said, and retreated back around the corner from the direction Walters and Vanderman were likely to come at us. I hoped it gave us a more defensible position. It would at least give us some warning before the two werewolves launched an attack. "We need backup for this."

The soldiers should have contacted Colonel

Stafford, who would be here any minute now, but I wanted to make sure. Then I realized I didn't have the first idea how to get ahold of Colonel Stafford. So I pulled out my cell phone and called Dr. Shumacher.

She answered before the phone had finished ringing. "Hello? Kitty?"

"Hi, Dr. Schumacher. I was wondering, could you give me Colonel Stafford's phone number? I mean, if he even has a cell phone. Or if he has a secretary who has one. Or whatever." My phone voice sounded like my radio voice, I realized—I came across far peppier than I was really feeling.

"Kitty, where are you, what's happening, what's going on?"

I hesitated a beat. "I expected Colonel Stafford would have called you the minute I showed up."

"No, he didn't," she said, sounding frustrated. I couldn't blame her for being put out. She probably thought she and Stafford were partners on equal footing. Stafford probably wasn't thinking about her at all.

I sighed. "Fort Carson's under lockdown. I managed to talk Stafford into letting us through because I thought I knew where to find Walters, and I was right."

"He's at the hospital," Schumacher said. "He's trying to release Vanderman."

"Yeah," I said. "He already has."

"I should be there, I should have found a way there, this never should have happened."

"Are you snowed in in Denver?"

"The news says it's a storm of the century."

"Hey, we usually get those every ten years or so," I said. Ben was watching me, smirking—so I was still being too chipper. Tyler was braced like he was going to pounce on the first thing that came around the corner. He hadn't drawn the gun yet. Maybe he wanted to do this with his bare claws. "Doctor, I need to get ahold of Stafford. I need to tell him what's happening here."

"I'll call the colonel," Shumacher said firmly, determined to be back in charge. I wanted to growl at her. That wasn't what I asked, that wasn't what I wanted to have happen.

"Doctor, how are you going to know what to tell him? You have no idea what's going on here—"

"It's my project. I'll call him." She hung up.

We were all going to die. I slammed my phone closed and shoved it back into my pocket. I didn't want to think about what version of the story Shumacher was going to tell the colonel. He might just gas the place the place and call it a day.

"Someone needs to go outside and catch Stafford on the way in, tell him what's happening," I said.

Tyler said, "If we get to a land line we can call the front gate. They'll be in radio contact."

I smiled. "That's so low tech it's cool."

"And in the meantime, we do what? Wait for our guys to stroll along and ask them to stop by for coffee?" Ben smelled twitchy, sweat breaking out despite the chill. He tapped his leg and looked like he was ready to start pacing.

"We have to keep them in the basement. We can't let them get out." We'd probably have to shoot them, which made me angry. And hopeless. I turned to Tyler. "Can you go tell Stafford that Walters is here and Vanderman's out?"

"Kitty, you should just go upstairs and wait for him. You can explain it all when he gets here," Ben said.

"I don't think Stafford would even listen to me. He'll listen to Tyler."

"He won't have a choice. Would you please just go upstairs?"

Ben wanted me out of here—he didn't want me to face down Walters and Vanderman. We looked at each other, and I saw so many unspoken words. So much fierce protectiveness. I had a sudden urge to throw myself at him and wrap all my limbs around him. My hands itched from wanting to grab him.

"Ben, you should go," Tyler said. "Stafford will listen to you."

"Like hell. I'm not leaving Kitty here," Ben said.

"Kitty has the best chance of talking them down," he said. "And if she can't talk them down, there's me. So you have to go talk to Stafford."

"I hate to say it, but we're way past talking," I said. It wasn't just Vanderman who'd be up on murder charges now.

"You have to try," Tyler said. "It can't be too late."

He wasn't worried about Walters or Vanderman; he was worried about himself. He had to believe it was possible for them to come back from that dark place. Because then it would be possible for Tyler.

Ben said, "I'm not leaving you."

I grabbed hold of his collar and pulled him to me. He cupped my face in his hands. Our kiss tasted hot and anxious after all the cold and stress of the day. It melted me, just a little. Enough to keep going until we cleaned up this mess.

"I'll be okay," I said, a statement made mostly on faith .

Ben nodded, but his frown wracked his whole face. "There's got to be a phone in one of these offices. Shout if you hit trouble."

"Hell, yeah," I said.

Ben trotted back down the hallway and ducked into the first unlocked office. I almost yelled at him to close and lock the door behind him—but he did so without me having to tell him. Couldn't have anyone sneaking up on him.

Tyler and I continued, toward Vanderman's cell, looking for the rogues.

"Where else could they go?" I asked in a whisper.

"There's the elevator."

The elevator was at the other end of the hallway, around the next corner. "They wouldn't take the elevator, would they?"

Werewolves on the edge of wild, on the hunt, would follow the trails of human scent. Their animal sides at the fore, they might not think of taking an elevator—the scent trail would be cut off. And even if they did think of it, they wouldn't want to get trapped in a tiny steel box. At least, I wouldn't.

"I don't know," he said. "If they know the stairs are cut off because we're here—yeah, they might."

"So we should go lock the elevator."

"I don't know," he said. "It all seems so futile."

"Don't say that. Remember, we're here to save Walters." *We're here to save you.*

He shook his head. "Captain Gordon would have hated this. Hated what we've all turned into. It wasn't supposed to be like this."

"I'm sure he was a very nice guy, but right now I'm royally pissed off at him."

Tyler actually chuckled.

A crash rattled the hallway behind us, like a door breaking—I thought it was behind us, but these hallways looped back on each other, and with all the tile, they echoed. It might have come from the office where Ben had locked himself—or it might have come from around the next corner. Tyler and I were looking in opposite directions.

"That's gotta be Van," Tyler said.

"And Walters, right?" I said. "They wouldn't have separated, would they?"

Or maybe they would. They were a wolf pack on the hunt—hunting us, the rival pack in their territory. They'd be moving to flank us.

"Go," I said, and Tyler ran, back to where we'd left Ben.

So, either we'd split them up, or they'd split us up. We wouldn't know which until it was all finished and we figured out who won. Except no one was going to win this thing.

Another crash sounded, and this time I was pretty sure it had come from the next hallway, where the elevator was. Maybe I could shut down the elevator. I stepped carefully, a Wolf creeping in this mad human forest—and smelled werewolves all around me, hunting, spilling blood. I had to listen, watch, smell, feel.

I turned the corner to find Vanderman throwing himself at a locked door. He was naked, as if he'd just woken up from shifting back from wolf and hadn't bothered with clothing. He looked primal, his muscles flexing as he shouldered into the door, rattling it in its frame. Teeth bared, snarling, he grabbed the handle and wrestled with it, twisting, wrenching, looking for all the world like a dog with a chew toy.

The dead bolt cracked the frame; the door wrenched out of place. On the other side, two women screamed. Their footfalls pattered as they scrambled away from the door, and two sets of heartbeats raced. Vanderman doubled his efforts to break in.

"No!" I shouted and ran at him. I didn't think about it. If I had, I would have run the other way. Of course, then he would have chased me. Wolves love nothing better than chasing after prey. This way maybe I had a fighting chance.

He jumped away from the door and faced me down. His eyes lit. Tendons and muscles stood out as he sprang at me with hands outstretched. Claws grew—he showed a sheen of fur. I scurried, trying to change direction midstride. Dodging didn't help. He tackled me, smashing me against the floor shoulder first. It hurt.

Kicking, clawing, I tried to get out from under him. My breath came out in a whine. I had to get off my back or he would claw into my belly, rip into my throat. An arm free, I swiped at him, catching his face, ripping my nails across his cheek. I didn't have claws yet. In a few more seconds, I would, like him.

He put his knee into my belly, pinning me. He was so damn heavy. But I didn't stop struggling. Pain throbbed in my shoulder; I could feel ribs popping under his weight. Panic tightened my lungs.

"This is all your fault," he growled into my face. His breath was foul, tainted with old meat. "You come into my territory, you steal my pack. I'll murder you, I'll—"

"Van, no!" Walters's voice echoed. He appeared at the other end of the corridor, behind Vanderman. Also naked, glaring, wild—as much wolf as human. He might have been looking for Tyler, where the hallway turned back around to the elevators. And where was Tyler?

Walters continued, pleading. "She's helping us, she's on our side. I came to get you so she could help you, too." The submissiveness of his posture was painful to watch. He was groveling, his back curled, his limbs bent, almost on all fours, only daring to take quick glances at Vanderman out of the corner of his eye. If he'd had a tail, it would have been between his legs and tight against his belly. In another moment he'd be on the floor, his stomach to the ceiling.

When Vanderman faltered, I snarled and kicked, hitting his unprotected crotch. He took it with little more than a grunt. Raking claws down his sides, across his ribs, I got him to flinch. I rolled to my belly and pulled myself away—his knee went into my back. If I shifted, I could get out of this . . . I tried to steady my breathing, tried to keep it together. I heaved, growling, and rolled away. Jumping into a crouch, I turned to face them. Wolf stared out of my eyes.

Vanderman stared right back. Pure hate, pure challenge passed between us. It was okay, I could take it. Sure, he was big and scary. But the more I looked at him, the angrier I got. He'd ruined things for the rest of his squad. They'd all be alive now if he'd been able to keep it together. I could blame him for the whole terrible sequence of events, since Captain Gordon wasn't around to blame.

I tried to talk him down, as I told Tyler I would. Even though breathing hurt. "Sergeant Vanderman. You need to get ahold of yourself. If you expect to get out of this alive, stand down. In a minute this place is going to be filled with soldiers carrying rifles with silver bullets. They will shoot you. Please."

"Van, come on," Walters continued, backing me. His body acted on its own to give every submissive signal it could, at once. He fell to the floor, exposing his neck and belly even more, putting himself as low as he possibly could. He was trying to get the sergeant to stop and listen, to feel some compassion for this pathetic creature. To evoke some of an alpha werewolf's instincts to protect the weaker members of his pack. "I came back for you—like we all promised. We're in this together. We'll get out. We'll get away from here. They can't stop us."

Vanderman wasn't listening to anyone anymore. The skin on his face furrowed as his nose wrinkled; his grimacing lips showed all his teeth. The expression was lupine. He was a very angry wolf. He stepped toward me, head leading, arms bent. On my hands and knees, I stepped backward. I just had to hold out until Ben or Tyler got here.

Walters whined. He'd tried to stop him the best way he knew, but Vanderman was too far gone to respond to the signals. So Walters attacked him. To protect me.

The smaller soldier jumped at Vanderman, and momentum shoved him over. In his next movement, Vanderman rolled Walters to the floor, pressing him down. The sounds they made weren't human. Walters barely struggled, as if he knew this was how it would turn out, as if he believed he didn't have a chance. Vanderman dived at Walters's throat, teeth bared, releasing a guttural snarl. Hands with claws gouged into Walters's belly. Blood spilled. Vanderman—partially shifted now, his face lengthening to contain wide, sharp teeth, capable of holding and ripping—clamped his jaw over the other's throat and shook, tore, mangled, until red covered his face, chest, shoulders. Walters squealed, half human scream, half animal shriek of pain. He kicked, bucked, and tore at Vanderman with his own claws. But Vanderman had all the leverage—his claws were buried under Walters's rib cage, digging for his heart.

I stayed out of the way, holding my aching stomach, favoring my hurt shoulder. Wolf knew better than to draw attention. Just stay calm, out of the way. I crouched low by the wall, one hand resting on the floor. But inside, I was crying out. Walters wasn't moving anymore.

Tyler came up behind me. I glanced at him over my shoulder. He wasn't looking at me, but at the scene of slaughter ahead. His lips were parted, his teeth bared, a sign of aggression. But the expression in his eyes was anguish.

He settled into a crouch and aimed Ben's semiautomatic, bracing in his left hand and sighting down the barrel. With no fanfare, he fired three shots. All three struck Vanderman in the chest and head. Vanderman didn't make a sound. He twitched and fell, rolling off Walters's body. Then he lay still.

I turned to Tyler. "I tried talking to him. I tried."

Grief furrowed his expression, his whole face taut to prevent tears from falling. His breath was coming in gasps, near to hyperventilating.

Then he squeezed shut his eyes and turned the gun to his ear.

"No!" I shouted. I flinched back rather than trying to go for the gun, to wrestle with that massive, professional arm. I didn't want to touch it and have it go off accidentally, doing as much damage as it would have otherwise. All I could do was beg. "No, Tyler. Please don't. Please."

He didn't put the gun down. But he didn't fire. "I don't want to turn out like him," he said, his voice a whisper. "Like either one of them. I'm too dangerous to be around you. Around anyone. I'm too dangerous to be."

"No, you're not like them, you've already come so much farther. Look at you—after all this you're still you. You're okay, you're going to be okay."

The hand holding the gun wavered, and my heart swelled.

"Please put the gun down," I said. "Don't waste all this work I've been doing with you. I need to save at least one of you."

Slowly, the arm dropped. The gun rested on the tile floor at his side. Carefully, I put my hand on it and pulled it away from his limp fingers, sliding it to the other side of my body.

"Thank you," I said. "Thank you."

I slid my hand up his arm, squeezed his shoulder, and pressed my face to his neck as I hugged him. With deep breaths I took in his scent, and with the language of wolves I tried to comfort him as he slumped into my embrace.

My ribs hurt with every gasp of breath. I didn't know how damaged I was, but I trusted that my werewolf healing would take care of me. My Wolf was still poised to fight; she wouldn't retreat. But she wasn't on the edge of bursting free anymore. I tried to concentrate on comforting Tyler, letting my own pain fade by ignoring it.

I heard noises. The women behind the door ahead of us were still there. I could smell their fear, their sweat. Around the other corner, a door smashed opened and several sets of boots clomped on the tile, running toward us.

Tyler immediately pulled away from me and straightened. His gaze had turned grim, but determined.

"Don't tell him," he said. "Don't tell Stafford I was going to . . ."

"But don't you think you can get some help, some counseling—"

Shaking his head, he cut me off. "I do anything like that, it's on my own. I don't want to give him any excuse to lock me up." Tyler drew a deep breath, gathering himself to get through the next few minutes. Then the few after that. And so on.

Right. Then at least for now, it didn't happen. I tried to stand, but pain shot through my guts and ribs. Breathing still hurt; I settled back.

Several soldiers paced up the hallway and stopped to crouch in defensive positions, their rifles aimed at us. I just looked at them. Didn't beg, didn't plead, didn't yell for them to stand down. Just looked. Surely they could see that it was over.

The one closest to me lowered his rifle first. The other four followed. Then they waited.

Colonel Stafford and Ben came up behind them. When I saw Ben, tears finally blurred my vision. He met my gaze, and I tried to tell him everything without speaking. I wasn't sure I could speak.

He gave my anguish back to me with his gaze, which I felt like a hand on my arm. His expression tightened, full of worry. But he didn't rush. Turning to Stafford, he spoke a few words.

The colonel nodded and spoke to his men. "Stand down. Back off and wait at the doorway."

The soldiers retreated, walking backward, unable to turn away from the tableau we presented: two people bent in despair, two ravaged bodies, a hallway spattered in blood.

Ben came to us first. I watched him, as if I could draw him forward with my eyes. He touched my shoulder, then Tyler's, and bent his face to my hair. His breath tingled on my scalp, and I melted against him, relieved. I could finally let go. We were going to be all right.

"You're hurt," he said.

"Yeah," I said. "Mostly bruised, I think. Maybe broken ribs."

"Can you stand?"

We'd have to get out of here sometime, I supposed. Tyler's expression had settled into a mask. The sadness hadn't gone away. He seemed so tired.

Holding Ben's arm, I started to pull myself to my feet, but sharp pains rippled across my ribs. I hissed and doubled over, and both Ben and Tyler were at my sides, grabbing me to keep me from falling. They settled me against the wall instead. Yeah, bastard had broken something.

"What the hell did you do?" Ben asked.

"She went up against Vanderman," Tyler said.

"You did what?" Then Ben rolled his eyes as though that didn't surprise him.

"I had to," I said. "He was trying to break into that room." I called to Stafford, who was still hanging back. "Colonel, there are a couple of people in there, they might need help." My lungs ran out of breath, my voice choked, and I started coughing.

Stafford looked like he wanted to argue, but he went to the broken door, called to the women inside, and after they answered, he shoved into the room. One more problem taken care of.

Ben and Tyler sat against the wall on either side of me. I leaned against Ben and let myself heal. Were-wolf healing was fast, but never fast enough when you were in the middle of it.

"Walters saved me," I said. "Right at the end. He got Vanderman away from me. I think he would have been okay. If we could have kept him safe, he would have been okay." I shook my head.

Ben kissed the top of my head, and I sighed.

I would have liked to have said that it was all over. But I expected there'd be a lot of excuses, finger-pointing, and rationalizing. Maybe for Tyler this would never be over. He'd have Walters, Vanderman, Gordon, and all the guys from his unit living in his memory for the rest of his life. He'd be asking himself how he was the one who got out alive. This moment might have felt like a victory. But it was a Pyrrhic victory. We were left with a lot of pieces to pick up.

Stafford returned to the hallway. The room's occupants were two women in fatigues, looking impossibly young and tiny. They glanced at the bodies, glanced at us, then hurried up the hallway and to the door. Two more hatch marks on the victory column. Were we even yet?

The colonel just stared at us.

Tyler pushed himself to his feet, stood at straight, formal attention, and saluted. He held his hand to his forehead in that salute for a long time while Stafford stared at him, apparently at a loss. My Wolf would have bristled under that gaze, accepted the challenge, and tried to throw it back to him. Tyler kept his gaze down. He stayed submissive, acknowledging that Stafford was the one in charge. Most people wouldn't recognize the body language. Stafford may not have recognized it as lupine body language. But he recognized it as military.

He returned the salute, and Tyler dropped his hand.

"At ease," the colonel said, and Tyler relaxed a fraction. "What happened here?"

"Sir," Tyler said, his voice heavy with exhaustion. "Sergeant Vanderman and Sergeant Walters aren't going to be causing any more trouble."

"And what about you?"

"I'd like to request a discharge, sir."

I expected Stafford to argue, to at least get huffy, to rant at the little bit of his world attempting to slip out of his control. But he didn't. He studied Tyler for a long moment, lips pursed, as if he wanted to say something but the words had stuck. Then he touched Tyler's arm, a quick, sympathetic pat, and turned away.

"Stick around for debriefing. All three of you," Stafford said over his shoulder as he continued on to lock down the floor.

My phone chose that moment to play "The Good, the Bad, and the Ugly." I answered.

Cormac said, "I need help. Now."

Chapter 21

"WHAT'S GOING on? What's happening?" I pressed my hand to my opposite ear and walked a few feet away to get some privacy.

"Franklin found himself some very weird ancient magic. He finished casting his spell and this blizzard is just getting started."

I had stopped questioning this sort of thing a long time ago. Weird ancient magic, check. Even worse blizzard, check. I wanted to go home and take a hot bath.

"Right. But can we stop him?"

"We can neutralize the spell, but we have to hit every Speedy Mart in town to do it. I can't do it alone."

That was a pretty big thing for him to admit.

Denver and the surrounding suburbs had thirteen Speedy Marts. Cormac had visited them all over the last week. Normally, getting to all of them would sound doable. Crazy, but doable. But now?

"Cormac, we're in Colorado Springs in the middle of a blizzard. How the hell are we supposed to get to Denver?"

"I don't know. Hijack a snowplow or something."

"Not helpful," I said. "How much time do we have?"

"A couple of hours before it's too late to break the spell."

"Let me call you back in ten minutes," I said.

"I'm serious, Kitty. We don't have time to screw around."

A snarl burred at the back of my throat. "Ten minutes." I hung up.

Cormac wouldn't exaggerate. He was talking the worst blizzard ever. A Katrina level of destruction blizzard. I couldn't imagine. That was the point. Hundred-mile-an-hour winds, subzero temperatures, a dozen feet of snow crashing through roofs, no power, no heat, and having it last for a week or more.

"What's wrong?" Ben said when I rejoined the group.

"The Franklin situation's blowing up. Cormac needs us back in Denver."

Ben blinked in disbelief. "He knows there's a blizzard on, right?"

"He suggested stealing a snowplow."

Another moment passed while Ben considered. "He's not doing anything that's going to break his parole, is he?"

That question wasn't highest on my list of current concerns.

"Can I help? What can I do to help?" Tyler asked. Guy needed a mission.

"Think you can get the army to issue us a Humvee?" I said, mostly joking.

Tyler glanced at Stafford, who was down the hall, conversing with a medical crew that had arrived to help clean up the mess. They were loading Walters and Vanderman into body bags. The place was becoming crowded, lots of people in uniform taking orders from the colonel, ducking in and out of rooms, clearing debris. Someone should call Dr. Shumacher to let her know what happened.

"The base is still under lockdown," Tyler said. "He may not let us out at all."

Who was I kidding? He probably wouldn't even let us out of the building, much less out of Fort Carson. But I'd never know unless I asked. The worst he could do was say no.

I walked over to the colonel, hands laced behind my back, trying to look harmless. The slight limp probably didn't hurt.

"Colonel Stafford?"

He turned and glared, but didn't tell me to go away.

"I know you want us to stick around, but I really have to get back to Denver. I've got a friend who needs help. I'll come right back as soon as I can, but

Tyler says that with the base under lockdown nobody can leave. I *really* need to leave."

If possible, his frown deepened. More than stern, though, he looked tired. He disguised the shadows under his eyes with sheer willpower. "I don't suppose there's any point in keeping the lockdown in effect. But you can't drive to Denver in this weather. You might as well stay."

He was right. We'd barely gotten here in Ben's sedan as it was. I had no other argument, except to clasp my hands to my chest and look up at him with my big brown eyes while begging, *Please?*

Even my dignity had bounds.

I crossed my arms. "What if I told you that this blizzard isn't natural? That it's the product of a magical spell designed to cause millions of dollars in damage and plunge the region into chaos. I know how to stop it, but I have to get to Denver to do it."

He crossed his arms back at me, and stared at me down his nose. "I'd say you were crazy." But the thing was—-he was still listening.

"You know that werewolves exist, right?" I said. "You ever think about what else is out there? If werewolves are real, what else must be real?"

"Actually, Ms. Norville, I've been trying not to think too hard about that."

I hid a smile. I understood the impulse. "I really have to get to Denver. You can talk to my friend and he'll explain the whole deal, if you want. Dr. Shumacher could probably back us up."

He considered me for an even longer moment. In my mind, a clock was ticking—I needed to call Cormac back. By this time, Ben and Tyler had inched over to listen in. Tyler's brow was arched, possibly in amazement. Ben was just smiling.

Then Stafford said, "So you came down here to try and help my men before chasing down this other situation?"

"Yes," I said. Of course I did.

"Sir," Tyler said, stepping forward to interrupt. "If you have a Humvee with chains you can spare, I can drive it."

Tyler was bigger than Stafford, who might have been that fit earlier in his life. So it was strange seeing Tyler defer to him—he still stood at military attention, but his shoulders slouched, just a little, and his gaze was down. I held my breath.

"Are you going to be okay, Sergeant?" Stafford asked.

Tyler glanced at me, and nodded. "Sir. For a little while, I think so, sir."

So. Stafford let us go.

I called Cormac while we waited for Tyler to find our Humvee with tire chains. We were in the glass-fronted lobby of the hospital. Ben was grinning wide enough to split his face.

"What?" I said while I waited for Cormac to pick up.

"You're awesome, you know that?" he said. "You just talked an army colonel into loaning you a Humvee."

"It was that or try to steal one, right?" I said. I tried to be happy, but I was getting tired. "And I couldn't talk Vanderman into anything."

Cormac answered before Ben could say anything to that.

"Hey," I said. "What did I tell you? Ten minutes."

"It's been twenty," he said.

"Whatever. We found a ride. We're on our way. Now what's going on at Speedy Mart? What do we have to do?"

He paused while he adjusted the phone. At least that was what it sounded like. "He's using them to anchor power. Each one is a focal point in a ritual, and he strings them together in a kind of circuit. He can extend the effect of the ritual over an entire region that way—a hundred miles in every direction. But if we can neutralize each location, we can stop this."

"Right, cool, and how do we do that?" I imagined it involved burning incense, sprinkling some sort of concoction, or chanting. The usual stuff.

"There's a symbol, the *gromoviti znaci*, the thunder mark. People in Slavic countries used to carve it into their doorframes to protect against lightning strikes. Franklin's power is associated with the weather because he's invoking thunder gods, gods of storms. But that's his problem—he's not limiting himself to a particular magical tradition or set of symbols. He's invoking as many as he can, thinking it will gain him more power. That's why I had trouble identifying the magic, because it's a mishmash of different systems. He's using the power outside of its cultural contexts. The Norse god Thor doesn't correspond exactly with the Slavic Perun, or the Hindu Indra, or the Yoruban Shango, or Sumerian Ishkur. They're all thunder gods but they mean different things to their respective cultures. Some of these gods were meant to combat chaos, not cause it."

He'd slipped into full-on lecture mode. I'd never heard him speak more than a couple of sentences together at a time. It almost freaked me out more than the blizzard. "Cormac, where the hell did you learn all this? You never used to talk like this."

When he stayed silent, I was afraid I'd lost the connection. Then he took a breath, and his voice sounded calm, but there was tension—temper—held in check. "I'll explain it all later. I promise."

"But what—"

"It's complicated."

I bit back a million questions. Cormac wasn't right. Something had happened to him in prison, and it was beyond my ability to guess what. His stubbornness hadn't changed—he wouldn't explain until he was ready to.

"What do we need to do?" I asked.

"We need to put the *gromoviti znaci* on the doorway of every Speedy Mart in the area. It should neutralize Franklin's power."

"Should?" I said, a little wild.

"This isn't an exact science."

I almost laughed.

Between tracking down Franklin and the research I'd done for the show the previous week, I knew where the Speedy Marts were located. In my mind, I tried to map an efficient route between them all. Denver was a sprawling city, its suburbs reaching out for miles. The southernmost location was in Parker, in the southeastern corner of the metro area. The northernmost was in Lafayette, closer to Boulder than to Denver. It would take an hour to drive straight from one to the other, without any detours, in the best of weather and with no traffic.

"We can't do it," I said, at a loss. "It would take all day, even if the weather was perfect. Maybe if we had a dozen or so people to help—"

What was I saying? I had resources. I had a wolf pack that lived all over the region.

"What is it?" Cormac asked.

"We can do this. Can you e-mail this symbol of yours? Or do you have a URL people can link to?

We have to do this before the power goes out—or do it by phone." I didn't know if everyone had phones that could receive photos. Shaun did—he could help cover gaps, maybe.

"Yeah, I think I can send out a photo. Who am I sending it to?"

"Shaun. You remember Shaun, from New Moon?" He did, and I gave him the number. "Give me a minute to call him and warn him it's coming."

"What's this going to accomplish?"

"I'm sending my pack out to do the legwork. I need to look at a map, but I should be able to get someone to every location within an hour."

Cormac breathed a relieved sigh. "Good."

"I gotta run for a sec." I hung up. Tyler had just pulled up in a beige Humvee.

Ben said, "That sounded like a plan."

"Yeah. I sure hope so. We need a map of the city, to mark down the addresses of all the Speedy Marts and figure out who in the pack is closest to each of them. We can hit the ones on the way into town."

"I think I can handle that. Just a sec." He went outside, ducking before the driving snow, and headed toward his car.

Tyler's Humvee seemed to be going awfully fast as it rounded the corner. I braced, waiting for it to slide and spin out on the ice—but it didn't. He brought it right up to the curb, where it stopped cold.

The vehicle was squat, low profile, low center of gravity. It had four doors, and I could see a stark interior through the windshield. The tires had chains on them. Maybe we could get to Denver after all.

Ben returned with supplies: phone, a blanket, road flares, a bottle of water, and a ragged city map. Tyler was waving to us from the cab of the Humvee.

"You ready for this?" Ben said.

I hadn't stopped to consider whether I was ready for this. I took a deeper breath—my ribs still hurt, my stomach was sore. They hurt less if I didn't think about it. So, time to power through.

"Yeah," I said, brushing back his mussed-up hair.

Tyler drove, and Ben and I sat in back where we could plan. We got moving, heading east, back to state Highway 83 rather than the interstate, which we assumed would still be closed farther north. We were hoping to see little to no traffic. Tyler assured us that with the vehicle's four-wheel drive and the chains, we ought to be able to make good time. The highway went straight to Parker.

The Humvee was rough and noisy. Between the rattle of the chains on the tires, roaring engine, the uninsulated steel cab, and wind beating against the windows, I couldn't hear much of anything, and every little bump jostled us. But I had to make these calls.

"Hey, Shaun?" I shouted into my phone.

My werewolf hearing was the only way I heard

his reply, a clear voice under all the rattling. "Kitty? What's going on? What's all that noise, I can barely hear you."

"It's a long story. I'm in a Humvee heading north. You feel like saving the city?"

"Does it involve stopping this snow?" he said.

"Yeah, actually."

"Then I'm totally in."

"Cool. This is going to take footwork and phone calls. Where are you?"

"I'm snowed in at the restaurant. They weren't predicting this. I thought we were going to get the usual snowy day lunch crowd looking for coffee and a bowl of soup. This is epic."

"Yeah, more than you know. Look, Cormac—you remember Cormac? He's going to be sending you a photo of a symbol. We have to put that symbol over the door of every Speedy Mart in town."

"And that'll stop the snow? That's kind of crazy." He chuckled.

"Shaun, we're werewolves, we don't get to judge crazy."

Ben had the map spread out over his lap. We didn't have anything to write with, so he'd poked holes in the Speedy Mart locations. "Here, I think I got them all."

I double-checked his work and found a couple he missed. Now we had to figure out who lived closest to where and start making assignments.

A couple of members of the pack—such as Rachel, who lived in the foothills west of town—were too far away to be any help. With the weather like this, they were probably socked in under a couple of feet of snow by now. But with a few of the other locations, we were in luck—Becky lived a couple of blocks from the store in Littleton. Trey lived up north in Broomfield and ought to be able to reach the two northernmost locations. Shaun would cover the one downtown, after calling everyone and passing along the symbol.

"Have them call me if they argue. This isn't a request, it's an order from on high." I rarely pulled rank in the pack. Instead, I usually cajoled and prodded. I was hoping the rarity of me issuing orders would get across how serious this was.

I was also hoping that Cormac was right, and that this would work.

"This isn't going to be easy," Shaun said.

"No," I agreed. Even with help, we might not cover all the locations. But this seemed like the best chance. "Our other option is to call all of the Speedy Marts and see if we can talk the clerks into posting the symbol themselves." What were the odds?

"It wouldn't hurt to have someone on that as backup," Ben said. "We just need someone with a phone book and a phone."

"Okay, let's get Rachel on that, since she's probably snowed in anyway."

Maybe we'd covered all the bases.

We raced on. Tyler sat straight, both hands on the wheel, focused ahead and concentrating. There wasn't any traffic, not anymore, though we passed abandoned cars that had slid off the shoulder and gotten stuck. Every now and then I saw flashing lights through the driving snow—the yellow warning lights of snowplows, the red and blue of a police car once. I expected us to get pulled over by a cop wanting to know what the heck we were doing out here. But maybe you saw a military Humvee driving with purpose up the highway in a snowstorm, you figured it was on a mission.

I called Cormac. "Did you get ahold of Shaun?"

"I did. He's got the picture. I'll send it to you next."

"You think this is really going to work?" I asked.

"I guess we'll find out," he said, his wry fatalism from the old days showing through. "I—I think it will. I have faith."

I'd never known Cormac to have much faith in anything except the gun in his hand and his ability to shoot. Now that he'd lost the guns, what did he have faith in? And why did that make me worry? "Cormac. Seriously. Are you okay?" Frowning, Ben glanced at me.

"I'm fine. I'll explain everything when this is all over." He clicked off.

"That just means there really is something to explain," I said, staring at my phone.

"He is okay, right?" Ben said. And I really didn't know.

My phone beeped—photo coming through.

The *gromoviti znaci*, the thunder mark, looked like a wheel, or a very stylized flower. Six spokes radiated from a space, with a circle in the middle. On the wheel's outer ring, between each spoke, was another circle. I knew enough about magic to know circles were powerful, often used as symbols of protection. This was one of the more intricate, beautiful versions of the pattern I'd seen.

Ben leaned over to look at the screen on my phone. "That's it, huh?"

"Yup."

"I'm trying to figure out if 'saving the city' would fly as a defense for vandalism charges," he said.

"You're always the practical one." I kissed his cheek.

The storm around us was morphing from a pale gray to a dark gray—the sun was setting. I wondered if twilight or nightfall was part of Franklin's spell, and if that was how much time we had to stop this.

"How's it going, Tyler?" I said.

"It's nice having a job to do," he said, smiling a little. "A mission."

I was glad someone was enjoying this. I'd have been happier at home, safe in our den.

We approached the lights of Parker.

Chapter 22

I NAVIGATED TYLER to the Speedy Mart, which was on the corner of a wide intersection between subdivisions. The snowplows had given up awhile ago, and the wind had blown drifts across the streets. We only made it through because Tyler gunned the Humvee, and the chains bit into the snow. The streetlights were on; sheets of huge snowflakes—golfball-size chunks of icy, clinging snow, really—fell through the orange beams. It would have been beautiful—if I'd been watching it from inside a heated room.

A single car, half covered by a drift of snow, was parked in the lot. A light was on inside the convenience store, but I didn't see anyone behind the counter. The place might not have been open, but that was okay—we could put the symbol on the outside. I hoped.

Tyler swerved to a stop by the curb in front of the door.

"I don't suppose anyone has a pen and paper? A can of spray paint?" I said.

"Why don't we ask him?" Ben said, nodded through the window.

A scruffy-looking guy in his early twenties was pulling himself to his feet. He looked like he'd been lying down behind the counter.

Ben and I piled out. Tyler waited, keeping the motor running.

The door was unlocked, and a tinny bell rang as we pushed in. The guy behind the counter, fully upright now, stared at us. Ben and I must have been a sight: still in jeans and T-shirts, we'd been soaked wet and dried off a couple of times over. My hair felt like a nest and my eyes had shadows under them. I might have had a fading bruise or two left over from the fight with Vanderman.

"Hi," I said. "I wondered if you had a marker that we could borrow, or for sale, or something." I smiled in a way that I hoped was cheerful rather than crazed.

He pointed down one of the aisles. "We have a few office supplies there."

"Thanks." I ran. Sure enough, I found a package of Sharpies. The nice, thick, stinky kind. I picked up three and brought them to the counter. Ben got out his wallet to pay.

"That's it?" he said. He sounded numb.

"No, wait." I made a quick tour of the store,

grabbing sodas, a package of beef jerky, a box of cookies. This ought to get us through. "Anything else?" I asked Ben.

"Permission?" he said.

"Ah. Not just yet."

The clerk dutifully scanned our items. "Would you like a bag?"

This was getting kind of surreal. A gust of wind rattled the door and snow pelted the glass. "Yes, please."

The transaction completed, the clerk, still blinking dazedly, said, "Thank you for choosing Speedy Mart."

I grinned, teeth showing. "I didn't choose Speedy Mart. Speedy Mart chose me. Oh, and I'm really sorry about this."

I ripped one of the markers out of the packaging before handing the bag back to Ben. We both looked at the door, and the clear space of wall—a clean white canvas—above it. There didn't seem to be any convenient footstools or chairs around.

"Can you lift me up?" I said.

"I think so," Ben answered.

First, though, I flipped open the phone so I could look at the picture. I'd never taken an art class in my life. I hoped the thunder gods were forgiving of my lack of talent.

Kneeling, Ben held my legs while I sat on his shoulder, and he stood. Werewolf strength meant he didn't even wobble, but I had to grab his other shoulder to keep my balance.

"You okay?" he said.

"Yup." I started drawing.

"Hey, what are you doing?" the kid said, rushing around the counter. He didn't get closer than about ten feet. He just stopped, hand outstretched, watching with an expression that resembled hopelessness.

"Breaking a spell. I hope," I said.

"Huh? But—you can't—I mean—"

"The blizzard? Not normal. We're here to save the city."

The guy started laughing, hysterical. "This sucks! I mean, who are you? What the hell—" He sat down and put his head in his hands.

I was almost finished drawing the thunder mark, just adding the circles.

"Hey, are you okay?" Ben asked him.

"No. I was supposed to be off my shift six hours ago, but I can't get home, and no one else can get here. The manager said I should just stay open as long as I was here. I've been here for fourteen hours!"

What could I say? That really did suck.

"Okay, I'm done," I said to Ben, and he let me slide to the floor. We regarded my artwork, comparing it to the image on my phone. It looked like it was supposed to—the distinct wheel-like symbol, as big as my face. And if I wasn't mistaken, the wind seemed to have died down a little. It may have been my imagination.

"It just seems way too easy," Ben said.

I stared at him. "We just drove eighty miles through a blizzard in a Humvee—you call that easy?"

Ben made an offhand shrug, and he had a point—that was actually one of the easier things we'd done today.

"Who *are* you people?" the clerk shrieked. "What am I supposed to do about *that*?"

"Please don't paint it or wash it off or anything. At least for a couple of days," I said.

"But—"

"Seriously."

He clenched his hands and drew himself up with new resolve. "I'm calling my manager." He marched to a phone behind the counter.

We both ran to beat him to it. Ben lunged over the counter to grab the base and pull out the cord. I went right for the receiver in his hand and snatched it away. The clerk yelled and scrambled away from me to press himself against the wall, panting for breath. We must have looked pretty aggressive—a couple of wolves on the run. And he'd acted a lot like prey. Smiling, I glared at him and resisted licking my lips.

"How about we give you a ride home?" I said. "We've got a Humvee with chains."

He only took about five seconds to say yes. Ten

more minutes ticked off the clock while we waited for him to get his things, shut off the lights, switch on the alarm, and lock up. We waited in the Humvee.

"What's up with that?" Ben asked, looking at me. "Giving him a ride?"

"It's the only thing I could think of," I said.

"Oh, I'm not complaining, it's not a bad idea. It's not a *great* idea. Especially if the kid finds out we're all werewolves."

"What's going on?" Tyler asked.

The kid hauled open the front passenger door, which creaked on its hinges, and climbed it. He needed a couple of tries to make it up to the seat. When he had to lean way over to close the door again, I was afraid he was going to fall out, but he managed the stunt.

"Whoa, I've never ridden in one of these before. This is, like, a real one. Not a Hummer. Right?" He looked around. We were all glaring at him. He leaned away from the large and intimidating presence of Tyler and looked like he was maybe reconsidering the ride.

"Uh, hi." The clerk said. "I live just a couple miles away. A block or so off Keystone. Um, thanks for the ride, I guess."

Tyler shifted into gear and the Humvee crunched forward on a new layer of snow.

"You think it's getting better?" Ben said, craning his neck to look up out the window.

It would be easy to fool ourselves into thinking so. The snow was still falling in giant flakes. But it was falling straight down in lazy drifting patterns now, instead of driving horizontally.

"I don't know," I said.

"Um, turn left here." The clerk pointed to an intersection, and Tyler drove through. The streetlights might have been red, but we couldn't tell because they were covered with a layer of white.

Away from the store, the wind started blowing again, kicking up eddies and whirlwinds of snow around us. It could have been my imagination.

We stayed quiet; we didn't want to talk in front of the kid. I didn't even want to call Cormac until he was out of here. Ben was right. What had I been thinking? But it meant he wouldn't mess with the thunder mark.

"This thing doesn't have a heater, does it?" the kid said.

"It's pretty stripped down," Tyler answered. I swore the kid flinched at the sound of his voice. Tyler sounded like a movie badass, which was pretty cool unless you thought he was maybe going to kill you.

Tyler followed the kid's directions until he turned onto a side street in an unassuming neighborhood of tract housing. It hadn't been plowed, and the Humvee barged into a three-foot drift. Snow flew everywhere.

"Here's fine. It's just a couple of houses up." He probably lived with his parents.

"You sure?" Tyler asked.

"Yeah, yeah." The door was already open, and the kid fell out and into a drift. He probably would have run away, but he sunk to his knees with every step and had to shuffle. We waited until he reached the front door of his house—two up, like he said. We could barely see him through the whiteout.

"There," I said when the door closed behind him. "Good deed accomplished."

"I thought it was a bribe," Ben said.

"Hey. Win win all around." I grinned.

Tyler backed out of the drift he'd driven into. I got out my phone and called Cormac.

"Hey," I said. "One down. We're headed to our second stop. How are we doing?"

I heard a noise in the background, like he was rearranging the phone, or like I'd caught him in the middle of something. "You did it? You got the symbol up? What happened?"

"Uh . . . nothing?" I winced. "Was something supposed to happen?"

"I don't know," he said, sighing with frustration. "Becky got the one in Littleton, Shaun hit downtown. I'm still waiting for the others. I'm thinking we ought to know by now if it's working."

And if it didn't work, what then? "Where's Franklin? He's got to be masterminding this from somewhere."

"I'm tracking him down right now. I'll be in touch." He hung up.

Ben was navigating Tyler to the Tech Center location. The world outside was getting darker as night fell. Buildings were shadows in a fog, and the glow from streetlights shone strangely, diffused by the snow. We might have been barreling across an alien world.

"Any progress?" Ben said.

"I can't tell. He seems distracted. But he says two other locations are done."

"That's good, right?" he said.

I couldn't say.

Our visit to the Speedy Mart at the Tech Center went better than our first stop had. Mostly because the store was closed and locked up, with no one to hassle us. Once again, Ben held me up while I marked on the painted concrete above the door. The overhang sheltered us a little. Once again, I imagined that the wind diminished when we were done.

Then we were off again. After sunset, it was hard to tell if the weather was changing. The sky could be clearing and we'd never know.

"Back in Afghanistan," Tyler said, thoughtful, distracted, "patrols would head out sometimes and get ambushed. They'd lose one or two guys, but we wouldn't find any sign of attack—no explosions, no gunfire. Not even footprints. The captain and I went out once to try to find out what was happening. I smelled it—and it wasn't human. But we didn't know what it was. It shouldn't have surprised us—we aren't really human, right? But it's hard knowing how to fight something when you don't know what it is. The guys got real superstitious about it, saying it was some kind of magical curse. Some of them started carrying around charms—four-leaf clovers, St. Christopher medals, things like that. Who knew if it did any good? Kind of like this. But if it makes you feel better, is it really so bad?"

We drove for another mile, tires crunching on ice, before I figured out how to ask, "Did you ever find out what happened?"

He shook his head. "Not really. Not officially. But some of the locals told stories—they said there was a demon that lived in the desert. The ghul. It could change its shape, turn into a deer, or a wounded dog, or whatever it needed to lure people into the canyons. Then it would attack. Maybe it was a person, some kind of lycanthrope. But we could have tracked it down then. This thing—we never saw a sign. Just the bodies it left." He looked over his shoulder at me. "You ever hear of anything like that?"

I shook my head, and once again felt daunted about how much I didn't know.

We arrived at the South Broadway location, the one we'd trailed Franklin to, which seemed appropriate. Like we'd come full circle. The clerks had bailed here as well, which left the parking lot empty.

We put the thunder mark over the door, same as the others. I thought I was getting better at it—faster, anyway. Had to stay positive, right?

Back in the Humvee, Tyler was holding my phone out to me. "It's your friend."

I grabbed it and said, "Hello? Cormac? Where are you?"

"Just a sec—there's four more down," Cormac said. He told me the locations—Trey and Dan had teamed up to hit two stores up north—and I crossed them off on the map with the Sharpie. They made bold, satisfying *X*'s across the region. This was like marking territory. I was so proud of my pack.

"That's great," I said. "We're halfway there."

"Not quite. Franklin's leaving town."

"In this weather? How?"

"That Hummer he rented. This follows his pattern—he sets the storms in motion and leaves before he gets caught up in it."

"So . . . we're stopping his spell, right? What else do we need to do?"

"I want to get him," Cormac said.

Yeah. So did I. "What do you need?"

"Meet me outside the Brown Palace." And he hung up. No plan of attack, no clue about what we were actually going to do when we confronted Franklin. We'd get to that point soon enough.

"We're heading downtown," I told Ben and Tyler.

"The interstate's closed," Ben said. "We'll have to take surface streets."

"That just keeps the adventure going," I said with false cheer. My nerves were vibrating—what if we went through all this and it didn't work?

My phone rang again. Shaun this time. "Hey," I said. "How's it going?"

"I was going to ask you that," he said. "Is this actually working? It's stopped snowing here."

"It has?" I looked outside, peering at the odd streetlight to catch a hint of movement. I couldn't see snow falling. Maybe it really had stopped.

The line clicked. "I have another call coming in," Shaun said. "Lance, it looks like. I'll talk to you later."

"Awesome." I closed the phone and looked at Ben. "I think this is working."

"It ain't over yet," he said.

We drove on, Tyler leaning forward to navigate the snowdrifted street, with stalled and abandoned cars left as obstacles every block or so.

"How are you doing?" I asked him.

"Good," he said. "As long as I have something else to think about, I'm good."

I patted his shoulder, and he flashed a smile.

The phone rang again—another Speedy Mart marked, I assumed. Excited, I answered and waited for Cormac's voice.

"Change of plans—he's heading east on Colfax. We've got to stop him."

Not exactly what I was expecting. "Stop him how?"

"I don't know. But we can't let him leave town."

"You're following him, I take it?"

"Yeah. You think you can cut him off?"

Well. We could certainly try. "Sure. Why not? See you in a minute."

This was going to get ugly. I slipped the phone into my pocket.

"I heard that," Ben said.

"Where are we?"

"Broadway," he said.

"We have to hustle," I said, shaking my head. "We'll never make it."

"Just tell me how to get there," Tyler said, and gunned the motor. I fell against the backseat and grabbed the door to steady myself.

"Head east on Alameda," Ben said, grinning. "Two lights up."

Tyler ran the next red light. But we were the only vehicle in sight. Tyler sped through the next three red lights, which was kind of cool. Racing on, we managed to approach Colfax without sliding out of control. I kept expecting to see flashing red and blue lights reflecting off the snow and fog—the one time you don't expect any cops around, Murphy's Law said they ought to be here.

Ben navigated until Tyler swung the wheel and fishtailed onto Colfax. I studied the way ahead of us for a black Hummer barreling along. It was hard to see anything through the snow, which was still falling here.

"There he is," Tyler said, shifting hard and swinging the steering wheel. The Humvee lurched sideways, the chains biting into the ice covering the street. We blocked most of the road, now, and could move forward or back as needed to stop Franklin. The Hummer was a black hole moving through the mist, getting closer. We all expected him to stop.

"Guy's not slowing down," Tyler said.

"Maybe he can't stop on the ice," I said, doubtful.

"He's speeding up." Tyler's hands kneaded the steering wheel. He bared his teeth. "This is just like a roadblock. He ain't slowing down."

Roadblock, car bomb—Tyler was in another place at the moment. I squeezed his shoulder.

"Asshole," Ben muttered. "Thinks a monster car like that makes him invincible."

"We can still stop him," I said. "It won't hurt us."

Tyler's breathing steadied. "Permanently, rather. It's still gonna hurt. You sure?"

We didn't have any time for further discussion. Tyler hunched over, bracing. In the backseat, Ben and I curled up on the floorboards, hanging on to each other.

Then came the crash.

Near as I could figure before I shut my eyes, Franklin's Hummer T-boned us. Steel crunched and tore. A shockwave slammed through us and we skidded, even with the tire chains. I flew, bounced—hands grabbed me. My vision went upside down for a minute. Then, silence.

I'd been holding my breath. Wolf was shrieking through my gut, claustrophobic and crying to get out. I pulled her in, locked her down tight, made my breathing slow and calm. Only then could I assess. Sore—lots and lots of sore. I had a bruise on my head where I'd run into something hard. But no shooting pains. No blood or broken bones. All in all, I didn't feel much more beat up than I had after Vanderman worked me over.

Ben's hand closed on my arm. I grabbed it and squeezed back. We'd ended up on the seat, him pressed up against the door and me sprawled in his lap. I peered through the window and got a look at the hood of Franklin's Hummer, which was only slightly rumpled. The engine had smoke coming out of it.

We took a moment to stretch our limbs and extricate ourselves.

"Everyone okay? Still human?"

"Barely," Ben said, voice tense. "You?"

"Shaken. Fine," I said.

"That sucked." Rolling a shoulder, he winced. He opened and closed his hand as if he expected it not to work.

"Tyler?" I asked. I could hear him breathing in the front seat, but he hadn't spoken yet, which worried me. If he shifted, this would get messy. Messier. I straightened, feeling a muscle in my back spasm. Yeah, if I'd been fully human this would have hurt. Leaning over the front seat, I got a look at Tyler.

Hunched over, muscles trembling, he was still gripping the steering wheel, like it was a life preserver. I took a breath—full of wild, full of wolf. I also smelled blood. He was on the edge. He'd been hurt, and his wolf would blaze forth to protect him.

I pulled myself into the front, grunting when my battered muscles complained. Moving close so he could smell me, so he would have to listen to me, I put my arms around him. My embrace seemed small, unable to contain his powerful frame.

His eyes were clamped shut. Blood dripped from a cut on his forehead.

"Tyler, listen to me. Keep it together. Pull it back in. You don't have to shift, we're fine, we're going to be fine. Stay with me. Breathe . . ." The litany went on. Stay human. Stay with us. Breathe slowly, in and out.

I could usually get wolves to listen to me when they were on the edge like this. Just hold them, wrap them up, keep talking to them so they would remember human voices. But those were wolves I knew. How well did I know Tyler, really? "Please," I begged.

And his breathing slowed. The muscles in his back relaxed, some of the tension going out of them.

"There's Franklin," Ben said, looking out the window at the man stumbling out of the other crashed car. His own voice was sounding low and rough, and I wondered how close he was to losing it. He shoved open the door and stalked out like he was on the prowl.

"Tyler, you okay? I gotta go back him up," I said.

The soldier shuddered through the shoulders and straightened, like a dog shaking itself out. "Let's go," he said.

Ben had paused outside the Humvee, waiting for us. Together, we moved around to Franklin's Hummer, to face the man himself.

He wasn't dressed for the weather. His trench coat would be more at home on the streets of New York City or London. He probably wore his usual suit underneath. The maroon wool scarf wrapped once around his neck didn't seem to do much to hold back the cold. The snow came up well over his dress shoes. He was tense, shivering.

When he saw us, he backed away, stumbling. He must have seen something inhuman in us. Something ferocious, animal. A pack of beings who wanted to tear him apart, and very much could if they got to him. One wonders if he saw anything but the threat. He knew what I was—my identity as a werewolf was very public—and could guess that Ben and Tyler were also werewolves.

He raised a hand over his head; he was holding something, a metal artifact as big as his fist. "Stay back! I have defense against your kind! *Stay back!*"

The object he held was made of silver and shaped like some kind of hammer—a broad T with rounded edges. A Scandinavian charm, with an intricate design stamped into it. Gleaming, it threw back what little light shone on it, and almost writhed in his grip, like it was a living thing trying to break free. Some twisting force of nature—lightning, maybe.

"Stay away from me!" he shouted again.

I smelled blood on him—such a sharp, sweet scent. My mouth watered. He'd skinned his cheek in the crash, and the red dripped along his jaw to his chin. He may not even have noticed. Ben curled a lip and growled, teeth showing. "Wait," I murmured. Yeah, Franklin was asking for it. That didn't mean we were going to give it to him. Guy wasn't in his right mind.

Still, I wanted to get in his face. Not to do anything to him. Just to scare him a little. "Who hired you?" I shouted. "Who are you working for? Who wants to destroy my city?"

"This is bigger than you, little girl!"

I stepped forward, imagining I was stalking on

wolf's paws, snow and ice crunching lightly under my feet. I held his gaze, staring hard, and wondered if he understood the challenge.

"Back!" he shouted, waving his little charm. Then he said something in a language I didn't understand. Couldn't even guess what.

Thunder bellowed, the ear-shattering crack of a powerful summer thunderhead striking right over-head, along with an atomic flash of light. The sound was wrong in the middle of a snowstorm. I ducked, arms wrapped around my head. We'd all dropped to the ground—except for Franklin, who grinned at me. The talisman in his hand seemed to glow.

I straightened, angry that he'd made me put myself lower than him. Lightning had struck, right on top of us—maybe one of the vehicles or a streetlamp. I couldn't tell where, but smelled sulfur and burning.

"You think that makes you tough?" I said. "You're all powerful and stuff because you can destroy entire cities?"

"You wouldn't understand. You have no faith! You're an *animal*!"

Oh, why did I bother? I put my hands on my hips. "We'll stop you. We've already stopped you." I didn't know if that was true. Shaun and the others had five more stores to mark. I hoped they were doing that now.

Franklin wore the triumphant expression of a con-queror. "You can't stop us!"

From the darkness up the street, another vehicle appeared and skidded to a stop, enough behind Franklin's Hummer that there was no danger of a collision. Cormac's Jeep, hunched like a creature in the fog. Cormac slid out of the front seat and strode forward without a pause, until he stood about ten yards behind Franklin.

"Hey," Cormac said. "If you're done with them, you come deal with me."

Franklin turned and slipped, nearly toppling over. He windmilled his arms to recover and then stood unsteadily, legs braced, arms outstretched. Straightening quickly, he faced down Cormac with his former air of superiority.

That he turned his back to me—that he thought I wasn't a threat—made me angry. I wanted to snarl and pounce on him. But I also wanted to see what Cormac was going to do to the guy. I still wasn't sure we had him cornered; he could call the cops on us and it would be just like the libel suit. Sure, I was right that he was a bad guy, and he really was using his Speedy Mart franchise to work magic, and he really was working on a spell to put Denver under ten feet of snow. And I would prove all that, how?

"You're too late!" Franklin said, right out of the bad-guy handbook, as if there were any remaining doubt. "The divine power lives on, through me!"

"We'll just see about that," Cormac said.

Franklin thrust his amulet at Cormac, as though

brandishing a cross at a vampire, and repeated the phrase he'd used before. I cringed, ducking, expecting a crack of thunder to crash over our heads. It didn't. Franklin also seemed surprised, and he tried the gesture again.

Cormac seemed amused when he pulled his own amulet, a metal disk, out of the pocket of his leather coat. He studied it a moment, then threw it at Franklin, underhanded, as if he expected the guy to catch it.

Franklin didn't catch it. He flinched in a panic, and the amulet hit him, then fell into the snow. Maybe we all expected an explosion, for flames to burst forth and devour him, but nothing happened. Franklin pawed in the snow for the object. When he found it, lying it flat on his hand, he stared at it with as much terror as if it really had rained physical destruction on him.

It showed the *gromoviti znaci*, wanna bet?

"Told you," I said at him. I'd about decided we had to take him down and damn the consequences, if he didn't just admit defeat and crawl away.

Then clouds parted. It seemed to happen suddenly, but more likely it had come upon us gradually, the clouds thinning, fading from gray to nothing, until fissures appeared, and a dark sky showed through, edged by lingering curls of mist. I felt as if a blanket lifted off me, like I could breathe freely again. Which meant that Shaun and the others had succeeded, and the spell was broken. While the blizzard had caused havoc, it wasn't any worse now than the usual impressive winter storms that struck Denver every couple of years. People wouldn't be talking about this one as the storm of the century.

Franklin stared up at the clearing sky with the rest of us. I couldn't see his expression, but his shoulders sagged.

He put the amulet in his coat pocket and turned back to Cormac. "It's your fault, isn't it?"

"I guess so."

Cormac and Franklin faced each other down like a couple of Old West gunslingers. Cormac even stood ready, arms loose, hands at his hips, ready to yank pistols from holsters. He looked wrong without his guns. But he didn't look worried.

"What are you?" Franklin's tone was both frightened and angry. He'd probably never been defeated. He was used to a world where few people knew anything about magic. "Who do you serve?"

"No one. I'm just a guy," Cormac said, a tilt to his head.

That seemed to infuriate Franklin. He began chanting, not a one-phrase curse, a moment of power, and then done. He didn't have an amulet this time. Above, clouds that had been clearing began to coalesce again, sinking low, as if drawn toward him. The temperature dropped—to even feel it at this point meant it was plummeting, going from freezing to arctic. And all the power gathered toward Franklin, who was pointing outstretched arms at Cormac.

"Kitty, what's he doing?" Ben said, standing close behind me, taking hold of my shoulder. "Does Cormac need help?" Nearby, Tyler was breathing deep, fogging breaths.

"I don't know," I said, and my voice sounded thin, lost. I had seen magic at work before. I hadn't seen anything like this.

I had a professor in college who read Anglo-Saxon like he'd grown up with it. This was the language of *Beowulf*, a rolling, singsong way of speaking, full of portent. Like thunder, rumbling for miles over a windswept plain. After the passage of time, this professor explained, ancient languages become the language of magic, the meanings forgotten but the power of them remembered. The Catholic Church could chant Latin, and it didn't matter that no one knew what the words meant a thousand years later. He'd been speaking metaphorically. But he was right.

Franklin was drawing on that power now, gathering it to launch at and smash his enemy, and I couldn't understand why Cormac was just standing there, why he didn't look worried. But did he ever?

A white glow was growing around Franklin, seeming to light him from within. His hair was standing on end, as if he were gathering a static charge. The whole area looked like an electrical

KITTY GOES TO WAR

experiment gone awry. His voice increased in volume and pitch, a sign that the spell was drawing to a close. Then, as the words broke down into a primal yell of power, a static discharge, a bolt of lightning, crashed from Franklin to Cormac.

Cormac raised both hands, set his legs apart as if to brace, ducked his head—and a blue flare encased him. It was like someone lit a torch under him, and he was all flame—hot, intense, dangerous. Franklin's lightning bolt disintegrated in a wave of sparks—which doubled back and caught him in the backwash.

I shielded my face; Ben and I ducked together, sheltering each other. The crash of thunder seemed to last for minutes. Then, silence. I could hear my heart pounding. Even Wolf was quiet, trembling in my gut, waiting to see which way we had to jump.

Finally, I looked around.

Harold Franklin was lying flat on his back, half buried in snow, and not moving. Cormac stood exactly as he had before the light show started. He didn't even look singed. He pursed his lips in a thin smile and appeared satisfied.

"What the *hell* just happened?" Ben asked. His hand dug into my arm. He looked at Cormac, then looked at me. "Kitty?"

I just blinked at him. Cormac brushed his hands together in a dismissive gesture, like he'd just taken out the trash.

Overhead, stars shone. It was going to be a very cold night, the kind that froze eyelashes together and turned the snow into a glass-hard icy crust. Worst kind of weather. I still felt a lot better than I had a few hours ago.

I checked on Tyler. The cut on his head had stopped bleeding and was healing, closed over with a pinkish scab. Otherwise, he seemed fine. A little startled and wide-eyed like the rest of us. But he wasn't about to lose it.

"Is he dead?" Tyler asked, looking at Franklin.

The heat was leaching from Franklin's body as if he was dead or dying—but he was also lying in the snow, in freezing weather. I started forward to check, but Ben slipped in front of me and got there first. Franklin didn't stir when Ben crouched to touch his neck and said, "He's just passed out, I think."

If I listened carefully, I could hear his heart beating slowly. So he was alive, but we had to get him out of the cold if we wanted him to stay that way. I could be forgiven for hesitating a moment on that one.

"We should get him inside before he freezes to death," I said with a sigh.

"He'll be fine," Cormac said.

I stared at Cormac: Mr. Mysterious, minding his own business, keeping to himself, didn't need guns anymore badass. I thought I'd known him. Or rather I thought I had a pretty good interpretation of the face he presented to the world. Even after he got out of prison I thought I had a little bit of a bead on him. Not so much, it turned out. And after all I'd been through over the last few years, all the people I'd met—psychics and magicians among them—I thought I knew enough to make some guesses. Maybe not.

"Right. No more dodging. Time for a straight answer. You're a wizard. You learned how to be a wizard in prison."

In a moment of sheepishness he ducked, looking away. Scuffed a boot in the snow. Then he studied the sky as if we were discussing the weather, which we sort of were, but still. Tyler and Ben had gone to get Franklin out of the snow, and they stood by him now, watching Cormac, waiting for his answer.

"Cormac?"

"I'm not the wizard," he said finally. "Amelia Parker is."

"Amelia Parker—"

About a year before his release, halfway into his sentence, Cormac asked me to find some information on a woman who'd been executed a century earlier at the Colorado Territorial Correction Facility, where he was serving his time. I'd discovered Amelia Parker: an odd woman, British, a world traveler and collector of exotic knowledge, something out of a Victorian adventure story. This just got even more odd.

"Amelia Parker is?" I said. "She's not dead?"

"Not all of her is," Cormac said.

"Just so we're clear, we are talking about a woman who was hanged a hundred years ago," I said. "She was a wizard. She had powers. And now she's . . . possessing you? Is that it?"

"I guess you could say I met her ghost while I was on the inside. She needed a body and I needed . . . I don't know. Company, I guess."

"So, what, you guys just hooked up? So now you're some kind of possessed zombie wizard?"

He gave me a look. The "you talk too much" look.

Ben had the most precious, adorable, totally confused look on his face I'd ever seen. His brow was furrowed, his mouth open, like he was trying to decide between screaming at Cormac, laughing him off, or asking if this Amelia woman was hot.

"I think I need to sit down," Ben said. He looked at the drifts of snow around him, growled a little, and looked back at Cormac. "Are you okay? It's still you in there, right? You're not *possessed* possessed, right?"

"I'm fine," Cormac said, sounding tired.

"But you have her power? Her knowledge?" I asked, trying to understand. Not that the situation could ever be clear cut or described in a straightforward manner.

"No," Cormac said. "It's all her. Sometimes, she's in charge. That's all. Don't ask me to explain it. It's just one of those things."

We stood in the cold, glaring at each other, uncertain how to move forward.

Tyler cleared his throat and pointed at the unconscious man in the snow. "We really should get this guy out of here."

Tyler and Ben hauled Franklin up and brought him to the Humvee, covering him with blankets. He made a noise, so he was still with us.

"I guess we should take him to a hospital," I said. I didn't know how we were going to explain this at the emergency room. I couldn't prove anything that happened. And after everything, I might still be sued for libel.

"Are we done here?" Ben said to Cormac. "Spell broken, no more crazy weather?"

"Yeah," he said. "It's over."

"We're not done with this conversation," I said to him, pointing. "You still have explaining to do."

He shrugged, as if it didn't matter to him one way or the other.

The Humvee was pretty smashed up, the whole driver's side crunched in, but it was still drivable if you ignored the disturbing clacking noises in the engine. But that was what this vehicle was designed for, getting beat up and still going, right? I wasn't looking forward to telling Colonel Stafford about it, though.

Franklin's Hummer started up, but the noises it made sounded pretty sickly as well. We pulled it over to the curb and left it.

Cormac helped with that much. He also patted

down Franklin and cleaned out all the charms and amulets from his pockets. He must have found a dozen of them. The look he gave me said he wasn't going to explain what he found. But I couldn't argue—Franklin was powerless now.

"I'll catch up with you later, then," Cormac said, waving himself off. He went to his Jeep and drove away, just like that.

"I don't even know what to worry about anymore with him," Ben said, watching him leave.

"I don't know what to tell you," I said, hooking my arm around his. "This is a new one for me, too."

He sighed. "Never a dull moment."

WE TOOK Harold Franklin to the emergency room at St. Joseph's. The place looked understaffed—the waiting room was crowded, and the official-looking people in scrubs all wore exhausted, vacant stares. But there were a couple of orderlies with a gurney to help pull Franklin out of the Humvee. I gave them his name and the phone number for his office, and told them we'd found him in the snow, passed out and close to freezing. They didn't ask us to stick around, and I didn't offer.

Then, finally, we went home. I remembered to call my mother. I wasn't sure she believed me when I told her that everything was fine, but what could she do about it? "Mom, trust me, you don't want to know," I finally told her. That, she couldn't argue with.

I'd coped well enough with the cold of the last two nights and day. I'd been uncomfortable without being in outright pain. But as soon as we got inside, I changed out of my damp clothes into sweats and a big wool sweater. We still had power, and I really appreciated access to a hot shower and central heating.

The next morning, the sun shone on a brilliantly crystalline world. A thick layer of snow covered everything—cars, buildings, trees, streets. Even power lines had fluffy, glittering strips of snow balanced on them. Cleanup began. Plows caught up with the backlog, power lines were repaired, tree branches cleared away, and the world came back to life. The talking heads on the news shows kept saying that this should have been so much worse, that the weather radars had been tracking a vast storm system that had suddenly coalesced over the city, but that it had somehow dissipated overnight, as abruptly as it had appeared. Not that anyone was complaining. Weather reporters gleefully described a rare case of thundersnow over downtown Denver and seemed very impressed. If only they knew.

Cormac came over for coffee.

Tyler was still asleep on the sofa. Last night, he'd seemed inordinately happy at the sight of a sofa in a real living room. He said this was the first time he'd had a chance to sleep in a normal house—not outside, not in barracks, not in Shumacher's werewolf-proof cells—since before he left for Afghanistan. I'd wanted to hug him. Instead, I smiled and wished him sweet dreams.

Ben, Cormac, and I sat at the dining room table nursing mugs of coffee. Maybe we could finally have a real conversation. The pack of three, I called us sometimes. These two knew me and my weird life better than anyone else. They'd been there for some of the more pivotal moments of it. They'd both pulled my ass out of the fire more than once.

We waited for the explanation. Cormac drew a breath, held his mug in both hands, and got started.

"Before she was hanged, Amelia worked a spell that moved her consciousness into the stones of the prison. And she wasn't alone; there's all kinds of freaky shit going on there. Hauntings, demons—I couldn't get out of there fast enough. But to escape, she needed a living body. Once she discovered she couldn't just replace the person already living there, she had to find someone who could put up with her." He spread his hands as if to say, *ta-da*.

"So you were the crazy one," I said.

He shrugged.

"It had to be the right kind of crazy, I'm betting," Ben said, shaking his head in disbelief. But he was smiling. As though now that we had an explanation for why Cormac had been acting funny, we didn't have to worry anymore. Except that where Cormac was concerned, we'd always worry, for one reason or another.

"How does it work?" I said. "I mean, she's there right now, right? Can you talk to her? Does she talk to you? Is she, like, listening right now?" Were there four of us around the table? I might never look at Cormac the same way again. At the same time, I was a little bit in awe. Oh, the questions I would ask a nineteenth-century wizard.

"Yeah," Cormac said. "She hears what I hear. Sees what I see."

"So she's using you," I said, ready to be defensive and huffy on Cormac's behalf. Not that he wasn't perfectly capable of defending himself, even from a disembodied Victorian wizard woman. And did that even make sense?

"It's not that simple," he said, sighing, looking away, frustrated.

"You wouldn't have figured out what Franklin was doing without both of you working together," Ben said. "Right?"

Cormac pursed his lips and nodded. "I like to look at it as a partnership. That's how she sees it."

I stared. "This is very weird. Even for me."

"Amelia likes you," he said, leaning back in the chair. "She likes that you speak your mind."

Not sure what to say to that, I looked away. I didn't want to ask any more questions just yet. I wasn't sure I was ready to know more. I wanted to talk to Amelia Parker—but I didn't want to hear her speaking with Cormac's voice. Then I realized, I probably already had talked to her. The lecturing voice, when we were on the phone and he told me about Franklin, the spell, the thunder mark—that had been Amelia.

I could deal with it later.

"What now?" Ben asked.

"Stay out of trouble, like you keep saying," Cormac said. "Nothing's changed. Not really."

"Have you considered a career in paranormal investigation?" Ben said. "You seem to have developed a talent for it."

He just smiled.

I kept staring. In wonder, awe, confusion. It wasn't a werewolf stare, the challenging stare, or the "trying to figure out what someone was going to do next" stare. It was like, if I didn't turn away, I might figure it out. But all I saw was Cormac. I could have dismissed everything he'd just explained as impossible, unprovable. Except that it explained everything that had happened so well.

"Kitty?" Ben prompted. It had been so long since I'd said anything.

"I have so many questions," I sighed. "For you. For *her*."

"I think that's my cue." Cormac pushed the mug away and stood, retrieving his leather jacket from the back of the chair. "Thanks for the coffee."

Oh, grrrr. He was still Cormac. Still dodging me.

Ben just smirked. He was more patient than I

was—he'd been putting up with Cormac his whole life. And he knew that Cormac would come back. He always did. He didn't have any other family, and we were a pack.

"Is he going to be okay?" I asked after he'd left, not for the first time, a little more desperately than the last.

"Kitty. Are any of us going to be okay?" Ben said, spreading his arms to encompass him, me, the door Cormac had left through, Tyler lying on the sofa, the window, and the city outside.

I knew what he meant. For the moment, we really were okay. But what about tomorrow? What about the day after that? Would we be okay then? I kept asking the question because the answer was never permanent. And that would be true even if we weren't werewolves, ex-cons, traumatized war veterans, and possessed wizards.

I reached for him, and he took my hand and kissed the inside of my wrist. We were going to be okay.

Chapter 23

T HE SNOW melted faster than you'd expect, as it always does in Colorado. Temperatures the following week reached sixty. Rivers of melting snow flooded the streets. I went out without my coat, and the blazing sun felt like a treasure.

A couple of days after the blizzard, we went back to Fort Carson to return the Humvee and retrieve Ben's car, and for Colonel Stafford's debriefing. I was worried about the damage, but the soldier at the motor pool seemed bemused by the condition of the vehicle rather than upset. "What the hell could do this to a Humvee?" he said.

"Evil corporate Hummer," I answered.

"Huh," he replied, and that was that.

Originally, Stafford wanted to hold the meeting at the hospital. I had visions of him trying to get Tyler back into the cell. That probably would have broken Tyler. Broken him more, at least, past all repair. I suggested to Stafford that he find a more unassuming office or conference room in a different building. One with windows. I'll never know why he didn't argue. He could have, but maybe he suspected what I did about Tyler.

The three of us entered the conference room, me in the middle, the men flanking. I could feel the tension that bound us, that made us a pack at least for now. We didn't know what we were about to face, but we'd be ready, standing up for each other, protecting each other. Ready to fight if we needed to, or run if that was what the situation called for.

Stafford, official in his army uniform, was standing across the table. Dr. Shumacher was there as well, clipboard in front of her, gaze downcast. Her back was stiff; she smelled sweaty.

Tyler took a step forward and saluted the colonel, who returned the gesture. They both looked tired. At Stafford's invitation, we sat at the table, lined up across from him and the doctor. It looked like some kind of tribunal.

The final toll: Vanderman and Walters were dead. Two other military personnel were dead. Walters killed one, both Walters and Vanderman the other. The post had remained under lockdown for the rest of the day while Stafford's people cleaned up the mess. Tyler was not only cleared of any wrongdoing in Vanderman's death, but Stafford was recommending him for a citation.

Stafford seemed to be trying to record the incident

as clinically and objectively as he could, avoiding pointing any fingers—lest any be turned back at him, presumably. Ben and I were asked to give our own version of events. Ben was the lawyer—his retelling was also awfully clinical. When my turn came, Ben gave me warning looks whenever my adverbs got too sensationalist. But *somebody* had to get some appropriate emotion into the situation.

I thought it was over. Stafford had closed the manila folder that contained his notes and printouts and pushed it aside. Shumacher had set down her clipboard.

Then Stafford looked at me and said, "Ms. Norville, in your expert opinion, what is your assessment of the potential for the use of lycanthropes as soldiers in the military?"

I tried to argue. "I'm not an expert—"

"You've testified before the Senate on the subject. You're all I have."

That was a scary thought.

I had actually thought about this. The record spoke for itself. "I think people who are already werewolves—experienced, well-adjusted werewolves—could make excellent soldiers, with the right training and a good support structure. Captain Gordon proved that. But I don't think that means the military ought to recruit lycanthropes, and they especially shouldn't go around creating them. You had six men, highly trained and experienced, who are all gone now because of a situation that never should have happened. You didn't understand all the implications of what it means to be a werewolf, to be part of a pack. Gordon didn't understand and he should have. Almost by definition, we're monstrous, out of control. We're where the berserker stories came from. You can't just put that in a box and think you have control." I spoke quietly, steadily. The alternative would have been screaming. Losing control and giving them a demonstration.

Under the table, out of sight, Ben rested his hand on my thigh, a touch of comfort. I straightened and regained my breath.

"Thank you, Ms. Norville," Stafford said. "Sergeant Tyler? Where do we go from here?"

"I'd like to request a discharge, sir," he said, meeting the colonel's gaze. "On medical grounds."

"You're not hurt. You look just fine to me."

Look harder, I almost growled.

Ben rested his arms on the table, leaning forward. "I'm not qualified to comment on military law, but I did some reading. Sergeant Tyler should qualify for a medical discharge under any circumstance. The U.S. government, through the National Institutes of Health, has identified lycanthropy as a chronic disease. The sergeant acquired this disease in the course of duty. I think you could make a good argument. I can give you the NIH references if you want them. Or Dr. Shumacher could."

I glanced at Tyler, who was holding himself still, quiet and expressionless. But I thought I saw a gleam of hope in his eyes.

"We could really use a soldier like you over there, son," Stafford said.

"I don't think I'd be any good to you without the others, sir," Tyler said, a heartfelt plea.

Stafford bowed his head and nodded. "I'll submit the case to the Medical Evaluation Board. It'll be up to them."

WHERE ELSE could we end up but at New Moon, toward midnight, having drinks—beer this time— and food in a muted celebration? The place was almost empty—everyone was still digging out, or enjoying the night by staying wrapped up nice and cozy at home. But Ben and I were there, along with Cormac, Tyler, and Rick.

The vampire arrived last, coming through the door and stomping snow off his shoes. Cormac watched him, his expression blank. Who knew what he was thinking? Either one of them. I kept seeing the old black-and-white photo of Amelia Parker floating behind his shoulder. By all appearances, he was just Cormac. It was going to take time to wrap my brain around it.

Tyler gripped the table and parted his lips in a snarl. "What's wrong with that guy?" he said.

Rick smelled dead—not rotten, just cold. Frozen. He had no heartbeat.

"He's a vampire," I said. "Don't worry, he's nice."

I made introductions—Rick hadn't met Tyler or Cormac, at least not in person.

"I've heard a lot about you," Cormac said when he shook the vampire's hand. Rather ominous.

"Likewise," Rick said.

"Is that going to be a problem?"

Rick smiled. "I try not to make more problems for myself than absolutely necessary."

Cormac still seemed to be sizing Rick up, as if judging how best to take him out. I had an urge to sit between them.

"Sergeant Tyler," Rick said.

Tyler shook Rick's hand, but didn't say anything. The soldier was wary—staring, his shoulders tensed. I might have done the same the first time I'd met Rick. Rick didn't seem bothered; he just took a chair and joined us.

"I got your messages," Rick said. "I'm sorry there was nothing I could do to help, but you seem to have done well. The city is safe again."

"Yeah. Didn't need you to ride to my rescue this time," I said, grinning.

Cormac slid the picture of Franklin and his blurred compatriot across the table. "Kitty said you'd want to take a look at this."

"Is it Roman?" I said.

Rick studied it, shaking his head. "It's a vampire. I can't say exactly who it is. But Roman's the only one who has a reason for dropping this kind of destruction on Denver—it would punish both of us for standing up to him."

"Is it time to call Anastasia?" I said. I told Anastasia I'd call her if I heard from Roman.

Rick rubbed his chin for a moment, staring thoughtfully at the image. "Call her, tell her what happened. But don't raise any alarms. If this is Roman, this wasn't part of his plan. This was just a . . . a test."

Ben said, "Well, did we pass?"

The vampire smiled. "I think Roman underestimated your resources yet again." He glanced at Cormac and Tyler, without whose help Denver would currently be under a dozen feet of snow.

"Go team," I said, raising my glass for a toast. We clinked glasses, except for Rick, who sat back, his expression amused.

Tyler kept himself apart, leaving space enough for extra chairs on either side of him—the places where Vanderman and Walters should have been sitting. Maybe he saw his whole squad sitting around the table. I worried, but all I could do was look after him.

"You okay?" I asked, failing my attempt at subtle inquiry.

He shrugged. "I'm alive."

"That's good, right?" I said.

"Yeah," he said. "Eventually."

"Amen," Cormac muttered. I considered that the two of them might be able to talk to each other about adjusting to life on the outside.

Rick asked, "What's next for you, Sergeant Tyler?"

He took a long drink. His smile was wry. "We just have to wait and see."

Epilogue

KNOB's LAWYER successfully bucked Franklin's lawsuit. She would have done a fine enough job of it without my help, but I helped anyway. I wrote up a report of everything we'd discovered about Franklin, his thunder-god cult, the spells he used and power he wielded, about the storm that had threatened the Denver area and what we'd done to stop it. Ben still muttered about the possibility of us facing charges for vandalism, but I avoided the word. Ben, Cormac, Shaun, and Tyler all agreed to testify that everything I reported was true, no matter how crazy it sounded. I left out suspicions that Franklin was working with or for someone else. As Ben said, I didn't want to inadvertently paint targets on my friends. In response, the lawyer wrote me a very nice note, saying something along the lines that while such evidence might not be admissible in court, she certainly appreciated my perspective on the situation, given my profession as an entertainer specializing in supernatural topics. It didn't *quite* sound like a brush-off.

It turned out that Franklin had enough wacky stuff going on that my claims about him on the show, while extreme, were not in fact outright lies. There were statements from former employees indicating that Franklin would only conduct meetings under certain circumstances—specific times of day, the chairs arranged around the table in a certain way—that could be perceived as ritualistic. He was an enthusiastic collector of archaeological artifacts and would lose his temper if his collection was shifted out of place in the slightest. He'd once fired a custodian for failing to replace each artifact in the correct spot after dusting. I had to ask—were the artifacts connected to thunder or weather gods from various cultures? Why yes, the lawyer answered.

And the final bit of information: Franklin had been known to place good-luck charms at various Speedy Mart franchises. He personally visited each new building at least once during construction, and the lawyer had a signed statement from the foreman on one project saying he'd seen Franklin placing strange items in the foundation. He didn't know what. The specifics weren't important at this point. Franklin really was doing freaky magical stuff at Speedy Marts all over the country. It wasn't libel. Franklin's lawyers tried pressing the case. The judge threw it out.

Franklin himself sold his company and retired, citing health concerns. By all accounts, he returned home from Denver a broken man, physically damaged by hypothermia, mentally wracked by vague nightmares. I never got Cormac to say exactly what he—and Amelia—had done to him. Probably just as well.

A MONTH after the storm, Tyler got his medical discharge and even qualified for disability benefits. He'd done enough, sacrificed enough, it was decided. Ben and I took him home to Seattle.

Werewolves are territorial. Tyler couldn't just fly home and set up shop without ruffling a lot of fur with the local wolves. With his intimidating stature, he would set the locals on edge. They might see him as a threat, someone who was powerful and who might try taking over. We all knew that wasn't what Tyler wanted, but the Seattle pack would need convincing. He'd have to tread carefully and give plenty of warning.

I knew a little bit about the Seattle pack. It was supposed to be one of the safe havens, one of the packs that was willing to take in runaways and refugees, to take care of wolves who needed a little extra help. I hoped they wouldn't look at Tyler and decide that he was too much of a threat to help. Instead of making Tyler navigate the situation on his own, I decided to act as an intermediary.

I called my contact, Ahmed, the werewolf in Washington, D.C., who ran the local lycanthrope scene there. He passed along the contact information for Christopher, the alpha of the Seattle werewolves, and I called him to explain the situation. As I'd feared, he was wary about taking on Tyler, a Special Forces veteran. I couldn't really blame him; this was uncharted territory for all of us. "Just meet him," I'd said, trying to sound confident and reassuring rather than pleading. He agreed to a meeting, and I liked to think it was my incredible powers of persuasion that convinced him. The fact that Christopher turned out to be one of the good guys and willing to take the chance probably had more to do with it.

Ben, Tyler, and I drove straight through to Seattle a week after his discharge. Ben and I took turns driving; Tyler spent most of the drive napping or looking out the window, face right up to the glass, taking in the world. He'd spent most of the last month or so locked up in a hospital room, with occasional excursions. Driving the interstate with the scenery sliding past had to feel as much like freedom as anything.

We reached Christopher's meeting place, a regional park northeast of Seattle, at dusk. I'd called a couple hours out to let him know our ETA. He'd directed us to a parking lot and picnic area, against a backdrop of a thick pine forest. Even in the middle of winter the place was green, and I could smell the rich scent of evergreens touched with icy snow. He and a number of his pack were already there, waiting for us. I'd have done the same thing if our positions had been reversed. Stake out your territory, show your strength, take the high ground, and so on.

I didn't know all that much about werewolf packs. I'd heard a lot of stories through the radio show, and through rumor and hearsay. My own experience was mixed—my pack was part of the best of times and the worst of times, as they say. Some cities didn't have packs at all, just loose confederations of like-minded lycanthropes. I'd been warned away from some areas entirely because a chaotic, warlike environment dominated. There were almost as many different kinds of werewolf packs as there were individual werewolves.

I'd never really met another werewolf pack with a solid alpha male and his followers lined up behind him. This was going to be educational. I was nervous but tried not to show it. Confident, suave, hip—that was me.

The three of us got out of the car. "Wait here a minute," I said to Ben and Tyler. "Let me talk to them first."

"I should be with you," Ben said. He was looking at the leader, standing out in the grass, and at the men and women arrayed in a semicircle behind him like an entourage. "You can't face that all by yourself."

Tyler tipped his chin up a little and took a deep breath. "I can smell them. This whole place smells weird. Different."

Alien. Another pack's territory. I could sense it, too.

"They can see you," I told Ben. "Let 'em think I don't need backup, right?" I grinned. Ben looked like he was biting his tongue.

Christopher was a handsome man, older, close to fifty, maybe, with thick graying hair swept back from his face. Really fit. He had his arms crossed, showing off sculpted muscles. He wore jeans and a short-sleeved, button-up shirt. Among his entourage, a woman stood at the end, red hair twisted up in a braid, laugh lines creasing her eyes. She looked at Christopher rather than at me, watching for his reaction, his cues. His alpha female, then. Everyone else was young, tough, glaring, their shoulders tense, on the verge of bristling like hackles. He'd brought his fighters with him, rather than any older, wiser wolves that might be part of his pack. They smelled like pine trees and salt air, as well as musk and wild.

I stopped about a dozen feet in front of Christopher and stayed relaxed, loose. Tried not to feel small and vulnerable. They were trying to intimidate me, because that was just what werewolves *did*.

"Hi!" I said, way too cheerful, as if I was about to offer them Girl Scout cookies.

Christopher gave a huff, like a silent chuckle. "So you're the notorious Kitty Norville."

"Hey," I said. "I thought it was more like infamous."

Then he did chuckle, amused. "Kitty. It's very nice to finally meet you."

"Yeah, likewise." I glanced at the rest of the pack, watching to see if they relaxed. They seemed to, nominally. But if I breathed on Christopher wrong they'd be on me in a second. I wondered: would my pack look like that, if our places were reversed? Hm.

The alpha female stepped forward to join her mate. "This is Sarah," he said.

"Hi," I said simply. She smiled a wry greeting, as if she was saying, *Nice to meet you, but I could totally take you*. I wasn't going to argue. If all this went well I'd be gone by morning and the point would be moot.

None of us shook hands, which wouldn't have been normal werewolf behavior. When you approached a werewolf with your hand outstretched, you looked like someone getting ready to take a swipe with claws. This was more natural for us: we looked each other up and down, took in each other's scents, and didn't stare into each other's gazes, which would have been a sign of challenge.

This wasn't so bad after all.

"And your friends?" Christopher said, nodding toward my two companions.

"This is Ben, my mate." I looked back, and Ben came forward at the cue, until his shoulder touched mine. He kept his head up and looked over Christopher and all his wolves, meeting each gaze before moving to the next. All he had to do was get across the message that he wasn't worried and he wasn't weak. He might have been channeling his inner lawyer as much as his inner wolf. Christopher nodded at him in acknowledgment.

"And this is Joseph Tyler," I said, looking to the soldier. Christopher waved Tyler over.

In contrast to Ben, Tyler slouched as he walked to join us, and he kept his gaze down. Showing as much deference as a six-three guy who'd just gotten out of the army could show. He came to stand at my other shoulder, and I brushed my hand against his arm, a brief touch of comfort. The anxiety was transmitting. The wolves around us watched him, waiting to see what he'd do.

I glanced at Christopher for his reaction. Did Tyler make him nervous? Would he have to struggle to hide it?

No to both. If he was nervous, he hid it really well. He seemed relaxed—not a hint of hackles rising. But then that was how he got to be alpha of one of the country's more stable packs. He gazed at Tyler calmly, appraisingly, without a hint of challenge. His stance made me relax—Tyler would be okay here.

"Joseph?" Christopher said. "What is it you want here?" The question had a tone of formality, of ritual to it. He wanted to put Tyler on the spot, to see how he would react.

"My family lives here. My mom, sister. They don't—they don't know what I am, what I turned into. They don't have to know. But I want to be close. I want them to know I'm okay."

It was a true answer. Christopher nodded.

"If you're going to live in my territory, you need to live by my rules. We can give you a safe place to spend your full moons. We can help you cope. But you have to do your part to keep the peace. You must help when I call on you. Don't cause trouble."

"I don't want any trouble," Tyler said. "I . . . I just want to come home."

"I know. Sometimes it doesn't always work out that way."

"I need help," he said. "Can you help?" His voice was bleak, tight with sadness, like he expected Christopher to say no and send him away. I would take him back to Denver, I would let him into my pack, he had to know that. But this was home to him, before he'd gone away and traveled through hell.

Sarah looked up at Christopher, her lips pressed into a line, as if she wanted to say something but was waiting for him. We were all looking at him, waiting for a response. His expression was thoughtful.

"I think we can," Christopher said. Tyler bowed his head and sighed. I let out my breath, too.

Ben took my hand and squeezed. "I think it's time we go."

He was right. We'd done what we came here to do, delivered our charge to his new home, and done it peacefully. And now we were invading someone else's territory. Christopher and Sarah probably would have let us stay for a visit, maybe even given us the tour of Seattle if we'd asked. But making a clean break seemed like the thing to do. Let Tyler join his new pack without us around to divide his loyalties.

When Tyler looked at me, he had an expression I'd never seen on him—the tension was gone and he smiled. He was relieved. "Kitty. Thank you."

"I'm not sure I did all that much. I think you'd have been okay eventually."

"But it's been nice having a cheerleader around telling me that," he said.

We hugged tight, cheeks to ears. And I let him go. After shaking hands with Ben, he moved forward to his new pack. Sarah took his arm, held his hand, and led him to the others. One at a time, they touched him, putting their scent on him, adding his scent to theirs. I heard names, introductions, and Tyler smiled through it all.

I turned back to Christopher. "Be careful with him. He's had a rough time."

"Is that a warning?"

"No. I don't know. I just don't know what your next step is, and he's not really ready to be on his own." I didn't want Tyler to ever think he was alone, to fall into that hopeless place again.

Christopher shrugged. "A bunch of us will probably head to my place, grill some steaks, sit around and talk."

I brightened. "Hey, that's how I'd handle it."

Ben put his hand on my back. "She's always worried that she's doing the pack alpha thing wrong."

"The way I look at it, if no one's flying off the handle and getting killed, you're doing it right," he said. "If it makes you feel better, call me any time. If you want to check up on Joseph, or just to talk."

"Thanks." And my network got a little bigger, which made me feel a little better. I turned to Ben. "Ready to go?"

"Yeah, that sounds good."

Christopher offered his hand then, and we both shook it in turn, like normal human beings. We could pretend to be regular people.

Ben and I drove south and east for a couple of hundred miles, until the knots in our shoulders faded, and we could step outside the car and not smell foreign wolves. We got a room at a motel near Boise, to sleep for a few hours.

Ben and I lay on top of the bed, leaning against each other, still in our clothes, too tired to move, too wired to sleep. I was at that stage of exhaustion where closing my eyes hurt. My body still vibrated from the road. Ben must have felt the same; he stared at the TV, flipping channels slowly, rhythmically, without seeming to comprehend what he was looking at.

I was thinking too much to really take in what was on TV. Settling more firmly against Ben's shoulder, I started rambling.

"I've been thinking about history," I said. "Werewolf soldiers aren't a new thing. So I'm wondering where else they've shown up. What other wars. If we peeled back the veneer, what else would we find?"

"I sense a research project coming on," Ben said. Flip, news show. Flip, sports channel. Flip, a twenty-year-old movie I couldn't remember the name of.

How would I even begin such a project? The evidence would be circumstantial: military units or individuals with a reputation for aggression, viciousness, and for possessing supernatural abilities. Bloody battles happening on nights of the full moon. How intriguing. There had to be a way to find out.

"Do you think Tyler's going to be okay?" I asked after another five minutes.

"Eventually," Ben said. "I think he's going to be living one day at a time for a while."

Yeah. I knew how that went. I sighed. "I wonder if this is what it's like to send a kid to college."

Not that I was ever going to find out what that was like for real. But I could imagine: a mix of pride and sadness. Was Tyler going to be all right? Would he write?

I couldn't have children—no female lycanthrope could because embryos didn't survive shape-shifting. Some days, I thought I had no business even thinking of having kids, the way my life went. The late hours, the supernatural politics, the death-defying, injury-producing escapes. I could hear the phone call now: "Hi, Mom? Could you look after Junior while I chase a rogue werewolf across half the state?" And who would look after a baby on full-moon nights? So maybe it was just as well.

It still made me sad. I could find a way. I could adopt, I could hire a baby-sitter. I'd made the rest of my life work pretty well, hadn't I? I wiped my eyes before the tears could start.

"Hey," Ben said. "You okay?"

I felt stupid. Whiney, needy, and stupid. I ought to be able to cope without dumping all this on Ben. And I knew what he'd say to that: who else could I talk to, if not him?

"Do you think I'd be a good mother?" I said.

He glanced at me. Then he shut off the TV and set the remote aside. "That's a bigger question than you're making it sound." I must have frowned, because he put his arms around me. "I think you'd be an excellent mother. You'd drive your kids crazy, but you'd do it excellently."

"Really?" I said.

He grabbed me, one hand lacing into my hair, the other settling on my hip, and pulled me into a long, startling kiss. And then some. And then some more, before we both came up gasping for air. I had on a silly grin.

"Really," he said.

Suddenly, being too wired to sleep seemed like a good thing.

Acknowledgments

A big thank-you to Kevin McLean, who read the first draft for me and gave me suggestions for which I'm grateful. Thank you also to the usual suspects— family and friends and writing cohorts—for listening to me complain a lot, getting me out of the house, feeding me, and taking me on vacation. Thank you also to the people who helped make this a book, rather than just a bunch of notes on my hard drive: Ashley and Carolyn Grayson, Stacy Hague-Hill, David Hartwell, Jaime Levine, and Kim Hoffman. And thanks to Craig White for the iconic artwork. I'm the luckiest kid in the world.

VAMPIRES, MURDER, INTRIGUE . . .

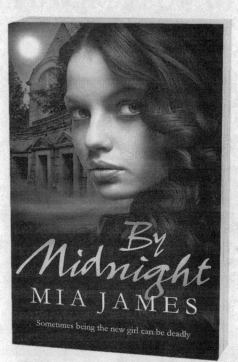

April Dunne is not impressed.

She's had to move from Edinburgh to Highgate, London, and leave behind all of her friends. Then there's Ravenwood, her prestigious new school that seems to have something sinister going on behind its glamorous façade. When the mysterious Gabriel Swift saves April from . . . something . . . . in Highgate Cemetery, she has to wonder if she will survive her new school's deadly secrets.

WELCOME TO RAVENWOOD, THE SCHOOL WITH BITE.

For a closer look at April's world visit Ravenwood at:
www.orionbooks.co.uk/ravenwood

GOLLANCZ V/A
Fierce fiction for young adults

For more information, proof giveaways, exclusive competitions and updates please visit: **www.orionbooks.co.uk/gollanczya**

BEAUTY
IS THE MOST DANGEROUS
WEAPON OF ALL

Set in a world of stunningly beautiful, exceptionally
dangerous monsters, Fire is one of the most dangerous monsters
of all – a human one. Aware of her power, and afraid of it,
Fire lives tucked away in a corner of the world. Until the day
comes when she is needed and has to take a stand not only
against her enemies, but also against herself . . .

NEW GIRL.
NEW SCHOOL.
SAME OLD MONSTERS.

As the new girl at the elite St. Sophia's boarding school,
Lily Parker thinks her classmates are the most monstrous things
she'll have to face. When a prank leaves Lily trapped in the catacombs
beneath the school, she finds herself running from a real monster.
This is a world of magic, vampires, demons and secrets.
Get ready to join the Dark Elite.

IN A WORLD SURROUNDED BY THE LIVING DEAD, WHAT DO YOU LIVE FOR?

The Unconsecrated are never alone.
You are . . .

THE FOREST OF HANDS & TEETH

CARRIE RYAN

THE INTERNATIONAL BESTSELLER

In Mary's world there are simple truths. The Sisterhood
always knows best. The Guardians will protect and serve.
The Unconsecrated will never relent.

But Mary's truths are failing her. When the fence that surrounds
and protects her town from the Unconsecrated is breached her
world is thrown into chaos and she must choose between
her village and her future - between the boy she loves and
the one who loves her.

GOLLANCZ Fierce fiction for young adults

For more information, proof giveaways, exclusive competitions and
updates please visit: **www.orionbooks.co.uk/gollanczya**

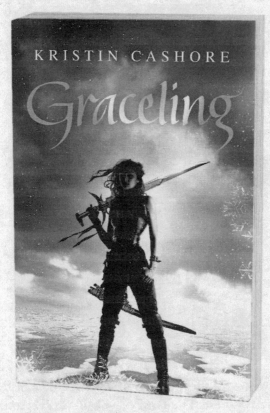

WHAT IF EVERYTHING YOU TOUCHED WAS CURSED?

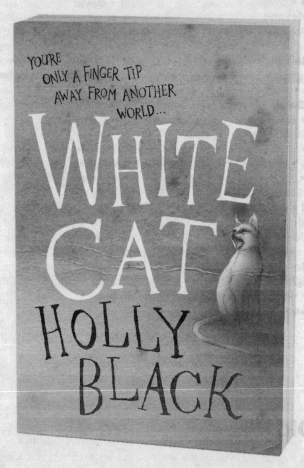

YOU'RE ONLY A FINGER TIP AWAY FROM ANOTHER WORLD...

WHITE CAT

HOLLY BLACK

Cassel is cursed. Cursed by the memory of the fourteen year old girl he murdered. No-one at home is ever going to forget that he is a killer or that he isn't a magic worker. But Cassel is about to discover a dangerous family secret that will change everything.

www.orionbooks.co.uk